Ben Hovik. Tall, dark and handsome.

He was also one person in town she went out of her way to avoid.

"Olivia." The way he said her name seemed like a caress.

Her heart cramped, as if she hadn't already felt like a walking advertisement for Prilosec. Why did he have to look so damn good?

"I need to get back to work," she said, desperate to avoid him.

"You don't look like someone who should be going in to work. Is it your dad? I saw you were with your mom."

Olivia laughed, a corrosive sound that had his eyebrows climbing. "Dad? Oh, sure. And Mom, who is apparently ready to throw off the old life and begin a new one." Now, finally, she tried to shuffle sideways to go around him. "I'm sorry. I shouldn't have said that. Really, I need to go—"

"You need to vent," he said firmly. "I'm here and willing. Plus, I'm discreet." He looked momentarily rueful. "On my job, you get good at keeping secrets."

Dear Reader,

Ages ago I read about a teenage girl being found dead and how, when she remained unidentified, the folks in a small town decided to consider her theirs. If there was any follow-up to the story, I don't remember it. I have no idea why this particular snippet of a story stuck with me, but it did. Maybe it was ready-made for me. As I've said before, I'm always interested in the aftereffects. You know, those ripples spreading outward from an event that might have seemed momentous, or really trivial, but that set something in motion.

In this case, the discovery of this girl is a catalyst in a small town, where a whole bunch of people start wondering guiltily whether they might know something, or might have done something that played a part in her death. Nothing like the uncomfortable tweak of a conscience, and especially when those same people decide to keep quiet!

You may have noticed that I most often set my stories in small towns. The truth is, I've never lived in a city. My parents moved often when I was growing up, but even when my father taught at big-city universities (Mexico City College, San Francisco State University), we always lived in a small town. I love going into Seattle, my closest big town, but have chosen small-town and rural life myself. I like the quiet, and as I was raising kids I also liked the sense of community, knowing other people kept an eye out for my kids, too, just as I did for theirs. When everyone knows everyone, though...well, gossip is, in some ways, an indication people are interested in each other and care, but it can also be destructive.

Ripe ground for a novel about secrets... And all the more ironic when the holiday season is upon these characters and they celebrate goodwill toward all even as they bury their own uneasiness.

Please visit my website at www.janicekayjohnson.com! I love hearing from readers.

Janice Kay Johnson

USA TODAY Bestselling Author

JANICE KAY JOHNSON

One Frosty Night

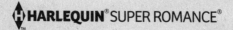

Recycling programs
for this product may
not exist in your area.

ISBN-13: 978-0-373-60880-5

One Frosty Night

Copyright © 2014 by Janice Kay Johnson

www.Harlequin.com

Printed in U.S.A.

ABOUT THE AUTHOR

An author of more than eighty books for children and adults, *USA TODAY* bestselling author Janice Kay Johnson is especially well-known for her Harlequin Superromance novels about love and family—about the way generations connect and the power our earliest experiences have on us throughout life. Her 2007 novel *Snowbound* won a RITA® Award from Romance Writers of America for Best Contemporary Series Romance. A former librarian, Janice raised two daughters in a small rural town north of Seattle, Washington. She loves to read and is an active volunteer and board member for Purrfect Pals, a no-kill cat shelter. Visit her online at www.janicekayjohnson.com.

Books by Janice Kay Johnson

HARLEQUIN SUPERROMANCE

SIGNATURE SELECT SAGA

*The Russell Twins
**A Brother's Word
+The Mysteries of
   Angel Butte

Other titles by this author available in ebook format.

PROLOGUE

WHERE WAS THAT damn dog?

Marsha Connelly stomped into the woods, swearing when she noticed the laces on her right boot were straggling and now snow-crusted. Grunting, she bent over far enough to tie and double-knot them. After she straightened, it took her a minute to regain enough breath to bellow again.

"Blarney!" she bellowed. "You come right this minute!" *Blarney.* She only hoped neighbors thought the blasted dog's name was Barney. What was *wrong* with Barney or Riley or Felix? Or even just Dog? But, no, she'd had to let the grandkids name the new puppy back a couple of years ago, when he'd been charming and small enough he couldn't yet bowl people over in his enthusiasm.

She could see his footprints in the snow; that was one good thing. Otherwise, she wouldn't have a clue where he'd hightailed it off to. On the other hand, it was aggravating to have snow on the ground in October. *October!*

"Blarney!"

Marsha wouldn't have admitted it to anyone, but

she was starting to worry about the dumb-as-a-box-of-rocks dog. And they said golden retrievers were smart! Well, not this one. Still, it wasn't like him to take off like a rocket and not come back. He was pretty willing to please, on the whole. Just big and energetic and cheerful. She didn't like to think he might have slipped on icy rocks into the creek or, who knew, not so long ago there'd still been some trappers around here. Imagining the steel jaws crushing his leg made her swear some more.

She had to stop every couple hundred yards to catch her breath. Could be that young doctor was right, saying she needed to get some exercise. Except how could you exercise when you couldn't breathe? *Answer me that, huh?*

What with everyone using their woodstoves and inserts, the smell of smoke was sharp in her nostrils. The air was so still today, she had no doubt a gray pall hung over the valley, clinging to the lowland between the mountains rising sharply to each side.

She stopped dead, cocking her head. Had she heard a bark? She called the dog's name and definitely heard an answer this time. She kept calling, and he kept barking, but he wasn't getting any closer. So he'd gotten himself stuck somehow.

Mumbling about dumb dogs, she kept right on through the woods, tripping a few times, getting snagged by a sharp blackberry cane disguised by snow in a small clearing. Every so often she called, "Blarney!" and the dog answered.

He didn't sound as if he was hurt, so maybe he'd just gotten his collar caught on something. Only why had he taken off like that in the first place? And gone so far?

She remembered how restless he'd been during the night, wanting out. He'd stood at the window whining until she'd grabbed the book from her end table and threw it at him. Then the minute she *did* open the door this morning, he shot out.

At last, she saw his plumy tail waving furiously just the other side of a mature cedar with low, sweeping boughs. Her puzzlement grew as she circled the tree, because he didn't look to be snagged on anything at all. He had all four feet planted as if he'd grown there like the snowberries and ferns.

"All right, what is it?" Marsha grumbled.

Blarney dipped his head as if to bury his nose in the snow, which she'd seen him do in play, only whatever snow there was here in the woods was thin and crusty.

And then she saw what he guarded, and her mouth dropped open.

It was a woman, curled up as if to sleep and lying on her side, wearing only jeans and athletic shoes and a sweatshirt. No hat, no coat, no gloves or scarf. And she was dead; there was no mistaking that. Her skin was bluish white, her lips and eyelids a deeper blue. Ice rimed those lips and glittered on her eyelashes.

And, oh, dear merciful God, she was a girl, not a woman. Maybe fourteen or fifteen. Slight and immature.

And frozen to death, here in the woods approaching Crescent Creek, which Marsha could hear burbling in the not-too-far distance.

"Oh, sweet Jesus," she whispered, tears burning in her eyes. This poor girl hadn't been here but overnight. Marsha had looked at the outside thermometer before she went to bed, and it had registered thirty-nine degrees. The snow had been slush these past few days, until another cold spell hit during the night. If she'd let Blarney out when he'd asked—

Assailed by guilt, she said roughly, "Good dog, Blarney. You stay while I get help."

He barked, and stayed where he was when she turned and hurried as fast as her old legs would carry her back the way she'd come.

CHAPTER ONE

SNIPPETS OF CONVERSATION from surrounding tables in Guido's Italian Ristorante came to Olivia Bowen as she waited to find out why her mother had wanted to have lunch with her.

Lunch out, when they'd sat at the breakfast table this morning without exchanging a single word. Dinner last night, too, without anything important being said. And, yes, status quo the day before that. They were living in the same house, and she had been trying to get her mother to talk to her for weeks. Months.

"…can't believe a film crew was here again." Arnold Hawkins, his self-important voice unmistakable.

"…don't understand why the police…" A woman's voice.

"At least, thanks to this town, she has a respectable resting place." Claudia Neff, an insurance agent. Also sounding smug.

Olivia was glad the town of Crescent Creek had cared enough to raise the money to bury the still-unidentified girl found dead in the woods. She just wished they'd been motivated by genuine philanthropy rather than the self-conscious awareness that they were acting on a world stage for the first time in their lives. The mystery of the girl who had seemingly appeared from nowhere, died for no apparent reason and been buried by a community of people who had tenderly taken her to their collective hearts was still an internet sensation.

Jane Doe's death was a watershed for this town, one that made Olivia uneasy more than anything.

Maybe because her father had died only a month later, as if—

There was no *as if,* she told herself firmly. What possible connection could there be? They all knew Dad's heart had been damaged by the first attack. It had only been a matter of time. She'd come home to Crescent Creek to take over Dad's hardware store and lumberyard to give him peace and to spend time with him.

Listening to the receding footsteps of the waitress who had taken their order, Olivia decided she'd been patient enough.

"So, what's up?" she asked, looking questioningly at her mom.

Marian Bowen's mouth firmed and her eyes met Olivia's. "I've decided to sell the house."

Olivia gaped. "Dad hasn't even been dead two weeks." Or in the ground for one. They had buried Charles Bowen on the Sunday of Thanksgiving weekend, and today was only Thursday.

"I know what I want to do, Livy. Please don't argue."

"But…it's *home*."

Her mother's face softened. "I know it was. But that doesn't mean I have to stay in it for the rest of my life."

"You know it's too soon to be making decisions that big."

"I can't stay there. I won't."

The misery that had been balled in Olivia's chest for three months now—the same three months when she had seen her parents' marriage failing—intensified into active pain. "Mom, what's wrong? Please tell me."

"Nothing's wrong that you need to know about. I'm a widow now, and I'm ready to downsize. Is that so bad?"

"But…where will you go?"

"I'm considering a house at The Crescent."

The Crescent was a new and very nice senior citizen housing development. Technically, they were condominiums with the outside maintenance handled by the association. Olivia had been surprised to see anything like that in Crescent Creek, a small town nestled deep in the Cascade Mountain foothills, but the homes seemed to be getting snapped up as fast as they were built. Lloyd Smith, who managed the lumberyard side of the Bowens' business, had even mentioned that his wife wanted him to take a look at them.

If Mom had suggested the move six months from now, Olivia might have thought it was a good idea. But as it was—the decision had been made purely out of anger, not practicality. Her husband had died before she could leave him, but she was determined to go through with it one way or another.What's more, it occurred to Olivia that this felt an awful lot like receiving an eviction notice, given that she lived in the family home right now, too.

"Does that mean you intend to sell the business, too?" she asked. The one she'd thrown herself heart and soul into revitalizing?

"I don't know. I can't expect you to run it forever."

"Apparently you *have* made up your mind."

"You sound mad."

"A little taken aback," she said truthfully. "When do you want me to move out?"

Her mother's expression changed, showing a hint of shock and some vulnerability. "But…you know it's going to take time to make decisions about everything we have. I hoped you'd be willing to help."

This had been a really lousy few months. Mom and Dad suddenly, overnight, refusing to talk to each other. The house seething with everything they wouldn't say aloud, at least within Olivia's hearing. Dad's face, tinted blue. The oxygen tank kept beside the big chair in the den. The slow way he moved, struggling for breath. The shock of Marsha Connelly finding a teenage girl frozen to death in the woods. Dad insisting on going to the funeral despite his fragile health. Mom's angry absence obvious to anyone paying attention.

And then Olivia waking up in the morning to her mother telling her Dad had died sometime in the night. Mom didn't know when, because she had been sleeping in the guest bedroom, which meant he'd been alone.

Another funeral, held only eight days later.

Olivia had been hanging on by her fingernails since.

Those same fingernails were biting into her thighs right now. *Yes, Mom, I am mad.*

"I don't know what to say." She sounded a thousand times calmer than she felt. "You've hardly spoken to me in weeks. You don't care about the business. I'm not so sure you care about Dad dying. Now you're rejecting everything that represents our family and my childhood." She blew out a breath. "What do you expect me to say? Gee, Mom, that sounds like fun. Let's dig right in. How about a garage sale? Ooh, I love garage sales."

Marian Bowen sat so utterly still, she looked like a wax effigy. Only her eyes were alive, with a whole lot more than a hint of shock now. Apparently Olivia had betrayed more of her own pain and anger than she'd realized. In fact, out of the corner of her eyes she could see that other diners had turned to look. And, oh God, the waitress was bearing down on them with a tray holding their entrees. Bad time to jump up and say, "I'm not in the mood for lunch."

Instead she kept her mouth shut until the waitress had come and gone again, probably wondering why neither woman so much as glanced at her, forget thanking her.

Then she said, "We need to talk about this later," and reached for her fork. She wasn't sure she could so much as put a bite in her mouth, but she could pretend.

BEN HOVIK DIDN'T know what had possessed him to take a long detour by the cemetery.

Until a few weeks ago, he hadn't given it a thought. Growing up in Crescent Creek, he'd been as oblivious as any child was to the reality of death. Yeah, Grandma Everson was buried there, but he hardly remembered her. However, after the two recent funerals, the cemetery held a grim fascination to him.

He felt good about the first funeral. Not the death, of course, because that still left him stunned. How was it possible that a kid no more than sixteen had been too sick or injured or just plain scared to seek help on a freezing cold night? Why had she wandered so far into the woods, lacking even a coat? Then just lay down and died, like an animal that had lost hope?

And how was it that a girl that age could go missing with, apparently, no one who cared enough to be looking for her? The police had been unable to identify her, despite nationwide interest in her life and death. She was entered in missing persons databases that could be accessed by law enforcement from any agency. A drawing of her face had appeared in newspapers, on Seattle television news and even on the internet. There'd been calls, tips; none led anywhere.

The fact that the community had come together to pay for her burial was the part he *did* feel good about. It saddened him that she'd become theirs too late, when all they could do for her was give her a headstone, but at least they'd done that much.

Having Charles Bowen die so soon after Jane Doe, that hit hard, too. Ben had gone to his funeral because he'd known Mr. Bowen his whole life and had once loved Olivia Bowen. It had been all he could do to see her grief and not be able to do more than shake her hand at the end of the service and murmur condolences, the same way everyone else was. To see how blindly she looked at him, as if he were a stranger.

That was the moment when he'd given up.

His decision to apply for the job of principal at Crescent Creek High School, a return to his hometown, had awakened the seed of hope that he would see Olivia. That maybe they could reconnect.

The first time he saw her after the gap of years had been like a hard punch to his belly. She was only home on a brief visit that time, but she must have gone into work with her dad, because when Ben walked into the hardware store, Olivia was mixing paint and laughing at something a customer said. And, damn, she was even more beautiful than she'd been when he'd so stupidly broken up with her. At five foot ten, Olivia had gotten her height from her dad. That and her natural grace had made her a star on the girl's basketball team in their small high school league. She still had the most amazing legs he'd ever seen—long, slim, but strong. And, man, he knew what it felt like to have those legs wrapped around his waist.

Thick, shimmering hair the color of melted caramel was from her mother, as were those hazel eyes, a complex of colors that changed depending on the light or what she was wearing.

He had stood, stupefied, a few feet inside the hardware store, seeing only her. Inevitably, she'd turned and seen him. Her eyes had widened; there had been a flash of something remarkably intense, then...nothing but a pleasant, slightly puzzled smile. "Ben. Goodness. It's been forever. Do you need some help?"

Whatever that intense something was had kept his hope alive, even though she wasn't receptive on the few occasions he managed to meet up with her during her visits home. When she had moved in with her parents ten months ago, to take over her dad's business, he'd thought, *Now I have a chance.*

But apparently he'd been fooling himself, because she kept treating him like the merest acquaintance, not someone who'd once been a friend, never mind her high school boyfriend and first lover.

His fault, he knew, but still he kept thinking—

Didn't matter. It was time he quit thinking about Olivia. Unless he wanted to spend the rest of his life alone, maybe he should start noticing other women. Much to his mother's dismay, he hadn't so much as gone on a date in the two and a half years since he'd come home to Crescent Creek with his stepson.

I should change that.

He gave a grunt of unhappiness and took one more look at the cemetery in his rearview mirror. A fresh bed of snow covered the graves, new and old. Only the headstones showed. The one he pictured most vividly said, "Jane Doe, Much Mourned," and gave the date of the girl's death.

Usually he ate at his desk or in the cafeteria with the kids. The one student he stayed far away from was his stepson. Most students likely knew Carson's dad was principal, but the two didn't share a last name, and Ben figured it was just as well not to remind anyone. Today Ben had felt the need to get away. Ever since Marsha Connelly had found the girl dead, he'd felt unsettled. No, that was putting it too mildly. He'd felt a gathering sense of foreboding, as if the one tragedy was a harbinger of worse to come. His worry increased with the second death following so soon, even if it was unrelated. He didn't like the atmosphere at school. Sure, he'd expect kids to be disturbed about the death of a girl their age, but— This felt like more. Not whispers, he wasn't hearing those. More like silence, unnatural for hormone-driven teenagers. Especially such sustained silence.

He frowned. *Foreboding?*

Slowing when he reached downtown, he thought with near amusement, *Right.* He was dramatizing his own depression. Call a spade a spade.

And then, right in front of him, he saw Olivia and her mother come out of Guido's, the town's one Italian restaurant. His foot lifted from the gas. The hesitation was enough to make him miss the light, which allowed him to watch mother and daughter walk side by side for a block without speaking, if he wasn't mistaken. Both backs were stiff. They stayed a good two feet apart, careful never to so much as brush arms. Then they parted, with Marian Bowen looking both ways and crossing the street to her car, while Olivia continued on toward her father's hardware store.

No, her *mother's* store now, he supposed.

And there was a parking spot a half a block from the store. It was meant— He put on his signal, pulled into it and jumped out, his timing perfect to intercept Olivia.

Well, shit. Maybe he hadn't given up hope after all.

HEAD BENT, SHE walked fast. Her eyes burned, and she thought seriously about not going back to work at all. Except...where would she go? Not home, that was for sure.

Home for how much longer?

Oblivious to her surroundings, she smacked right into somebody, who then grabbed her arms and kept her upright when she bounced back. Even before she lifted her head, Olivia knew who it was. Her body knew.

Ben Hovik. Tall, dark and handsome. The lanky boy who had, to her dismay, acquired muscles and matured into a man who would turn any woman's head.

Except hers, of course. *Been there, done that.*

He was also the one person in town she went out of her way to avoid.

"Olivia." His deep, slightly gritty voice was as gentle as it had been at her father's funeral when he'd taken her hand in his. His expression was kind.

"I...excuse me. I wasn't paying attention to where I was going."

"You looked upset."

She smiled weakly. "It hasn't been the best of days."

Her feet should be moving, but they weren't. He

stood there looking down at her, apparently in no hurry even though it was the middle of a school day.

Her heart cramped, as if she hadn't already felt like a walking advertisement for Prilosec. Why did he have to look so damn good?

She had always noticed Ben. Mostly from a distance, until her first day as a freshman at the high school. He'd turned away from his locker and smiled at her, and she'd stumbled, dropped the backpack she'd just unzipped and spilled everything in it on the floor right in front of him. Lunch, pens, new gym clothes and athletic shoes. The rings on her binder had sprung open, compounding the mess. Her finest moment. When he'd helped her pick everything up and asked if she was all right, her crush metamorphosed into something a lot scarier.

The amazing thing was, he seemed to feel the same. He asked her out, she went. They fell in love. Made love. Talked about the future. Only, of course, she still had two years of high school left when he graduated, so he went off to college first, where there were lots of pretty girls his own age. She should have expected it, but she'd been stupidly naive and hadn't. He'd broken her heart, and, nope, seeing him right at this particular minute in time was not making her feel better.

"I need to get back to work," she said. Feet still not moving.

His dark eyes were penetrating, and his hands hadn't left her upper arms. "You don't look like someone who should be going in to work. Is it about your dad? I saw you were with your mom…"

Olivia laughed, a corrosive sound that had his eyebrows lifting. "Dad? Oh, sure. And Mom, who is apparently ready to throw off the old life and begin a new one." Now, finally, she tried to shuffle sideways to go around him. "I'm sorry. I shouldn't have said that. Really, I need to go—"

"You need to vent," he said firmly. "I'm here and willing. Plus, I'm discreet." He looked momentarily rueful. "On my job, you get good at keeping secrets."

Somehow she was letting him steer her to his Jeep Cherokee, which was right there at the curb. He must have just gotten out of it.

"Wait." She tried to put on the brakes. "Where are we going?"

"Somewhere we can talk. We can run through the Burger Barn drive-through and get drinks, then go park."

The last time they'd parked… Not going there, she decided. They had "parked" a lot during their two years and five months as girlfriend-boyfriend. But the last time was when he'd said the devastating words: "I've met someone else."

"No, I really should—"

"Olivia, you don't want to go back to work looking the way you do."

She closed her mouth on her protest. Even if she locked herself in her office, someone was sure to track her down. And she'd have to walk through the store to get to the stairs that led up to the loft where the offices were. She'd be waylaid ten times before she got that far.

Yes, but Ben Hovik…

There were worse people to talk to. Despite everything, she did believe he would keep a confidence. And he knew her parents, so he'd understand her bewilderment.

After a moment, she nodded and got in once he'd opened the door. From habit, she fastened the seat belt as he went around and got in, too.

Out of the corner of her eye, she saw her mother backing her Saab out of a curbside slot—which so happened to be right in front of the Home & County Real Estate office. Had she already listed the house?

Olivia's coal of anger burned hotter.

Ben saw her mother driving away, too, after which his gaze rested thoughtfully on Olivia's face and her hands clenched on the seat belt. Without saying anything, he put his SUV into gear, signaled and then slowly pulled out, going the opposite direction from her mom.

Neither of them spoke until he stopped in the Burger Barn drive-through. She was suddenly starved. Anger was apparently good for her appetite, when shock hadn't been.

"I want a cheeseburger and fries. Diet cola."

His eyebrow quirked, but he ordered for her and added a coffee for himself.

"You've already eaten," she realized.

"At home," he said.

"Did you have an errand in town?" she asked, suddenly suspicious.

"Nope. On my way back to the high school. Just spotted you and your mother, both of you freely projecting hostility."

"We weren't."

"If it wasn't hostility, it was a close relation." He turned his head when the young woman reappeared in the take-out window with bags. He handed over money before Olivia could reach for her wallet, accepted the food and drinks and started driving forward.

"Thank you," she said stiffly.

"You're welcome."

She asked if he minded if she ate; he said of course not. He took a few turns but, thank heavens, didn't head for any of the popular parking spots. Instead, he chose a lane that led to a now snow-covered field, turned around and set the emergency brake. He was nice enough to leave the engine running so they still had heat.

They sat in silence for a while, until she noticed he was amused by the way she was gobbling her French fries. Flushing, she wiped her fingers on a napkin.

"I noticed at the funeral that the two of you

weren't standing near each other," he said, instead of remarking on her gluttony. "I figured you were both trying to keep your composure and were afraid you'd set each other off. But that wasn't it, was it?"

She both wanted and didn't want to talk. Why was Ben the only person who'd noticed something was wrong? Or had other people, but he was the only one with the nerve to be so nosy?

Or the only one who cared enough?

No, she couldn't believe that. Whatever relationship they'd had was long past. Those words, *I've met someone else,* had been said sixteen years ago. Half a lifetime, for her. They'd hardly spoken since.

If she could just think of him as a high school friend...

"You know what Mom and Dad were like," she said. "So obviously in love even after all these years."

Ben nodded. Everyone noticed.

"It's probably why I'm not married. High expectations, you know?"

He nodded again, but she noted, when she sneaked a peek, that his face was particularly unreadable. Did he think she was slamming him for dumping her?

Ancient history, she told herself impatiently.

"After his first heart attack, Mom was so scared," Olivia continued. "But three months or so ago, something happened. They practically quit talking. Mom moved into the guest bedroom. Neither of them would tell me what was going on."

Now Ben looked surprised. "Your parents?"

"It was…weird. I think Mom was the one who was mad. *Is* mad," she corrected herself softly. "But what could Dad have done? I mean, he'd hardly left the house since they released him from the hospital. I was running the business, so it wasn't anything related to that."

"I can't imagine." Ben frowned. "Besides, your mother must have known he was living on borrowed time."

Olivia stared straight ahead through the windshield. "Even when he died, I could tell she was angry. Grieving, but not the way you'd expect. They'd been married thirty-eight years!" She shifted in the seat to look at Ben. "We buried him four days ago. Four! Do you know why we were having lunch today? So she could announce that she's putting the house on the market."

He stared. "Already?"

"That's what I said! Then *she* said, 'I'm a widow now, and I'm ready to downsize. Is that so bad?' We've barely washed the sheets from their bed!"

"Did she move back into their bedroom after he died?"

Olivia shook her head. "I think selling the house is her way of leaving him. Too late for a divorce, but she has to reject him somehow. And apparently, she can't stand to wait another minute."

He watched her, expression troubled. "You don't have any idea what it could have been."

"No." She looked away. "He died right after—"

"I know when he died." One large hand pried the small container of fries out of her hand, and she realized she'd been squeezing it in a fist. Ben set it between the seats. "Maybe attending the funeral got to him." He hesitated. "It was a cold day. That couldn't have been good for him."

"What you really mean is, he looked into that hole in the ground and saw his own mortality."

"It's possible," he said gently.

Olivia's shoulders sagged. "He was acting… strange. I tried to talk him out of going."

"Your mother didn't go."

She made a face. "They weren't speaking. How could she?"

"Is she mad at you, too?"

Olivia pondered his question for a minute and finally had to answer truthfully, "I don't know. She doesn't like me pushing for answers. But also…I was always kind of Daddy's girl. A tomboy." Like he didn't know that. "More interested in the business than I was in clothes or homemaking."

From the minute she'd been old enough, she had worked part-time at the hardware store, full-time in the summer all the way through college. It's why she'd been able to step in comfortably after his heart attack.

As a wounded sixteen-year-old, she hadn't been

able to help wondering if she just wasn't feminine enough to keep Ben's attention. In Crescent Creek, his options had been limited, but once he was surrounded by beautiful college girls, the girlfriend he'd left behind would have been cast in new relief. A giraffe—tall, skinny, lacking enough curves. Better with a circular saw than she was with a mascara wand.

Feeling impatient, she told herself it had been too long ago for her to still be wondering.

"So your mother believes you were on his side." Ben sounded thoughtful now. "Or thinks you'd be sympathetic to him on whatever their issue was."

"Issue?" she echoed. "That's a mild way of describing something that would split them, of all people, apart."

"Maybe they weren't as solid as they seemed."

"A few months ago, I'd have laughed at that suggestion. I *know* my parents." More softly, she amended, "I thought I knew my parents."

"You know she'll talk to you eventually."

"Do I?" Olivia sighed. "If she was only hurt, I'd agree, but she's harboring so much anger. And that's not like Mom."

This time he didn't say anything. After all, he didn't know her parents the way she did.

She turned her head and really looked at him. "You haven't heard anything, have you? You know... Rumors. If you have, please tell me. Don't think I'm better off not knowing."

But he was shaking his dark head long before she finished. "I haven't, Olivia. Not a word. People are feeling really bad for your mom."

She went back to staring out at the snowy landscape. "She wants me to help clean the house out. Get it ready to sell. I said, 'Gee, that sounds like fun. Let's have a garage sale, why don't we?'"

Ben gave a rough chuckle. "Bet that went over well."

"Oh, yeah." Her mouth curved into a reluctant smile. "So that's the story. Wow. Now I can't decide if I'm hungry enough for that cheeseburger after all."

He laughed again. "Didn't eat a bite at Guido's, huh?"

"I poked and stirred."

"Eat." The bag rustled when he reached into it, and he even partially unwrapped the burger before handing it to her. "Go on. You'll feel better."

Feeling calmer for no good reason, she did. Halfway through the cheeseburger, she felt the need to break the silence.

"What you did for that girl… It was nice."

His shoulders moved. From his profile, she thought she'd embarrassed him.

"If I hadn't started that fund, someone else would have."

"Maybe. I'm not so sure. The thing is, you did it for the right reasons. In Guido's I heard people talking, and it made me mad. It was all about TV coverage and feeling self-satisfied."

The skin beside his espresso-dark eyes crinkled. "You were already mad."

"Well...yeah."

"Damn, Olivia." The timbre of his voice had changed. "I've missed you."

"Sure you did." Appetite gone, she rewrapped the remaining half of the cheeseburger. "I really do need to get back, Ben. Thanks for listening."

She felt him studying her. Her skin prickled from her acute awareness.

"Okay," he said, in seeming resignation. He released the emergency brake and put the Jeep into gear. "I am sorry."

She bent her head in stiff acknowledgment, not daring to ask whether he was sorry about her present turmoil—or because he'd hurt her all those years ago. "Thank you."

Neither said anything during the short drive back to town. Only when he double-parked in front of the hardware store did she remember the lunch. "You should let me pay—"

Ben's expression shut her down.

"Thank you," she said again and hopped out, taking her drink and the leftovers in the sack with her.

"Good seeing you, Olivia," he murmured, and, once she'd shut the door and retreated to the curb, he drove away without looking back that she could tell.

Her heart slammed in her chest, and she felt a yawning emptiness deep inside.

CHAPTER TWO

CARSON CALDWELL LEAPED to knock the shot away; then, when the ball soared over his head, he turned to watch it sink through the net. *Whish.* Really pretty.

I should have stopped it, he told himself furiously. He'd hesitated too long, not starting his jump until the ball was already leaving Bearden's fingers. Too late, not concentrating.

This isn't a game.

No, but Coach was watching. If Carson wasn't careful, he'd find his ass sitting on the bench tomorrow night when Crescent Creek played Arlington High School.

He ran back down the court with the rest of the team, the sound of their feet thundering on the gymnasium floor. A shoulder jostled him hard, knocking him off balance. He flicked a glance at Coach, who paced the sidelines but didn't see. A lot of this shit had been happening.

Wham. The ball hit Carson in the chest and fell away. Finkel snapped it up and tore back down the court, making an easy layup.

The whistle blew, echoing shrilly off the concrete block walls. "All right," Coach called. "That's enough for today. Hit the showers. Caldwell, I want to talk to you."

Oh, shit, oh, shit.

Momentarily he was surrounded as they all walked over to grab towels and water bottles. There was another hard bump that had him cracking his shin against the bottom step of the bleachers.

"Mouth shut." For his ears only.

Dylan Zurenko, senior, starting center and all-around asshole. It was another senior, Dex Slagle, who'd jostled him on the court. The two were tight. Carson had been flattered when they had accepted him into their circle.

He knew why they'd decided now he was the weak link. Daddy the principal. Stepdaddy, actually, but what was the dif?

Hearing the receding footsteps, voices and friendly taunts, he mopped his face with the towel, then draped it around his neck and took a long drink of the now lukewarm water.

"Your head isn't on the court," Coach McGarvie said from right beside him.

He closed his eyes for a moment, scrubbed the towel over his face again and faced his coach. "I guess it wasn't today."

"Hasn't been since the season started."

"I scored fourteen Tuesday night." It had been only the second game of the season. The first game,

right before Thanksgiving… Well, he'd mostly been
shut out, but he thought he'd partly redeemed himself Tuesday.

"Good assists. You also fell over your own damn
feet."

He felt the flush climb his neck to his face. He
had. Right here, in this gymnasium, in front of the
entire student body. *He* had tripped and crashed
down. People laughed. Afterward, he'd pretended
his laces had come undone.

He couldn't blame Zurenko for that one. His feet
had grown two sizes since April. He was growing, too, but not keeping up with his feet. He wore
a twelve now, but was only six foot one. He had
dreams of the NBA, which meant he wanted to
keep growing, but lately signals seemed to be taking too long to get to his hands and feet.

He stayed stubbornly silent. Like he had a choice.

Coach was about his height, not a big man. He'd
played for some Podunk college—Ben said it was
actually a fantastic liberal arts school, just not
big-time where sports were concerned—and now
taught history as well as coaching boys' basketball. Last year, Carson had liked him. This year,
McGarvie was all over his ass.

"Are you going to talk to me?" his coach asked.

He clamped his mouth shut. He *couldn't* talk.
Not about what was bothering him. It was…too
big. And if he did, he'd be in deep shit. "Then I'm
starting Guzman," Coach said flatly. "You're not

concentrating, Carson. You've got all the ability in the world, but this season your heart isn't in it."

He couldn't seem to help the surly reply. "I thought you said it was my head."

McGarvie looked at him as if he was crazy, shook his head and walked away toward the locker room.

Carson went the other direction, past the bleachers, to where he could smack both hands on the porous wall of the gym hard enough to sting.

God. What am I going to do? he begged, with no more idea than he'd had since the morning after what he'd thought was the best night of his life.

Pride had him finally walking to the locker room. If he was lucky, everyone else would have showered and he could be alone while he took his.

BEN STOLE A glance at his stepson in the passenger seat where Olivia had been earlier. He could still smell her French fries and wondered if Carson could, too.

"Anything you want to talk about?" he said finally.

Carson shook his head, then grimaced. "I'm not starting tomorrow night."

"What?" Ben hoped he didn't sound as startled as he was.

"I've just been…I don't know," the boy mumbled. "Clumsy."

"You have been growing fast."

Head down, he shrugged.

"Let's stop and get a pizza. I'm not in the mood to cook." He'd almost suggested the Burger Barn, but that would make him think about Olivia, and he didn't want to right now. Something was going on with Carson, and he needed to find out what it was.

The boy's head came up. "Uh, sure. Cool."

Four and a half years since the divorce, and he and his stepson were still feeling their way, or sometimes that's how it seemed.

Ben waited until they'd been seated at Rosaria's Pizzeria, agreed on their order and received their drinks. Then he asked casually, "Heard from your mother lately?"

Carson looked surprised. "No. Not since…I don't know. Like, August?"

Ben had spoken to Melanie briefly that time, so he only nodded. Her life had been a mess, as usual. He refused to own any part of that, but he always worried that she'd succeed anew in sucking her son in. After her initial noble gesture—ceding custody to Ben—she'd tried a few times. Once, the second year, Carson had run away because he was sure she needed him. After he'd been hauled back, he and Ben had done a lot of talking, and Ben thought his stepson was doing well at letting go of an un- realistic sense of responsibility. Nothing in his ex- pression now suggested he'd even been thinking about his mother.

So that wasn't the problem.

He tried another not-so-random sortie. "You mad at Coach McGarvie?"

Hunching his bony shoulders, Carson didn't want to meet Ben's eyes. "Not really," he muttered. "I haven't been together. That's not his fault."

"Anything I can help with?" Ben asked. Years of practice kept his tone easy, not too pushy. Kids this age didn't respond well to pushy.

Carson sneaked a look at him before his gaze skidded away. "Nah."

Was that some kind of shame or embarrassment he was seeing? Ben wondered. Hard to tell in the dim lighting.

"You know, I'll listen anytime you want to talk," he said.

"Yeah. This is—" He hunched again as much as shrugged. What "this was" remained unsaid.

A girl? Carson was sixteen, a junior in high school. What could be likelier? Ben watched more closely than he let on, though, and he hadn't seen any particular yearning looks. Not the kind he'd been directing Olivia's way on the rare occasions when he saw her, he thought ruefully.

He heard himself say, "You must wonder why I don't date."

His son looked at him in alarm. Ben worked to keep his amusement from showing. A parental figure planning to talk about sex? What kid wouldn't be panicked?

"I figured, um…" Carson's throat worked. "It

was, you know, because things were so bad with Mom. And maybe because you have me…"

Ben reflected on what was actually a pretty darned perceptive answer from a teenager. "I guess at first it was because of your mother. And it's true I wouldn't want to set a bad example for you." He'd never been the woman-of-the-week kind of guy anyway, though.

"Grandma was whining the other day. She said she wanted, um, more grandkids."

Seeing the fleeting expression of pleasure on the boy's face, Carson gave silent thanks to his mother. Both of his parents, really. They'd accepted Carson without question as family. They openly called him their grandson. Even if Ben married and his wife started popping out the babies, neither of his parents would ever act as if the new, related-by-blood grandkids were any more important than the one he'd already given them. And because of that, he hadn't regretted for a minute returning to his hometown, even if it meant he had to keep seeing Olivia and face her complete indifference to him.

If she really was indifferent.

No, he was kidding himself. She'd retreated at warp speed today when he tried to get personal.

"Hey, here comes our pizza," Carson said, recalling Ben to the present.

They'd ordered an everything-but-the-kitchen-sink pizza that would probably have Ben suffering from regrets a few hours from now, but, damn, it smelled good. Carson fell on his first slice like a starving dog. Ben wouldn't have wanted to risk his fingers trying to take it from him. He grinned crookedly, remembering that age when it seemed he couldn't ever get full. And Carson, he suspected, might end up several inches taller than Ben.

Mel had never talked much about her son's father; in later years, Ben came to suspect she didn't actually know which of many men *had* fathered him. The fact that she hadn't put a name on Carson's birth certificate seemed to corroborate that theory. Whoever the guy was, he had to have been tall and likely a good athlete, too, since Mel had never seemed inclined that way.

Ben had taken only a few bites when Carson reached for his second slice. Unexpectedly, though, he set it on his plate rather than immediately stuffing it in his mouth. "So, how come you don't date?" he blurted.

Had there been a good reason he'd raised the subject? Ben asked himself. Oh, yeah—to open up the possibility of talking about girls and sex. It suddenly didn't seem like such a good idea.

"Waiting for the right woman, I guess," he said with complete honesty.

Carson's eyes were a bright blue, his hair a sandy brown that, like most of the other boys, he wore spiky. Right now, those blue eyes were sharp enough to make Ben feel like squirming. "There

aren't that many single women in Crescent Creek.
I mean, your age."

The last was a little condescending. Middle age
wasn't exactly looming, damn it; Ben was only
thirty-five. But what Carson had said was right:
most of the really appealing women his age were
already married. More so in rural Washington than
would have been true in the city, but he didn't get
to the city much anymore.

Ben braced himself for Carson to ask about
Olivia, since he did know they'd gone together in
high school, but instead his stepson picked up his
slice of pizza, then set it down again.

"Don't you ever, you know, want to have *sex?*"
His voice cracked at the end, and he turned his
head quickly, cringing at the possibility that anyone had heard him.

More than you can imagine.

Ben heard himself make a sound he couldn't
quite classify. A groan? Damn, he wanted sex…
but not with just anyone. With Olivia. He hadn't
been able to picture anyone else in his bed since
he'd set eyes on her again after his return to Crescent Creek. Two years and four months ago, to be
precise.

Carson suddenly blushed. "Or, oh, wow, maybe
you are and you're just making sure I don't know
about it."

"No." That came out so harshly, Ben had to clear
his throat. "I'm not. And, yes, I do. Want to." Was

he blushing? "Unlike a lot of men, I've just never been into casual sex." He hesitated. "I'm not saying that as a parental lecture, but to me, the whole thing is awkward when you're with a woman you don't feel much for. Sex with a woman who is essentially a stranger doesn't hold any appeal to me."

All the color left Carson's face. He looked... shocked.

And Ben had no idea why.

For a strange moment, they stared at each other. Then the sixteen-year-old gave an elaborate shrug and said, "You know that's totally abnormal, don't you, Dad?"

Ben let himself relax. Even enjoy the rare reference to him as "Dad" and not "Ben." "Yeah," he said, "but then I chose to spend my life working with teenagers, and what's normal about that?"

They exchanged grins and resumed eating. It wasn't until considerably later that Ben realized he still didn't have the slightest idea what was weighing on his kid.

THE MINUTE OLIVIA opened the front door and smelled dinner cooking, she realized her mother was trying to make amends. *Wonderful.* What she'd really like was to go straight to her bedroom. Now she had to be nice instead.

In a better mood, she'd have laughed at herself for her sulkiness. As it was... She sighed and went to the kitchen.

Mom even wore an apron as she tore lettuce into a bowl. At the sight of her daughter, she offered an uncertain smile. "I didn't hear you come in. I hope you didn't already have dinner."

"I'm just late. It smells good."

"Beef stroganoff."

"I can tell." She forced a smile. "What can I do?"

"Oh— If you'd like to set the table?"

Olivia did escape upstairs briefly to dump her messenger bag and change into slippers, but then she went back down. Were they actually going to have a real conversation?

Apparently. Olivia had no sooner spooned stroganoff onto her noodles than her mother said, "I'm sorry I took you by surprise today."

Olivia didn't know how to respond to that. *It's all right?* It wasn't. *Why didn't you tell me what you were thinking?* Now, there was the question.

"Lloyd's wife wants him to look at those houses, too," she offered.

"They're really very nice." Mom sounded so hopeful.

What could she say except "I'm sure they are"?

Both finished dishing up.

"I didn't stop to think how you'd feel," her mother said in a burst. "I mean, that this is your home."

"You forgot I grew up here?"

"Of course not!" Mom visibly settled herself. "It's just that it hasn't been home for you for a long time. Until these past few months, of course."

"I've been home for nearly a year now, Mom."

Little crinkles formed on her forehead. "But I never dreamed you'd stay. Or were even considering staying."

"I was focused on keeping things going for you and Dad," Olivia said honestly. "I...hadn't gotten so far as to think about what would happen when he was gone." Unlike Mom, who apparently had been revving her engine waiting.

"Would you consider staying?" her mother asked after a minute.

Would she? Olivia felt a tug both ways, and that surprised her. Newly graduated from college, she'd have laughed at the idea that Dad's hardware store was the sum total of her ambitions.

"I've been...happy at work since I came home," she said slowly. "Making changes. We're selling a lot of Christmas gifts." Thanksgiving weekend, never that big in the past, had been fantastic this year, despite the death of Charles Bowen only days before. "There's more that could be done to make the business even more successful."

"But there must be an upper limit."

"That's true," she agreed. "We can't draw a lot of new customers unless the population increases." Which they both knew wasn't happening. "But what we can do is meet the needs of locals so that they don't feel the need to drive to Miller Falls or even Everett to shop. We can be more competitive for builders, for one thing."

"How?"

"Initially, lower profit margin. Long-term, we'd be buying in greater bulk. No, we still can't compete directly with a Home Depot, say, but if we can come close, convenience will trump cost savings for local builders and remodelers."

Her mother nodded her understanding.

"What I'd really like to do is to continue to expand stock. Go way bigger into clothing."

That's where much of the boosted sales had come from; Dad had never carried anything but the most utilitarian of carpenter pants, work gloves and the like. Olivia had added rain gear, parkas, hats, gloves and socks. Flannel shirts for men, cute T-shirts for women and even some clothes for kids. Mostly outdoor and work related but attractive. The last clothing store in Crescent Creek had closed six or eight years ago, and its stock had appealed to the matrons, not younger shoppers or men.

"We've got the floor space in the loft to make clothing into a huge sideline. I see a possibility for gift items across the board. Garden art as well as shovels and wheelbarrows, for example. And then expand in every area. We have electrical—why not sell a line of lamps and expand the number of lighting fixtures we carry? Plumbing? More choice of sinks and fixtures plus add some extras, like bath mats and hampers. We can keep our core business but appeal more to women." She hesitated, the rush of ideas slowing as she broached the opportunity she'd been toying with. "You know that Swenson's next door is going out of business."

"Yes, I was sorry to hear that. Mr. Swenson's in poor health, you know."

"I do. My first thought was that we could use the floor space for some of my ideas." She eyed her mother a little nervously. It was supposed to be Dad she'd have to sell on the idea. "My second was that we could buy Swenson's and integrate it into our business. Appliances are pretty closely related to hardware and home improvement. Maybe we could pare down the stock to the bestselling brands and do both—sell appliances *and* use some of the floor space for other stock."

Mom was staring at her, either riveted or shocked. Olivia was a little startled to have heard the energy in her voice and to realize how enthusiastic she was.

So, okay, maybe she *had* been thinking ahead. Somehow it hadn't occurred to her that her mother would very likely want to sell the business once Dad was gone. As in, the minute Dad was gone.

Mom blew out a breath. "Well. I knew you'd made some changes, but I hadn't realized how many ideas you have. I've been...well, a little self-absorbed."

"Dad hasn't been gone very long."

Um...not the most tactful thing to say, when they'd both been trying to be conciliatory.

Without moving a muscle, Marian withdrew.

"No, of course not," she said with obvious reserve. "I suppose my instinct is to tell you to go ahead with your plans within reason. Even if we decide to sell, success should bring a higher price."

At least she'd said "we."

"Why don't you talk to Mr. Swenson so we can get an idea what it would cost to take over his business and lease?" her mother suggested. "After that, we can both think about what's best."

"That makes sense," Olivia agreed. "I can…help you with the house in the meantime."

Mom lowered her gaze. "Thank you. My goodness, our food is getting cold."

Prompted, Olivia picked up her fork. It occurred to her that eating together wasn't something they seemed to do very well anymore.

Several bites later, her mother said, "Did I see you with Ben Hovik today?"

She froze with the stroganoff halfway to her mouth. Mom could only have seen them in the rearview mirror while she was retreating.

"We talked for a minute."

"Such a handsome man. It's a shame you let him get away."

Olivia set down the fork. "*Let* him get away? He ditched me, Mom."

Her mother must have seen the gathering anger on her face, because she said hastily, "I didn't mean that the way it sounds. It's just that, well, I've had the impression he could be interested again."

"Would *you* want to open a second act with a man who'd dumped you the first time around?"

Her mother's mouth trembled, and after a moment she neatly folded her napkin and set it on the table to signify that she was done, although she hadn't eaten half of what was on her plate. "No," she murmured. "When you put it that way...no."

Upside of both losing their appetites? They had leftovers for tomorrow night's dinner.

OLIVIA'S HAND HOVERED over the telephone on her desk in the office. She already had the phone book open: Crescent Creek School District appeared in the government pages at the front. All she had to do was dial the number for the high school and ask to speak to the principal.

She wished she could be absolutely sure she wasn't using what she'd overheard as an excuse to talk to Ben. It was only yesterday she'd indulged in true confessions. What would he think, her calling the very next day?

Olivia moaned. Maybe she should call the police department instead... She got as far as starting to close the phone book before stopping and spreading it open again. No. This was really more Ben's bailiwick. He might even know enough to say, *No, the police investigated and there's no truth to it.*

Finally she dialed. When she asked to speak to Mr. Hovik, she had to give her name and was told, "I'll have to check to see if he's available right now."

Not a minute later, he came on. "Olivia? Is something wrong?"

"No, nothing like that. I mean, not really…" She rolled her eyes, then started again. "I heard something I thought I ought to pass on, that's all."

There was a slight pause. "Concerning?"

"The girl. Well, the night she died."

"Ah. Hold on a second, will you?" Muffled voices suggested someone else had been in his office. He came back on. "Olivia? Can you take time to have lunch and talk about this?"

Oh, heavens. *Had* she been hoping—?

Maybe, she thought. Then she remembered that sharp spike of anger she'd felt the day before when she'd said, *Would you want to open a second act with a man who'd dumped you the first time around?* No—she was doing what she believed was right, that's all.

"Sure," she said. "I didn't bring anything today."

"I won't suggest Guido's." There was amusement in his voice.

"Please don't."

"Not much privacy at the café or the Burger Barn." He sounded thoughtful.

"No."

They agreed on pizza. He'd pick her up.

She used the time before he came to study the loft space she was envisioning as an expanded clothing department. She tried to decide how much of a deterrent the long staircase would be. Maybe to some of the older folks. In this vast old building, installing an elevator wasn't all that feasible, and certainly not in the foreseeable future. They could seed the downstairs, so to speak, with some of the products available upstairs. Tempt shoppers, but also make some appealing items available to people who really couldn't climb the stairs. Of course, she'd have to hire extra help…

Ben called her mobile phone when he was a couple of blocks away, and she stepped out on the sidewalk just as his Jeep pulled up in front of the hardware store, meaning he didn't have to find parking. He leaned over to open the door for her. Her heart did some gymnastics at the sight of his lean, handsome face. Thank God he wasn't smiling. Given her history, she'd probably have fallen off the curb.

She was belting herself in when a horn sounded behind them.

Ben glared into his rearview mirror. "Makes me want to just sit here for about ten minutes," he muttered but immediately started moving anyway. "Downtown parking is grossly inadequate."

"You're telling me?" Olivia was glad for a neutral topic. "I've been campaigning for angled parking. I think the street is wide enough, and it would accommodate a few more cars on every block."

"Plus pleasing anyone who didn't master parallel parking."

"Right." She couldn't help smiling, even though

they both knew he was reminding her of the driving lessons he'd given her. She had been an exceedingly timid parallel parker. Still was; living in downtown Portland, she had rarely driven.

They talked about other possibilities, including a city-owned block not far away that could be converted to parking.

The pizza parlor turned out to be mostly deserted, maybe because the usual lunch hour had passed. The couple of other groups didn't pay any attention to their arrival. Not until she and Ben were seated in a booth and had ordered did he prompt her. "What did you hear, Olivia?"

"You know how many kids we have working for us."

He nodded. "I've sent a few your father's way."

"Right. He said you'd persuaded him to hire Tim Allard." A senior in high school now, Tim had shaggy hair and a sort of sullen, hulking mien. She'd blinked the first time she saw him, but he'd grown on her.

"He still working out?"

"Lloyd says Tim is his best worker. If Tim is interested, Lloyd would like to hire him full-time once he graduates."

"Good." Raising a questioning brow, Ben waited for her to go on.

"Anyway, I was out in the lumberyard yesterday afternoon and overheard a couple of the boys. They didn't see me in the next row. They were talking about a kegger, how lucky they were that word hadn't leaked out." She wished she didn't feel as if she was betraying a confidence.

His dark eyes were steady on her face. "What makes you think this kegger was that night? It's been almost six weeks."

She took a deep breath. "One of them was nervous—I could tell. The other one said, 'If anybody had talked, the police would have been all over us, and they haven't been.' No, a direct quote is, 'So far we've skated.'"

A nerve ticked in his cheek. "Damn," he said. "I've been afraid of something like this."

She stared at him in astonishment. "Wait. You mean...you *knew*?"

CHAPTER THREE

"Knew?" Ben shook his head. "No. I've just had an uneasy feeling that something wasn't right. Too many conversations that fell silent when I was seen approaching. Tension. Maybe—" he had to think it out while he was talking "—a different kind of shock than I'd expect at the announcement of the girl's death."

Olivia crossed her arms on the table and leaned forward, her vivid hazel eyes fixed on his face. "What do you mean?"

"I held an assembly." He waited for her nod. "A lot of the kids—freshmen and sophomores—reacted about how I'd expected. They were ghoulishly fascinated. Most likely thinking, Wow, horror movie awful, and she was, like, *our* age."

Olivia smiled at his mimicry, as he'd meant her to do despite the grim subject.

"But the juniors and seniors went really quiet. Not all of them. I saw heads turning, but also a lot of people not looking at anyone else. Definitely shock." This was the first time he'd put any of this into words. "I didn't necessarily have the sense they'd all gone on a rampage and were now afraid I knew. But I had to wonder whether a whole lot of them either thought they knew what happened or at least suspected something."

"You must have asked questions."

"In a subtle kind of way. Did a lot of eavesdropping, too."

She made a face. "Like I was doing."

"Yeah, sometimes I think it's a shame the architect didn't add a secret passage that leads behind the lockers." He waggled his eyebrows. "I could know all."

He hadn't heard that small choked laugh in an eon. Or seen the tiny dimple that flickered in one cheek. Mostly because he hadn't seen a lot of amusement or happiness on her face since she'd been back in town.

Her smile faded, though. "So you haven't learned anything."

He lost any vestige of humor, too. "No, and that's made me even more uneasy. High school kids aren't good at keeping secrets, not en masse, and not for so long. A girl being sexually molested at home, she's got it down to a fine art. But when more than one kid knows?" Ben shook his head. "After so many weeks, I'd almost convinced myself I was imagining things."

"I could be wrong," she offered. "I mean, it might just have been a party that got wild and didn't have anything to do with that girl. Maybe at somebody's house when the parents weren't home, and damage was done."

He shrugged acknowledgment. "You're right. But if it was that bad, wouldn't you expect the parents to have been bitching?" He shook his head. "I don't believe it."

He could tell Olivia didn't, either. From her quote, it was apparent the boys she'd overheard were scared, not just afraid someone's dad would be pissed. Nothing out of the ordinary had happened this fall in Crescent Creek—except for the one tragic death—so there had to be some sort of connection there.

Their pizza arrived. Different waitress than he and Carson had had, fortunately. He didn't tell her he'd eaten here last night with his son. He was glad to have gone with a veggie special today, for a change of pace.

They dropped the subject for a minute, but between bites, he asked about the boys she'd heard talking.

"Maybe you don't want to tell me who they were." She looked uncomfortable, and he nodded. "I assume they were juniors or seniors?"

"I think all the kids we employ are. I mean, they have to be sixteen."

"Right." He frowned. "Tell me one of them wasn't Tim."

Olivia chuckled. "No, Tim doesn't talk."

Ben laughed. "You're right. I don't know what I was thinking."

"I'll ask Lloyd to keep an ear to the ground, too," she offered.

Lloyd Smith was roughly the same age her father had been, early sixties. Growing up, Ben hadn't known him well, but his face was familiar. He had thinning white hair, a deeply creased face and brown eyes framed by crow's-feet. Days spent lifting heavy sheets of plywood and operating the forklift kept him lean and fit. He seemed like a good guy to Ben.

"He okay with you being in charge?" he asked.

"He seems to be. I half expected a problem, since I'd never worked with him before. He was at the lumber mill, you know, before they closed the doors."

Ben nodded.

"But he says he's happy running his side and letting me handle the hardware side. Claims he doesn't know much about keeping the books, but I've found him to be sharp when we sit down to try to figure out directions to go." She took a couple of bites before her next question showed that her thoughts had reverted to Jane Doe. "Have you talked to the police?"

"Sure." The Crescent Creek Police Department consisted of the chief and five officers, two of whom weren't that long out of high school themselves. It was the chief himself who had been to see Ben immediately, the morning Marsha found the girl. "Chief Weigand's first thought was that the girl had to have friends here in town. Why else would she be here? It was at his prompting that I called the assembly. He spoke to the kids, described her, asked for a call if she sounded familiar to anyone. He borrowed an artist from the sheriff's department, and they got out a sketch as soon as possible."

Again, Olivia nodded. Presumably they hadn't been able to make a dead girl look alive enough to want to flash around a photograph. Especially to kids, he thought, although he worried about the liberties the artist had had to take to give that illusion of life.

"Did he notice the reaction you described?" she asked.

"He didn't comment. I didn't, either. How could I, when I don't know anything?"

And, God—when he'd been excruciatingly aware that Carson had been out the night before. Supposedly spending it at a friend's house, but who knew? *He* was one of the students whose reaction to the news had been subtly off. Who had been more withdrawn than usual since. And until Ben knew what role, if any, his son had in the events being kept hushed up…he'd as soon the secret wasn't sprung open.

Seeing the slight crinkles in Olivia's high, usually smooth forehead, he was assailed by guilt. She thought they were having an open and honest exchange of information, and really he was holding something in reserve.

But how could he help it? His first loyalty went to Carson. It had to.

"So...what do we do?" she asked.

He was warmed by that "we" even as he shifted on the bench in renewed discomfort because he was holding out on her.

"I don't know what we can do but keep an ear out."

That dimple quirked again. "Thumbscrews," she suggested.

It felt good to laugh again, to let go of the guilt. "Keep some in my desk drawer."

He was pleased when she asked how he'd ended up in administration instead of teaching, and especially how he'd gotten himself hired as principal when he was younger than most of the teachers at the high school. He hoped it meant she was curious and not just scrabbling for a topic to get them through the rest of the meal.

He told her about going back for his master's degree even as he taught high school history and government, then making the decision to return full-time for a doctorate in education. "I always liked to be in charge," he admitted. He opened his mouth to say, *I guess you knew that*, but he changed his mind when he saw the way her eyes narrowed. "I wouldn't have had a chance at a position as principal anywhere but here, not so soon. I gather they weren't getting many quality applicants, and, well, I was the hometown boy."

"So that's why you moved back."

"Partly," he said, then shook his head. "Mostly it was for Carson's sake. You know I have a stepson?"

Her "I'd heard" wasn't very revealing.

"I thought he needed family." He shrugged. "This seemed like a good opportunity all around."

She nodded. He waited for her to ask about Carson—why he was raising a boy who wasn't his biologically—but she didn't go there. Either she wasn't curious, or she didn't want to admit to being.

So he asked what her plans were, and she told him she really didn't know.

"I never intended my return to be permanent. When I first came, I thought I was just filling in for Dad." She sighed. "Then I was so focused on him, I didn't think much about the future. It was just day to day."

She looked so sad, Ben wanted to lay his hand over hers, but he didn't dare.

"And now it isn't necessarily in your hands." He'd no sooner heard about Charles Bowen's death than he'd worried that it meant Olivia would be returning to whatever life she'd temporarily laid aside. That was when it struck him that her mother must now own the store. And Marian had never, as far as he knew, so much as worked part-time to help out. If she could get a good price for the business, why would she want to keep it?

The "if" was a big one, though; in small-town America, "Going Out of Business" signs were more common than transfers of ownership were.

"Yeah, you're right." Her smile was small and crooked. "That hit me about the same time she announced she was selling the house. I've been having fun running with some ideas—only suddenly, it was *bam.* Not my store, not my decision."

"Tough," he said with a nod.

She told him some stuff she and her mother had talked about—including the fact that they *had* talked last night. Made up after their lunchtime debacle. He liked all her ideas for the business and was impressed at how well thought out they were. The hardware store had always been solid, and, from all reports, her dad had made a success of the lumberyard, too. Ben couldn't imagine that Charles had done much to build the business into anything bigger and better in recent years, though, not the way she seemed to do by instinct.

"Was opening the lumberyard your idea?" he asked.

"Well…we talked about it." She showed some shyness. Didn't want to imply she was smarter than her father, he suspected. "Hamilton's went out of business the summer between my junior and senior years in college. So…I guess I might have prodded Dad some."

Ben nodded. "Your mother was receptive to your ideas?"

"Willing to think about them, anyway." Olivia made a face. "As she pointed out, the higher the receipts, the better price she'll get if she does decide to sell."

Was it possible the business had been in Charles's name alone, meaning Marian now had to wait for probate to sell it anyway? The house had presumably been in both their names, so she wouldn't be hampered the same way. Could that be why she'd so generously encouraged Olivia to try to build business? If so, Ben wished she'd been honest with her daughter. Otherwise, Olivia was going to be hurt when probate was complete and her mother brought down the hammer.

Damn, he hoped that wasn't the case.

"You'd be working for your mom," he pointed out.

She made a horrible face at him. "I am so trying not to think of it that way."

He laughed and didn't argue when she then decided she really needed to get back to work. A glance at his watch startled him; they'd been talking longer than he'd realized.

She was so insistent on splitting the bill, he had to agree. He reminded himself of his philosophy with teenagers: *don't push.* Olivia was as wary as any adult-leery sixteen-year-old.

He winced at the thought. Yeah, she had been

sixteen when he'd broken up with her. Not a good memory. *Leery* was probably a good word for what she felt, though, assuming it wasn't way stronger.

During the short drive, she said suddenly, "Chief Weigand has been really closemouthed about the girl. Everybody talks about her freezing to death, but is that really what happened? Was she injured? Sick? Drunk? Has he said anything to you?"

"I think it's clear the freezing to death part is accurate, but you're right. He hasn't wanted to say what else he knows. I'm actually surprised he's been able to keep so much information close to his chest."

Olivia would know what he meant. *Small town* translated to few secrets and gossip transmitted at a speed faster than light. Which made the mystery all the more shocking—and it all the more improbable that nobody at all knew anything. Nonetheless, Ben didn't like the idea that any number of people might know little bits of something, puzzle pieces that, if shared, would put together the whole picture. Yes, there was lots of talk about her death, but he'd have expected some of those puzzle pieces to be slotted into place by now. And yet not a one had been.

The girl had to have hitched a ride with someone, for example. And since the highway closed in winter only a few miles past Crescent Creek, that ride had been with someone going *to* Crescent Creek, not a trucker passing through. If she'd been in good health, not drunk, not injured, she wouldn't have died out there however cold the night. If she *was* drunk—she probably hadn't gotten that way alone. If injured—how?

And, God, he had a sudden thought he should have had earlier. The autopsy would have revealed whether she'd had sex recently before her death. Was there any chance Phil Weigand had some DNA and was waiting patiently for a suspect to emerge to whom he could match it?

No, I'm reaching, he told himself, trying to tamp down that anxiety. There'd been no suggestion of murder. Sure, everyone wanted to know how she'd gotten there and why she hadn't asked for help, but mostly they wanted to know who she was.

Still—damn, he wished he knew whether Carson had been at that kegger.

Olivia gave no sign of noticing his abstraction. The moment he braked in front of the hardware store, once again double-parking, she reached for the door handle. "I'll let you know if I hear any more," she said breezily and hopped out. "Thanks for listening."

He barely had a chance to say goodbye before she was gone. There was not the slightest suggestion she'd enjoyed talking to him, would welcome a call asking her out.

On his way to pick her up, he'd been worried about what she'd heard but had also felt...hopeful. Having her call the very next day after they'd talked... Now, half a block from the hardware store, he had to sit briefly at one of the town's four red lights. The hope had leaked out, as if it were air in a balloon she'd punctured.

What he'd been doing was dreaming, without the slightest encouragement.

Would they have made it, if he'd been patient and smart enough to wait for Olivia to grow up? He grunted. No way to know. Water under the bridge.

Besides, her mother might announce tomorrow that she was putting the business up for sale along with the house.

Maybe, Ben admitted, bleakly, for him that might be for the best.

SUNDAY MORNING, BEN woke to an astonishing silence. Frowning, he focused on the digital clock on the bedside table, groaning as soon as he saw what time it was. He'd overslept. Mom wouldn't approve if he didn't appear at church.

Thinking about it, he threw off his covers. Was Carson still asleep? And, damn it, given the hour, why was it so quiet out there?

His suspicion was confirmed the minute he looked out the window. The world was cloaked in white, and the snow was still coming down in lazy, gentle flakes.

Well, the Lord was going to be responsible for skimpy attendance at his houses of worship this Sunday morning.

"Hey!" Carson's voice came from behind him. "It's awesome!"

"Well, at least it's Sunday."

"Bummer," his son said. "If this was tomorrow, we could have had a day off."

"You may still get one off, although it's not coming down the way it must have during the night."

A storm had been forecast, but not the eight inches or more that already blanketed the front yard and street.

Now that he listened, he heard a snowplow working in the distance. He'd be able to get around with his four-wheel drive, but not everyone would. He and Carson could have their driveway shoveled in twenty minutes, but folks farther out of town with long driveways...

No surprise, it was Olivia he was thinking about. She and her mother would be trapped this morning. Unless—

"Let's have breakfast," he suggested, "then get out and clear our driveway."

"Do we have to?"

He laughed and clapped Carson on the back. "We have to. But I'm not making you go anywhere if you don't want to."

"We don't have to go to church?" the boy asked hopefully.

"We wouldn't make it in time if we wanted to." He had only a small moment of guilt at having implied he didn't much want to go, either.

As he mixed up pancake batter a few minutes later, Ben decided to wait until they were outside and their muscles warmed up before he suggested performing a good deed. He could pretend it had just occurred to him.

Yep. His kid wouldn't see right through that.

And...which part of *giving up* didn't he get?

As he watched butter sizzle on the griddle, Ben admitted that he wouldn't be giving up, not until he heard Olivia had left town again, and for good this time.

Worse came to worst, he and Carson could feel virtuous because they *had* performed a good deed.

"WHO ON EARTH...?" Olivia's mother exclaimed, setting down her cup of coffee. The two sat at the breakfast table, where they'd been making lists of supplies they'd need to begin packing.

Olivia's head came up. She'd heard the voices at the same time. "Maybe kids playing out in the snow?"

"That doesn't sound like kids to me."

And the voices should have come from farther away, too. The Bowen house only sat on an acre, but neighbors had at least as much land, and even if the people on either side had grandkids visiting, they wouldn't be right outside. There was no hill out front good for sledding, much to Olivia's regret when she was a kid. In fact, the closest hill that offered decent sledding was far enough away, she'd had to wait until one of her parents could drive her—which meant shoveling a very long driveway first.

Leaving pencil and list behind, she reached the front window with her mother close behind. Two men were shoveling their driveway. The voices were theirs, as was the laughter. As she watched in astonishment, one threw a snowball at the other, who dropped his shovel and bent to pack a snow-ball of his own.

"Oh, my goodness," Marian murmured. "Isn't that...?"

Olivia was gaping. "Yes. It's Ben and his son."

"They came all the way out here to make sure we could get out of the house." For just a moment, Mom looked like...well, like *Mom*, her eyes amused.

Olivia couldn't think of a single thing to say. A fist seemed to have closed around her heart, which might explain why she was breathless. *Say something,* she ordered herself.

"I should go out and help."

"That's a good idea," her mother agreed. She chuckled, watching as Carson whopped a gloveful of snow against his father's neck. "Dress warmly."

Suddenly energized, Olivia donned boots, parka, scarf and gloves faster than she could remember moving in quite a while. Just as she opened the front door, Marian called from the kitchen, "Invite them in when they're done. It never seems worth

baking just for the two of us, but I'll make a coffee cake."

Man and boy stopped wrestling when Olivia
stepped gingerly from the porch into snow that had
to be nearly a foot deep. Having started shoveling
down at the road, they were still quite a ways away.
She waved. "I'll grab my shovel."

She saw the flash of white teeth as Ben grinned.
"Guess we got distracted."

He looked...amazing. Even bulkier in quilted
pants and parka, the color in his cheeks high. The
dark shadow on his jaw told her he hadn't bothered
shaving this morning.

Carson might be a stepson, but with his height he
could have been Ben's biologically, too. Their coloring was the greatest contrast. His hair was sandy,
not dark like Ben's, his eyes light-colored...blue,
she saw, as the two tramped toward her. His grin
was as bright and friendly as his dad's.

Olivia hadn't felt butterflies like this in a very
long time. Ben hadn't decided to come shovel her
driveway because he felt sorry for the two lone
women. There were a lot of single women in town.
He might as well have presented her with a bouquet
of red roses. Which she'd have sworn she didn't
want him to do, but—

Dismay washed over her. Oh, damn, she was
more susceptible than she'd believed. The trouble
was, he'd gone from being the sexiest boy in her
high school to being...the sexiest man she'd ever

seen. No, it was more than that, she knew. The warmth flooding her also had to do with her realization the other night that, despite their past, she did trust him in many ways.

"I was just wishing we had a nearby hill for sledding," she said, because she had to say *something*.

"Yeah, cool," Carson exclaimed. "The one by the high school is perfect."

He was packing another snowball when Olivia let herself into the garage, but she was aware that Ben was watching her. When she reappeared, his dark eyes were still trained on the doorway. Hoping her blush wasn't obvious, she narrowed her eyes at Carson. "You weren't planning to greet me with that, were you?"

"Nah." He turned and slung it at his father, who dodged just in time and then grabbed the boy in a headlock. They were both laughing by the time Ben let him go.

"This is awesome," his son said.

"We could go sledding once we finish here," Ben suggested. "What do you say, Olivia?"

She hadn't felt even the tiniest spark of pleasure this morning when she'd looked out the window and saw the snowy landscape. All she'd been able to think was that they'd buried her father a week ago today. So it felt really good now to see the wonder in it.

"I say yes. Except first you have to come in and have coffee and a goodie Mom is baking right now."

Ben laughed, his teeth a brilliant flash of white. "I think we can manage that. We'll have worked up an appetite."

Olivia looked at the expanse of pristine snow marked only with their parallel tracks. "Maybe I should start on this end while you take up where you left off."

"No fun. We're here now. Might as well work our way back to the road." Ben yanked off the red fleece hat he'd been wearing. "Your ears will get cold." He put the hat on Olivia, tugging off one glove so he could smooth her hair beneath it. "There. I'm already warm."

Had his fingers lingered momentarily? She hoped the color in her cheeks could be explained by the cold. "Thanks." She turned a smile on the teenager. "I've seen you, but I don't think we've met. I'm Olivia."

"Carson." He grinned. "Dad said this was our good deed for the day."

"In lieu of church attendance," his father said with mock solemnity.

"Rescuing the little women," she said.

"Right," the boy agreed.

"Except the little woman isn't so little," she pointed out.

"Did I tell you Olivia took our girls' basketball team to a league championship her senior year?" Ben asked his son. "She was a heck of a center."

That caused a sting. Suddenly she wasn't smiling. "How would you know? You were long gone."

They stared at each other for a moment. "I...actually came to a couple of games. Anyway, Mom kept me up-to-date," he said.

He'd come to watch her? Probably only because his parents were going to the game anyway and he was home, so why not?

"You were a center?" Carson studied her with open interest. "I guess you are tall for a girl."

Olivia laughed. "And that's a compliment, right?"

He *really* looked like his dad right now. "Right." He spoiled his solemnity with a big grin. "Who likes little bitty girls anyway?"

Olivia mumbled, "Most men," at the exact same moment when Ben said something under his breath that might have been, "Not me."

His kid smirked.

"Work," Ben reminded them.

CHAPTER FOUR

THEY DID SHOVEL, working as a team except for the occasional impulse to pack a snowball and chase each other all over the yard. By the time they actually made it to the road, they were all breathing like dragons, red-cheeked and good-humored. Olivia, at least, was feeling the strain in her shoulders and upper arms.

She turned and surveyed their accomplishment as well as the trampled front yard. "If only it weren't still snowing."

"Yeah, but it's not coming down that hard." Ben groped in his jeans pocket and produced his keys. "Catch," he told Carson. "Why don't you move the Cherokee up here?"

"Me?" The boy's face brightened. "Yeah! Cool." He trotted toward the SUV.

"Does he have his license yet?" Olivia asked.

"No, but he's taking driver's ed this semester. I've been letting him practice." Ben grimaced. "Not so much in the snow, though."

Olivia suppressed her smile as they both watched Carson give a cheerful wave and hop into the red

Jeep Cherokee. "There's not much he can run into between there and here." She turned on her heel. "Except the garage doors, I guess. Mom might not appreciate that."

"Yeah, and us." Ben's hand on her arm drew her up the driveway. "Although I *have* taught him to brake."

"You were such a stodgy driver for a teenage boy." Olivia cursed herself the minute the words were out. Reminders of their past were not a good idea.

"That's a compliment, right?" he said, deliberately echoing her from a minute ago.

She had to laugh.

"He's doing okay for a kid. In fact, he's sure he has it all down pat, which means he's cocky."

She wondered at the shadow that crossed his face after that. What was he thinking as he watched Carson carefully maneuver the Cherokee up the driveway, braking neatly in front of the garage only a few feet from them?

"He's on the basketball team, right?" she asked.

"Huh?" He turned his head. "Carson? Yeah. He's not real happy because he didn't start Friday night. There's something going on with the team. I don't know what."

"You can't exactly go berate the coach because your kid didn't get enough playing time, can you?"

He made a sound in his throat that she recognized as frustration. "No, I have to step carefully. In this case…"

The driver's side door slammed. Carson ostentatiously stashed the keys in his own pocket. Ben's eyebrows rose, but he didn't say anything.

"Did your dad tell you he helped me learn to parallel park?" Olivia asked.

"Sort of," Ben muttered, and she elbowed him.

"I passed the driver's test, didn't I?"

"Pure luck."

Her elbow brought a sharp exhalation this time. "Skill."

Carson watched them with obvious interest. "You guys, like, hooked up when you were in high school, didn't you?"

"A very long time ago," Olivia agreed, not looking at Ben as she led the way onto the front porch. "I got together with a bunch of old high school friends Friday night. Nicki was in town," she said as an aside to Ben. "It got me thinking. I was sixteen years old when your dad and I broke up, and *that* was sixteen years ago."

"You were *my* age?" The horror in the teenager's voice made both adults laugh, although Ben's was more subdued than Olivia's.

"Well, I was a little older." Ben's tone was cautious. "Eighteen."

"Weird," his kid pronounced.

They stamped the snow from their boots, stepped inside and took off their parkas, hats and gloves in the entryway, laying them on the tile floor. Leaving boots there, too, they padded in stocking feet to the kitchen. The spicy smell of baking worked like a beacon.

"Mrs. B." Ben went to her mother and kissed her cheek. "Good to see you under better circumstances."

Marian's smile dimmed at the reminder that their last meeting was at the funeral, but she relaxed again when he introduced Carson. She cut generous slabs of a cinnamon-flavored cake, and they sat talking while they ate it and sipped coffee. Perhaps inevitably, Olivia's mother remarked on how proud she'd been of Ben for starting the initiative to bury that poor girl.

Carson ducked his head. Death, it occurred to Olivia, didn't often become quite so real to kids.

"It's so hard to believe no one at the high school recognized her," Marian said. "Are kids talking about it still?"

Ben's gaze rested inscrutably on his son's averted face. "Not as much as I'd have expected. Carson?"

He gave a jerky shrug. "There's not that much to say. I mean, since no one knew her."

"I suppose it wasn't all that different from reading in the newspaper about something like this happening elsewhere in the country." Marian gave a small laugh. "Or should I say, reading online?"

"Probably." Ben smiled at her.

"I almost wish people would quit talking about

her." Not until she saw the way the others all stared at her did Olivia realize how vehemently she'd said that.

"What do you mean?" Ben asked.

"Oh…I get the feeling a lot of people don't care about her at all. They're too busy congratulating themselves for their generosity to bother imagining her as a real person. Someone scared. Cold." Out of the corner of her eye, she saw Carson's body jerk and she wondered about that, but not much. She wasn't sure she hadn't shuddered herself. "And then there are the ones who got to see themselves on TV and haven't gotten over it."

Creases in Ben's forehead had deepened. "Don't you think it's normal for people to feel good after they've done something a little above and beyond?"

"Oh, I suppose." She knew he was right. The people who didn't want to talk about the girl at all bothered her just as much, but she knew that was dumb. Not everyone was given to brooding about a tragedy that didn't directly impact their own lives. A couple of times lately she'd caught herself speculating, though… But that was dumb, too. Just because someone was brusque to the point of being rude when the subject arose didn't mean a guilty conscience. "Where do you hear people talking?" Ben asked, seeming genuinely curious.

"Mostly in line at Bowen's." She rolled her eyes. "I swear sometimes our regulars come in to pick up something they don't even need just to have a chance to gossip."

Ben's expression lightened. "Aren't women supposed to be the worst gossips?"

She made a face at him. "Don't believe it."

"Come on." He was definitely amused now. "Men are strong and silent. You know that."

Olivia snorted. Ben laughed, but Mom didn't. In fact, she looked strained, making Olivia remember the silence that had run so dark and deep between her parents. Maybe this wasn't the best of topics.

"We were thinking about going sledding," she announced. "Although now that I can feel my toes again, I'm not so sure."

"Don't be a wimp." Ben smiled at her with warm brown eyes. "It'll be fun."

"I'll probably be the oldest person on the hill." Oh, she was pathetic, wanting to be talked into going.

"Nope. That'd be me."

"I don't suppose you want to come and be the oldest person?" she asked her mother, who shook her head firmly.

"Not a chance."

New widows probably didn't appear in public playing in the snow, it occurred belatedly to Olivia. Did grieving daughters?

Dad wouldn't mind. And the truth was…she'd been mourning him for almost a year already, knowing full well they were losing him.

Which was true of Mom, too, of course, which made it more reasonable for her to have decided already what she wanted to do about the house. Olivia discovered she didn't feel that forgiving, though.

And I won't think about it right now.

Instead, she was going to let herself have fun.

"Oh, fine," she said, getting up to take her dishes to the sink. "Do you know if we still have a sled out in the garage?"

"I think so," her mother said. "Did your father ever get rid of anything?"

The sharpness in her voice caused a silence that went on a moment too long. Mom must have heard herself, because in a different tone, she said, "Look up on the rafters. That's where the skis are."

"Ooh, do I still have cross-country equipment?" Olivia hadn't even thought to look last year. It had been a mild winter, for one thing, at least when she'd returned to Crescent Creek. And with Dad looking so much worse than she'd expected, and her having to take over the store, frolicking in the snow had been the last thing on her mind. "I don't know if I still have ski boots."

"Attic," her mother said. "I'm sure some of your winter clothes are still there."

"Oh, lord. I didn't even think of the attic." Their eyes met, and they were both thinking the same thing. *Packing.*

Not today.

Her mother ended up shooing them out after

wrapping most of the remainder of the coffee cake for Ben and Carson to take home.

This time Olivia dug out a hat for herself and found dry gloves to replace the ones wet from packing snowballs earlier. Ben followed her into the garage and used a step stool to pull an old-fashioned Radio Flyer sled down. Carson looked thrilled; apparently all he and his dad had was a plastic disc.

"Man, you can steer those."

"Kinda, sorta," she said, remembering some spectacular crashes. And a few runs down the hill with her squeezed between Ben's long legs and his arms encircling her, too.

Ben waggled his hand as he went to the back of the Cherokee. "Keys?"

Carson dug them out of his pocket with obvious reluctance. "I can drive, right?"

"I don't think so. Risking my life, that's one thing." A smile flickered at the corners of his mouth. "Olivia's, now, that's something else."

"Hey!" his son protested. "It's not that hard!"

"This actually might be a good chance for him to practice, if you feel brave," Ben said. "I didn't let him on the way here because I wasn't sure if the main roads were plowed. There isn't much traffic right now, though."

"I'm good with it," she said.

Grinning his triumph, Carson circled to the driver's side. Ben rode up front with him—so he could grab the wheel if he had to, she teased—and Olivia settled in the backseat.

Carson actually did pretty well during the short drive into town. Once he overcorrected during a skid, but he came out of it and nodded when Ben said something quietly.

She had known where they lived, but was just as glad Ben didn't suggest going in when they stopped at his house. He jumped out, going into the garage through a side door and returning with the bright blue plastic disc. Waiting, she studied the two-story house, modest like most in Crescent Creek, but one of the oldest in town. It was a simple farmhouse style with a porch that ran the full width of the front. The backyard was fenced. When she asked, Carson said he'd wanted to get a dog, but he was allergic so Dad had said no.

"It's dumb. I mean, I can be around them now," he was complaining, when Ben got back in.

"Around who?" he asked, fastening his seat belt.

"Dogs."

"Ah. The animals that sent you into full-blown asthma attacks when you were little. Attacks that meant you had to be *hospitalized.*"

"I've outgrown the asthma," Carson said sulkily.

"Maybe partly because we don't have any pets," his father said mildly.

Carson looked ostentatiously in all his mirrors before backing out onto the as yet unplowed street, then starting sedately forward. Olivia relaxed. If he crashed here in town, no one would die, not with a twenty-five-mile-an-hour speed limit.

They had to park a couple of blocks from the hill leading up to the high school, new since she and Ben had gone there. Once they'd parked and started stomping through the snow, Carson carrying the plastic disc under his arm and Ben pulling the sled by its rope, they could hear the whoosh of sleds coming down the hill. Excited voices rose.

Ben gazed upward. "You been to the new high school?"

"Not to go in," Olivia said. "I drove up one day just to see it." She'd actually been thinking about attending the Friday night home game, until her friend Polly had called to invite her to dinner. Maybe another night.

Ben and Carson called hello to people they knew, introducing Olivia to a few. She was astonished at how many of the adults she recognized—some who'd been recent customers at the store, but more who'd been her schoolmates and now had children.

"Why don't you try the sled?" she suggested to Carson, who demurred just long enough to be polite before sitting down on it, scooting forward with his heels, then gliding forward. He was really moving by the time he reached the bottom, letting out one delighted whoop.

She insisted Ben go next, accepting the accusation of cowardice and watching as he shot down the hill, spun out of control and crashed into a snowbank.

While she waited for him and Carson, she warmed her hands over a fire someone had started in a burn barrel hauled to the street for that purpose, and she joined the general conversation.

"Olivia!" a familiar voice called, and she turned to see one of the women she'd had dinner with Friday night. Autumn had been a good friend in high school. Unlike the others in their crowd, she'd gotten married right out of high school and now had three kids, the oldest almost a teenager. In fact, two of her kids were currently preparing to launch themselves down the hill on a sled.

"I can't believe you're here!" Autumn exclaimed. "I thought you'd still be snowed in."

"Um…Ben Hovik and his son came and shoveled our driveway. He just went down the hill."

"I saw him." Her eyes narrowed. "Friday night, you stayed totally mum about Hovik Stage Two."

"There's no stage two," Olivia said. "We're just having fun today."

"Uh-huh. Back in high school, you'd been out with Ben like half a dozen times before you told *any* of us— Ooh! Sabrina's here, too."

Thank goodness for distractions.

Both turned to include another of Olivia's friends, this one a basketball teammate who had become a nurse and returned to Crescent Creek. Although Autumn and Olivia hadn't stayed in close touch, Friday night had been all about updating each other. It turned out Sabrina had married a former logger turned builder who'd been several years ahead of them in school and therefore not on their dating radar back then. Her husband, Aaron, was a regular at Bowen's, so Olivia greeted him with pleasure, too, when he appeared pulling a plastic disc, their two-year-old son riding his shoulders, half strangling his dad and giggling.

She had a surreal moment, looking around and realizing how many of the people at this casual gathering she knew and even considered to be friends. In all the years since leaving Crescent Creek, she'd been a city dweller who had become accustomed to being surrounded by strangers. She had forgotten what it was like to be part of a whole instead of always standing apart.

A lovely, warm feeling filled her, except as she turned to watch Ben and Carson cresting the hill, she heard Autumn whispering to someone.

"With Ben Hovik, of all people..."

She never had been able to trust Autumn with a secret, Olivia remembered. If she'd confided in her the way she had in Ben the other day, everyone in Autumn's wide circle of acquaintances would know the Bowen marriage had been faltering even before Charles's death, and that Olivia and her mother weren't getting along.

So, you had to take the bad with the good, she reflected. Laughing at the sight of Ben still looking like the Abominable Snowman, she decided that, right this minute, the good was in ascendance.

Others started teasing him, but his gaze was fixed firmly on her.

"Bend your head," she told him, and when he obliged, she swiped at the snow clinging to his hat. "That," she told him, "is why *I* plan to stick to my sled."

"Yeah, but you've got to crash. What's the fun if you don't?"

Carson grinned at her, too. "Tall girls aren't afraid of crashing, are they?"

Man and boy let her go next. She steered herself right down the center of the hill, laughing in exhilaration the whole way, despite watering eyes and a face so cold her nose had gone numb. Oh, she'd missed doing things like this!

Inevitably Ben suggested they take a run together on the sled.

"Why not?" Olivia said recklessly. "Only who gets to steer?"

His face came vividly alive when he laughed. "Let's review. Which of us is the careful driver?"

"I haven't had a ticket in—" *Oops.* Seeing Carson's shocked expression, she said, "Um, quite a while."

"Right. *I'm* steering. Besides—" he gave her another rakish grin "—if you're in back, you wouldn't be able to see."

"I could sit in front and steer." If she could forget being in Ben Hovik's arms for the first time in forever. Okay, not really in his arms, but…close enough.

Ben sat down first and waited while she gingerly lowered herself on the sled, hesitated, then gave up and wrapped her arms around his thighs to hold on. Even through his quilted pants, she felt his muscles tighten as if in response. He took a good grip of the rope, Carson gave them a running push and they were off.

The rush of cold air and exhilaration were there this time, too. Hearing the rumble of Ben's laugh, feeling his rough cheek brush hers as he looked over her shoulder, made her heart do some stupid gymnastics.

The sled had just started to slow when he yanked hard on one side of the rope and steered them straight at a snowbank.

"What are you doing?" she yelled.

Wham. They both went flying, their bodies tangled together.

She ended up sprawled on top of Ben. For just a moment, she went utterly still, looking down at him. Past and present overlaid like transparencies. His face thinner, more boyish, but the laugh, oh so much the same. Crinkles beside those espresso-dark eyes that didn't used to be there. His mouth, more sensual now. A look on his face, both familiar and...not. The hunger was there, but something else, too.

She had to struggle for resolve but found it. *I am not doing this. Remember?*

His expression changed as she scrambled to get off him. "Olivia…"

"You did that on purpose," she snapped.

Ben sat up. "Yeah, I did. Is that so bad?"

"Ugh. Now I'm wet."

He rose a lot more lithely than she had and began to brush her off. "No, you're not. The snow is pretty dry."

And she was behaving badly. It wasn't like he'd tried to kiss her or anything.

But he was thinking about it.

The part that had her panicked was that *she'd* been thinking about it, too. And she knew maybe she was being unreasonable. Yes, he'd broken her very young heart, but *he'd* been very young, too. How many high school romances actually endured?

Autumn and Joe's had.

But how happy were they? Olivia had no idea, only that they were still together. But neither of them had wanted to leave town for four years of college.

Realizing she was doing nothing but standing there, staring at Ben, Olivia couldn't help thinking, *I could just as well have ended up breaking his heart, once I left for school.* That was reality.

So…why did he scare her so much?

"That was fun," she said, trying to sound natural. "Until you crashed us on *purpose,* anyway."

His face relaxed. "For old times' sake."

"Last time I let *you* steer," she declared.

He chuckled, a deep, slow sound that made her shiver. "You can steer anytime," he assured her, and it was not riding on the sled she pictured.

Not going there, she reminded herself, but this time she wasn't convinced.

OLIVIA WASN'T THE first to arrive at work Monday morning; Lloyd Smith's Chevy pickup was in its familiar slot. He beat her there almost every morning. She didn't know what she'd have done without Lloyd. The hardware business, she knew. Lumber, not so much, given that Dad hadn't added the lumberyard yet when she had worked for him. She'd have been in trouble trying to run that side without Lloyd.

The alley had been plowed, thank goodness, or they'd have both had to take up parking slots on the street. Even so, she slipped and almost fell on her way to the back door.

"Ugh," she mumbled, unlocking and entering. Snow had been way more appealing yesterday, when it was fresh. And, oh yeah, when she was playing in it with Ben.

Only a few of the lights were on. She turned on the rest as she went, including the Christmas lights strung along the eaves in front and the lights on the tree in the window. She did this even though she was dreading Christmas and would have preferred to skip the decorations this year here at the store as well as at home.

Home.

No, she wouldn't think about it, not right now.

Finally, she stopped to crank up the thermostat, too. The vast, barnlike building did not hold heat well.

The cluster of offices was in the loft: Lloyd's, her father's—at least temporarily hers—and the bookkeeper's. Olivia smelled coffee even before she reached the top of the staircase. Bless his heart, she needed another cup this morning.

He must have heard her footsteps, because he stood in his doorway waiting for her. His keen eyes searched her face. "No trouble getting into town?"

"Nope. Ben Hovik and his son came out and helped me shovel our driveway yesterday," she said, keeping her tone casual. "Otherwise, the roads were all plowed."

"You and your mom holding up okay? Anything new?" he asked gently.

She realized that, one way or the other, she and Lloyd had missed each other the past several days.

"Mom has already decided to sell the house," she told him. Everyone would know soon. Hard to hide a for-sale sign in the front yard. "I didn't know what to say. She's...not herself," Olivia said slowly, and that was the truth.

Well, part of the truth anyway.

"I'm sorry," Lloyd said, in that same kind voice, and this time she nodded and did succeed in smiling, if tremulously.

"We'll get through it."

"Sure you will." He cocked his head. "Sounds like Stu's here."

"Somebody is," she teased, despite the darkness of her mood. They had this conversation almost every morning. He was ridiculously good at identifying vehicles sight unseen from the sound of the engines, and Olivia gave him a hard time when he was wrong. This time she frowned, realizing it was a car engine she was hearing. "He hasn't driven his truck in forever. What's happened to it? Do you know?"

"All he'll say is it needs work."

Stuart Dodd's pickup had been his pride and joy. A Ford F-250, it couldn't have been more than a couple of years old.

"Shouldn't it still be under warranty?"

Lloyd shook his head. "No idea. He's being real tight-lipped, which makes me think he might have wrecked it and doesn't want to say."

She laughed despite herself. "That would be a blow to his pride, wouldn't it?" Stuart had worked for her father since a beam had fallen on his shoulder on a construction project, leaving him unable to do heavy lifting. His experience made him a godsend working with contractors. Olivia guessed him to be in his mid-forties.

Lloyd chuckled. "Yes, it would."

She let herself into her office and settled behind

her desk with a sigh, cradling the mug of coffee in both hands to warm them.

Most days she was glad to be here. Until she'd had to face the realization that Mom might sell the business, she hadn't let herself understand how much she was enjoying herself. Before Dad's first heart attack, she'd worked as an account manager at a major Portland investment firm. Dissatisfied, she'd been thinking about making a change, and she had quit without a second thought when her parents needed her. She could take some time off and help her parents, she had reasoned.

At the time, Olivia had expected to be here three or four months, tops. Now—she had no idea what she wanted to do next. She'd begun to wonder if she wasn't a small businesswoman at heart.

Something else, too. Thinking about what a tomboy she'd been had sparked a minor revelation. It wasn't like she'd make career decisions based on what she was required to wear to work every day, but…she wasn't missing having to wear suits and heels, do something elegant to her hair and put on makeup every morning. Jeans, flannel shirts, comfortable shoes, a ponytail—this felt really natural to her.

It's me, she thought.

She shook off the reflection, in part because, as Ben had pointed out, any possibility of her staying to run Bowen's Hardware & Lumberyard wasn't really hers, but also because brooding wasn't productive. She wanted to make time for sure today to talk to old Mr. Swenson about his plans for the appliance store. No point in starting to dream if it turned out he had a long-lost nephew planning to move to Crescent Creek to take over his store or already had a buyer.

Olivia spent the morning working the floor, as she frequently did, answering questions and helping people find the screws and bolts they asked for, pick out the best caulking material or identify the washer needed to stop that drip from the kitchen faucet. She loved the old building, with wood floors that creaked and weren't entirely level, those high ceilings and the cold drafts that came every time someone opened either the front or back entrance doors. Given a spare moment here and there, she considered the layout and eyed stray corners, trying to envision how she could expand the stock without aisles becoming claustrophobic or displays too cluttered.

The cash registers were the old-fashioned kind, although the credit-card machines weren't. Dad had modernized only as he had to.

"Nobody in Crescent Creek is interested in hurrying," he liked to say. In general, it was true. Like she'd told Ben, standing in line at the hardware store was as good a place to gossip as any.

This morning, passing by the short line at the front of the store, Olivia heard Bernard Fulton saying, "That damn wife of mine thinks we're going out to dinner tonight. Why can't she cook seven nights a week, I ask? She says, God didn't work seven days a week, either. I say, but this isn't Sunday—it's Monday. God liked Sundays, she says, I like Mondays."

Olivia stifled a laugh. June and Bernard had eaten at the Crescent Café every Monday night for as long as she could remember, and most Fridays, too. So did all their friends. Most of the men had once worked at the lumber mill. Lloyd and his wife would be there, too, just as they'd play bingo at the grange hall every other Saturday and plant their butts in the same pew every Sunday morning at the Grace Lutheran Church. Bernard and June were Presbyterian, if Olivia remembered right. Pete Peterson, currently listening tolerantly to Bernard, was Baptist. If your inclinations were for anything else, you had to drive at least as far as Miller Falls. Not many locals did.

Was this really what she wanted? she asked herself with some incredulity. By the time she'd graduated from high school, the predictability of every day, of everyone she knew, had begun to drive her crazy. She'd yearned for something different. For adventure. For a future different from the one that had been her dream, when it had included Ben.

And now here she was, taking a ridiculous sense of comfort from the very predictability that had once been such an irritant. Not minding gossip, because...oh, because it meant people were genuinely interested in each other's doings. Intrigued by the mystery of why Stuart wasn't talking about what was wrong with his Ford F-250, when her eighteen-year-old self would have pretended to be interested while really thinking, *Who cares?*

Discovering she did care gave her a funny ache beneath the breastbone, one that didn't want to go away no matter how busy she got.

CHAPTER FIVE

As yet unnoticed, Ben leaned one shoulder against the end of the bleachers and watched the boys' basketball practice.

Even though the weekend had been unexpectedly relaxed where Carson was concerned, he still felt the prickly grab of the burr that was his worry about him.

During the Friday night game, Carson had mostly sat on the bench with his elbows braced on his knees and his head hanging, his eyes downcast. His body language shouted, *I don't want to be here.* When he went in, he was a step too slow. Ben could see why McGarvie had benched him. The coach had probably had no choice. Ben had also seen the distance Carson was keeping from the stars of the team. Even when McGarvie called the team into a huddle to talk about strategy, Carson stayed on the outskirts, a careful arm's length from anyone else.

Something was wrong, above and beyond a rapidly growing boy's clumsiness.

He packed his observations at the game on top of Olivia's worries and his own, increasing that sense of foreboding. It might be an overreaction, but he couldn't shake the feeling. As a result, Ben had spent more time than usual today wandering the halls between classes, listening to snippets of conversation, talking to teachers and asking them to keep an ear to the ground for new rumors, and the only result by the time the last bell rang was that his uneasiness had grown, and he had not a grain of fact to base it on.

He didn't usually let himself watch basketball practice. Football, sure—but Carson didn't play football. Today, though, he had let his uneasiness drive him to the gymnasium.

He didn't like what he was seeing on the court, he knew that. Carson *wasn't* playing well, any more than he had Friday night. The ball bounced right off his hands a couple of times. He missed an easy layup. He let the guy he was guarding score, over and over.

But Ben also saw a couple of teammates take cheap shots at him. Hard rams with the shoulder. One tripped him, and Carson crashed to the floor. Other teammates had to notice, but they weren't saying anything. They didn't laugh when he went down, though, as they might have if it had been pure ungainliness; in fact, instead of taking off down court with the rest, Vadim Bukin stayed long enough to hoist Carson back to his feet.

Anger festering, Ben wondered how McGarvie could *not* be seeing what was going on.

And why the hell *was* it going on?

Had Carson gotten into it with those two guys, and this was payback time? They were teenage boys, loaded with testosterone. Sure, practice had gotten rough in Ben's time, too, but he didn't remember a time it wasn't two-way. This looked like a calculated attempt to intimidate Carson...or even get him to quit the team. Was that possible?

Is this my fault? Ben had to ask himself. But, damn, he hadn't done anything recently likely to impact the two seniors who were being such shits out there to his kid.

Had Carson gotten between one of the boys and something he wanted? A girl, say?

Ben grunted. Who knew? Apparently there was a lot going on in Carson's life he didn't know anything about.

He was even more baffled when he thought about the weekend, and especially Sunday. He'd felt remarkably close to Carson, who'd been so accepting of Olivia. Last night, when he wasn't exulting because Olivia had spent the day with him and seemed to have fun, Ben had let himself feel good about Carson. He'd imagined the constraint this past month or so, he almost convinced himself. Right now, they really felt like father and son, something that hadn't always been true. Still wasn't, he reminded himself, or Carson wouldn't fluctuate between calling him Dad and Ben. Ben wanted to be Dad 24/7.

Of course, whatever their relationship, Carson had to feel some push-pull because "Dad" was also the principal. Made sense he'd feel he needed to keep friends' secrets. Maybe that explained his recent silence. *Yeah,* Ben thought bleakly, *except I just saw* him *being the one with a problem.*

He left the gym and walked to his office, where he kept an eye on the parking lot out his window. The whole time he waited, his thoughts bounced between Carson and Olivia. The tension here at the high school…and her laughing face, cheeks made rosy by the cold, that sparkle of joy in her eyes. He'd forgotten how she transcended mere beauty when she was really happy.

It was long since dark by the time he saw the boys loping toward either their own cars or those of parents who'd arrived to pick them up. Not wasting any time, he made his way back to the locker room, glad to see the light was still on in Ray McGarvie's office.

In the act of shrugging into a parka when Ben appeared in his doorway, the coach looked surprised. "Ben. Thought I was the last one here."

Ben propped a shoulder against the door frame. "I watched practice today for a while," he said mildly.

McGarvie's eyes narrowed for a flicker. "You wondering why Carson didn't start Friday night?"

"It wasn't a surprise. He'd told me."

"That what you want to talk about?" The coach pushed a rolling chair toward Ben. "Have a seat."

"Thanks." He sat, trying to look more relaxed than he felt. "And, no, that's not why I'm here. You should know by now I try to keep my roles as parent and administrator strictly separate."

McGarvie lowered his greater bulk into the other chair. "What's up, then?"

What pissed Ben off was the air of caution the basketball coach couldn't hide. He knew what was going on, all right.

"I saw some aggression out on the court that I didn't like." He raised a hand. "I'd be saying this no matter what boy it was directed at. From where I was standing, I couldn't see you, but I kept thinking, McGarvie couldn't have missed that. Or that."

A great sigh gusted out of the coach's beefy chest. "No, I didn't miss a thing. But, damn it, Ben! You know the boys have to work these things out themselves."

"Even when it's the two team leaders conducting a vendetta on a younger boy?"

"Vendetta's a strong word. They've been a little rough with him, that's all. He hasn't gotten hurt."

"When did it start?" Ben asked.

"Pretty well from the minute we started practice." McGarvie rubbed a hand over his chin, expression thoughtful. "Surprised me, because I'd noticed Carson hanging out with them earlier in the fall."

Ben had noticed, too, and been less than thrilled. Dex Slagle seemed like an okay kid. He was a good student unlikely to be recruited to play basketball at the college level, but Ben knew his parents. He assumed Dex would at least be heading off to the University of Washington come next fall.

Dylan Zurenko was another story. He was smart, no doubt about that, but had a sly side Ben didn't like. He'd been accused last year of date rape, but it was too much of a he said–she said thing for an arrest, Chief Weigand had concluded. To Ben, he'd remarked privately that he thought the guy had done it.

"We need to watch that kid," the chief had said, voice hard, and Ben had agreed.

"It's not just Carson," McGarvie said finally. "Dylan doesn't like Asher Loomis, either."

"Have you called him on any of this?"

The coach sighed again. "Of course I have, but most of it's too subtle for me to be positive. You know this can be a rough sport. What I can't figure is why Carson isn't marshaling his own friends and fighting back. He's just taking it. Like…" He hesitated.

Like he thinks he deserves it, Ben finished silently. But, damn it, why?

"All right." He pushed himself to his feet. "I don't mean to criticize here. I just wanted to be sure you were aware that something is going on."

"I am, but so far nobody is telling me anything."

Ben grimaced. "Me, either."

"Harder being a parent than it is being a kid, isn't it?" McGarvie turned off the light and slapped Ben's back before locking the office door behind them.

Ben's answer was heartfelt. "One hell of a lot harder."

After Coach let himself out the side door, Ben strode back to the front of the school to make sure everyone else was gone. He checked locks on the way.

He had really believed he and Carson had finally achieved the kind of relationship that would stand up to the usual teenage troubles. This would teach him to congratulate himself too soon.

Sometimes he'd give almost anything not to be parenting alone. He had his parents, but this wasn't the kind of thing he could talk to them about. His mother especially wasn't good at keeping confidences. Before he knew it, she'd be hugging Carson and bursting out with, "We're so worried about you, honey. Your dad says…!"

He could talk to Olivia.

Ben shook his head in instant rejection of the thought. He was getting way ahead of himself. She'd listen, if only out of a sense of obligation, but how could he trust her to put Carson's welfare first? Especially if that girl's death turned out to be mixed up with the kegger that was being kept so quiet?

Ben wanted to think he was stretching there, connecting dots that didn't have anything to do with each other.

But if not…what was his kid hiding that was making him so miserable?

OLIVIA GRABBED SEVERAL flattened boxes, a roll of tape and a black marker, then started for the stairs. At the sight of her mother, framed by the kitchen doorway and looking stricken, Olivia's step momentarily hitched.

Mom still hadn't so much as taken a breath when Olivia started up the stairs.

She asked *me to do this.*

Yes, and Olivia knew why; going through Dad's closet and dresser, making decisions, would be less emotionally loaded for Olivia than for her mother. In theory. No, in truth. Think of all those years when she'd been home only for visits. There'd be clothes she wouldn't even recognize. Not every single garment would call up memories for her. Grief as a daughter was different than grief as a wife.

If Mom was grieving.

Trudging resolutely down the hall once she reached the second floor, Olivia knew better. Of course Mom was grieving, even if she was mad, too.

The bedroom didn't look any different than it normally did when empty, yet now the emptiness felt like the absence of oxygen. Like looking into a "bedroom" at a museum—the John Adams room—that had never actually been occupied by any human beings.

Ridiculous.

And, yes, she could have started somewhere else. She'd have to go through her own things she'd left behind, for example. But she'd told herself it made sense to get the hardest done first. Otherwise, knowing she had to deal with Dad's stuff would just loom over her.

Trying very hard to be matter-of-fact, she unfolded several of the boxes, double-taping the bottoms, then set them in a row. *Thrift store. Keep. Garage sale.* Because it did make sense to have a garage sale, whether she hated the idea or not. This was a large house; Mom wouldn't have room for half of the contents if she moved to something smaller. Olivia wasn't quite sure she could bring herself to put any of Dad's clothing in the garage sale box, though. She'd also brought a black plastic bag for trash.

When her parents had first bought the house before Olivia was born, they'd converted a small bedroom to a bathroom and walk-in closet. The original closet with double sliding doors had been Dad's, the larger walk-in one Mom's.

Olivia resolutely slid open one of the doors and made herself scoop up a bunch of his shoes.

Her eyes remained dry as she made quick decisions. The dress shoes weren't in bad shape and went in the thrift store box. Most of the rest went into the plastic bag. Dad had tended to wear his shoes until they ran over at the heel. No one would want them.

Her chest burned as she held his work boots, but in the end they went in the discard bag, too.

I can do this.

She moved on to the clothes hanging in the closet, patting to be sure pockets were empty. More of these went into the thrift store box. Dad hadn't often worn the dress shirts or sports jackets, never mind the nice suit Mom had chosen to bury him in. Olivia's only other memory of it was from her college graduation. Dad had looked so…distinguished that day, as handsome as any of the fathers who were attorneys or doctors.

She made herself keep working.

It was hardest when she got to his flannel and chambray shirts—his work clothes. Touching their soft fabric made her heart squeeze. *Oh, Daddy.* Some still hung in the closet despite tears or holes in elbows. He'd always be sure he could get some more wear out of a favorite. Each one gave her a flash of the kind of memory she'd known would be wrenching. Dad carefully guiding her hand as she learned to use a table saw. Carrying her then very small self on his shoulders as he waited on customers at the store. Once she was slightly older, letting her trail him as closely as a shadow. Always showing her what he was doing, and why. By the time she actually went on the payroll at the store, she was more knowledgeable than just about any other employee.

She buried her face in one of his T-shirts, smelling him as if he had wrapped an arm around her and held her close because she'd needed a hug from her daddy. The faint hint of sweat was there, reminding her of the hours they'd spent shooting baskets at the hoop in front of the garage and then at the outdoor courts at the middle school.

It was like the kind of family slide show that bored anyone but the people in the pictures. Daddy and her.

At one point, she discovered she was sitting on the edge of the bed, her hands fisted in that same faded T-shirt, tears rolling unchecked down her face. She hadn't made a sound. Unless her mother came upstairs to check on her, she'd never know Olivia's grief had finally broken free.

She'd shed most of her tears when a thought slid into her mind, taking her by surprise. None of those memories included her mother.

Because it wasn't Mom she was remembering.

But she went very still, thinking. No, it wasn't that simple. *I* was *a daddy's girl.* Marian Bowen was a very feminine woman, petite and beautiful. Her husband had always treated her as if she was delicate and precious. His gentleness and reverence was part of what Olivia remembered about her parents that was different from what she saw between other long-married couples. Mom would still blush at a certain look from him.

Yes, Olivia thought, but he had also excluded her from pretty much anything he and Olivia did outside the house. Mom gardened, but she didn't do the heavy digging. She certainly didn't operate the lawn mower or the weed-whacker or, God forbid, the chain saw, even though he eventually taught his daughter to use all the equipment. Shooting baskets? Unimaginable. Marian almost never set foot in the hardware store, and then it would be only to meet her husband for a daytime appointment or an occasional lunch date.

Maybe that's the way Mom wanted it, but Olivia wondered. Would she have enjoyed shooting baskets, too, even if she was inept at it? Bowen's Hardware & Lumberyard had become a family business when Olivia became interested. Mom could have contributed. Maybe they'd have picked up more business from women years ago if Charles had ever asked his wife's opinion.

And...what had she thought, when there was so much he enjoyed doing with his daughter but excluded his wife from?

Did her mother *resent* her? Olivia wondered, appalled. Could that be part of what had gone wrong between them, after her father's heart attack, when he'd needed Olivia to come home to take over the business? Why Mom was being so strange to her now?

Olivia sat very still, remembering these past months how conversation at the dinner table had been dominated by her telling her father about the day at work, who said what, how the new line of tools were selling, her ideas for small changes and his obvious approval.

Had Mom eaten her meal in total silence? Olivia couldn't remember and was ashamed.

She knew her parents would have liked to have more children, but her mother had miscarried several times and they'd eventually given up. It had never occurred to Olivia to wonder what would have happened if they'd had a boy. Would her relationship with her father have been completely different? With her mother?

She'd have sworn her parents adored each other. Sexual awareness had crackled between them as long as Olivia could remember. It had embarrassed her when she was at vulnerable ages. There had been odd moments when she'd felt invisible.

Mom, she thought, must have felt invisible even more often.

Or, God, am I reading a whole lot into nothing?

Wiping away the tears, she went back to work.

She decided to put off hauling down the boxes that sat on the shelf in the closet. They were likely to have contents she'd have to consult her mother about. Dresser, then.

Socks and underwear went straight in the black plastic bag. Undershirts and pajamas, ditto. One drawer held a man's small miscellany: everything from cuff links she couldn't recall him wearing to loose change and a pile of neatly washed and folded blue bandannas. She had a vivid picture of him pulling one from his chest pocket to dab at sweat or absentmindedly wipe oil or dust from his hand.

Olivia's chest was on fire, but she kept on, not allowing herself to hesitate about decisions. Trash. Garage sale. Thrift store. Only a very few things went in the keep box.

The bottom drawer held little-worn clothing. Nice sweaters—when had her father worn sweaters at all? A couple of dress shirts still with tags. A set of unworn slippers he must not have liked.

Then, near the bottom, she found some treasures: his basketball jerseys from high school and college. Those she held for a minute, smiling although her eyes stung, too. Keep. A sweatshirt from his alma mater. He'd worn that almost to threads, then tucked it away to save. Keep, damn it.

A bundle of letters, which she realized were from her mother and dated before their marriage. She set those aside, wondering if, in her current state, Mom would burn them right away.

Had Ben kept her few letters, written in the eight weeks he was gone before he came home to break up with her? Mostly, she'd emailed, but she remembered thinking he'd like to get some mail in his new college post box, too. Or had her letters and cards been an embarrassment, hastily disposed of before the cool college girls saw them? She wondered, suddenly, whether he'd ever admitted to having a girlfriend back home at all.

Stupid to care anymore.

She didn't.

Olivia lifted from the drawer a Seattle Seahawks T-shirt, which she had proudly given her daddy for his birthday. She'd been maybe twelve or thirteen. After that, he wore it most Sunday game days. She hadn't seen that shirt in years. Half smiling, half crying, she hesitated, then gently set it in the keep box.

For now.

The drawer was empty but for a greeting card. No envelope. How had it ended up here tucked beneath Dad's things? Puzzled, Olivia turned it over to find a bland picture of flowers. No "Happy Birthday" or "Get Well."

The "Dear Mr. Bowen" inside was in a childishly rounded handwriting, as was the rest of the short letter.

My name is Jessica, and I think you're my father.

Shocked, horrified, Olivia couldn't seem to read past that single sentence.

I think you're my father.

She lifted her eyes to the date at the top, written in that same hand. August 20 of this year. Three and a half months ago.

A day to mail it, two or three days for it to be delivered…

Mom had to have opened it.

Oh, yes. She knew now what had been wrong between her parents.

AFTER MONDAY'S PRACTICE, Carson turned off the shower and groped for his towel. He'd played better today, and nobody had slammed him. They were satisfied they'd made their point well enough. Which they had.

Walking out of the shower room, he scrubbed his hair with the towel, then wrapped it around his waist. He was careful not to turn his head when he passed the row of lockers where Zurenko and Slagle were getting dressed.

But Dylan Zurenko's voice stopped him. "Caldwell."

Carson wanted to ignore him. But he gritted his teeth and stopped, saying nothing.

"You want to come to a party Saturday night?"

"What?" He stared at Zurenko. Was this a setup?

"Ronnie G's parents are going to be out of town," Dex said. "His big brother has already ordered a couple of kegs."

Carson shrugged. "Didn't know I was still on your guest list."

"You've been a good boy." Zurenko planted a foot on the bench. Grinning, he pumped his hips a couple of times, making his dick swing. "Lots of bedrooms. Girls."

Slagle laughed and the two exchanged a low five.

They really were scum. In lieu of telling them so, Carson said, "I'll think about it," and kept walking.

"We'll expect you," Zurenko called after him. And, yeah, it sounded more like a threat than an invitation.

God, what do I do?

Make an anonymous call to the Graffs and say, "Do you know what goes on at your house when you're away? Maybe you don't want to go this time."

It would be just Carson's luck if they didn't actually *care* what went on when they were gone. Maybe they thought boys would be boys.

Claim his stepdaddy the principal had put him on restriction?

Sure, but why? And—reminding Zurenko and Slagle who his father was? Not a good idea.

Go, have a beer, slip away when no one was paying attention?

The thought made him feel sick. The morning after the last party, he'd puked his guts out, and not because he'd drunk too much. No, it was after he heard about *her*.

Bile rose into his throat as he stood here, unmoving, staring into his locker.

I didn't even know her name.

Nobody knows her name. Probably they never will.

In anguish, he thought, *I should have asked.*

There was no freakin' way he was going to a

kegger at Ronnie G's house with the idea of finding some random, probably drunk girl to have sex with. Carson didn't even know if it would be worse if she was a stranger, or if she was someone he'd have to see next Monday at school.

He wanted to have sex, but not like that.

Not again.

CHAPTER SIX

OLIVIA WAS FIERCELY glad the snow had kept them from going to church this week. In their family, Dad was the one who had faith. The church Olivia had attended all those years when she was growing up was really his.

And him a hypocrite.

Unfaithful, a man who broke his wedding vows and his wife's heart, too. The wife he had seemed to love so deeply.

Olivia didn't understand it at all.

And, no, she shouldn't hold Charles Bowen's failings against God, but she didn't feel reasonable today.

She hadn't said anything to her mother last night, or this morning, either. Mom hadn't asked how clearing out Dad's stuff was going, and Olivia hadn't volunteered any information. She had to process what she'd found first.

She'd brought a lunch today, but found herself wishing she and Ben really were friends and she could call and say, *I need to talk to someone.* They

could get burgers and park at that fallow field again.
Or get a booth at the pizza parlor.

No, she couldn't tell anybody, not even Ben. Not
yet. Maybe not ever. Who would it help?

So she ended up sitting at her desk Tuesday,
alone in the loft after Brenda the bookkeeper had
gone for the day and Lloyd was…well, either working through the noon hour or gone out; Olivia didn't
know. Muffled voices drifted up from below. And,
finally, she took the card from her bag and opened
it on the desk in front of her, reading it again.

Dear Mr. Bowen,

So polite.

*My name is Jessica, and I think you're my fa-
ther. My mother's name is Joanna Thomas.
She would never tell me who my father was,
but she died this year, and it's my grandma
who says Mom met you at a national hardware
show in Las Vegas. I am sixteen years old.*

Olivia hated the calculations she made automatically. Assuming this was all true, it meant her
father had had the affair when she was in high
school and dating Ben. So preoccupied then, she
doubted now she'd have noticed if her parents were
acting weird, or even having hissing fights behind
closed doors.

This maybe-sister was born the year Olivia was sixteen. The year Ben broke up with her. Half of her life ago.

She made herself keep reading.

If you don't want to meet me, that's okay. But I thought I would ask. I don't want to give you my grandmother's phone number since I didn't tell her I was writing you. I don't have my own phone. I got your number from Information. I thought I'd call this weekend. If you don't want anything to do with me, I don't mind if you say so. I won't bother you again. I promise.
Yours truly, Jessica Thomas

Olivia might have thought it was nonsense, if not for the reference to the hardware show—and for her mother's anger. Dad did go to one of the big shows every few years. Had to keep up with new products, he always said. Mom had gone with him sometimes, but not always. She wouldn't have wanted to leave her fifteen-year-old daughter alone for four or five days, especially when that daughter was getting serious about a boy. Olivia and Ben didn't make love until that summer, but they'd been coming close. Mom must have suspected and worried. No, she wouldn't have gone with Dad, not that year.

Had he felt obligated to invite his wife when he attended those things, but secretly hoped she wouldn't go? Oh, heavens—was he one of those men who went wild when he got away from home? He wouldn't have hired prostitutes, would he? *Please, don't let this Joanna Thomas have been a whore.* Although Olivia wasn't sure it made any difference if she wasn't, if she'd simply been another attendee.

How could you? she begged her father, even knowing she'd get no answer.

If Mom had opened the mail the day this card came, it wasn't hard to imagine her horror and disbelief. She must have hoped he'd be as shocked as she was. Maybe laugh it off. Point out that he hadn't gone to a show that year at all. Tell her that when the girl called, he'd say, *I'm sorry, but you've got the wrong man.*

Only, that hadn't happened. So…what did Dad do?

Kept the card, obviously. Tucked it away where his wife was unlikely to find it without a wholesale search—or the necessity of clearing out his possessions after his death.

The big question was: Had Jessica called? Had he talked to her? He could have said, *I'm sorry, but my health is poor and I can't explore what it would mean to be your father even if I am.* Or…Olivia's heart began to pound. Had he told her, *I remember your mother, and I'd like to meet you?*

And that was the moment where a firestorm of

fear roared out of nowhere, leaving her defenseless, waiting for it to sear over her.

What if this girl, this Jessica Thomas, had then come to meet her father? To surprise him. Only, she never got here. Or she got here, but never left Crescent Creek?

The biggest puzzle of all had been why the unknown girl had been here at all.

Jane Doe was the right age.

She had Charles Bowen's coloring, light brown, almost blond hair and brown eyes.

Against his daughter's and his wife's arguments, he had insisted on going to the funeral despite his fragile health. Olivia remembered her mother's biting anger at his decision to attend. She could still see his expression, bleak and withdrawn, as he sat in one of the few folding chairs at the grave site.

Had the girl shown up out of the blue and he turned her away? Or maybe they'd talked, and he hadn't realized she must have hitchhiked and didn't have transportation of her own to return to wherever she came from? Either way, if he felt he'd failed her, that *he* was responsible for her death—

She remembered Ben saying that attending the funeral might have precipitated her father's death. It could have been the cold, Ben had suggested.

Maybe it wasn't his mortality her father saw when he looked into that hole in the ground. Maybe it was his own terrible guilt. For what he'd done to this girl—and to the wife he'd betrayed.

What if that's my sister, buried anonymously at community expense? Olivia asked herself. *Do I leave it that way, for the sake of Dad's reputation and Mom's dignity?*

Immediate repulsion was her answer. *No.* They had to find out. Which meant…she had to talk to her mother.

And, dear lord, but Olivia dreaded it.

"CAN I ASK YOU something?"

Ben glanced at his son, then grabbed the bowl of broccoli to give himself a second serving. It wasn't his favorite vegetable, but the choices weren't great at this time of year. "Sure," he said. "Hey, you want more?"

Carson shook his head. It was a minute before he spoke. "Did you ever have sex with someone only then wished you hadn't?" he finally blurted.

Oh, damn. Ben struggled to keep his consternation from showing. He could say the right thing and open a dialogue, or he could blow it big-time and watch Carson clam up. He only wished he knew what the right thing was.

Just answer him straight-out, he decided, although this was one of those time it was tempting to lie.

"Yeah." It came out a little hoarsely "There was once." No, more than once—several times. But same girl, same reason for guilt.

Carson poked at his baked potato. "Can you, um, tell me? I mean, why you wished you hadn't?"

Were parents supposed to talk about their own sexual experiences with their kids? He had no idea. Yeah, and him the expert, he thought ruefully.

"I'm going to guess most adults would say yes to your original question, if they were being honest. There might be times they pushed a partner who was reluctant. That kind of thing. You know?"

Carson nodded. "Like, not rape, but almost."

Ben waggled his hand. "I wouldn't put it that strongly. Just…realizing what you felt wasn't entirely mutual."

"That's all?"

Seeing Carson's expression, Ben realized he wasn't going to slide that easily. "No," he admitted. "I guess the time I'm most ashamed of happened my first semester in college. I'd made promises to Olivia, and I didn't keep them."

"She still thought she was your girlfriend, and you were screwing around with some other girl."

The heaviness in his chest was composed of shame, disappointment in himself and just plain regret. "Yeah. As it turned out, the girl didn't mean anything to me. I think she just represented…freedom," he admitted. "Me being cool, out there in the big world, not tied to this hick town anymore." He grimaced. "I was an idiot."

"Did you…tell her?" Carson's voice was hushed. "The girl?"

"Olivia."

The weight on his chest became greater. He shook his head. "I told her I'd met someone else, that's all. I didn't tell her…"

"You kind of jumped the gun?"

"Yeah."

"She still doesn't know?" Carson asked.

"I imagine she guessed."

"Wow. You're lucky she speaks to you."

He felt his mouth twist. "She barely does. You saw her at her friendliest."

Carson bent his head and resumed eating.

"You must have had a reason for asking me all that," Ben said, trying real hard to sound interested and not demanding.

The boy sneaked a look at him before ducking his head again. His hair shouldn't be long enough for him to hide behind, but he managed somehow. "Just…I don't know."

Ben waited.

"Everybody talks about it. You know?"

Ben nodded. He did know. Men his age congregated in a locker room or bar still talked about sex. For all he knew, old men did, too. His mouth quirked ever so slightly. Maybe that was one of the main topics for the old guys in line waiting to pay at the hardware store.

"And I guess, um, most of them do it."

"The girls, too?"

Carson eyed him again, looking for…Ben didn't

know. Reassurance? Or was he suspicious that Ben in his role as principal would use anything he said against him?

"Some of them do. I mean, I don't *know*. For sure. Like…like, personally." The kid was panicking.

"Carson."

His son gave him a deer-in-the-headlights look.

"If you've had sex already and want to talk about it, that's okay. We can. If you have questions, I'll try to answer them. If you're not ready to talk about it, that's okay, too."

He bobbed his blond head.

"If you haven't had sex yet, I don't want you feeling like there's something wrong with you. I didn't until—" *Whoa,* he thought in alarm.

"Until Olivia," Carson said.

Oh, shit. He should know better than to have such a big mouth.

"That's…not something I should talk about," he said. "Let's just say, my first experience was with a girl I cared a whole lot about. It was the first time for both of us." The crushing sense of shame washed over him. "I didn't have casual sex until I was in college."

"You cheated on Olivia."

He closed his eyes for a moment. "Yeah."

Carson nodded. They both sat there looking at half-full plates of food, but neither took a bite.

Ben had the uneasy feeling he hadn't said the right thing. Had maybe even said the wrong thing.

Try again. "The last time we discussed this, I told you we're all different. You won't get that idea listening to locker-room talk. Most of the boys are swaggering and claiming they get some all the time, right?"

"Uh…yeah."

"The truth is, a lot of them aren't. They're all talk. Some have girlfriends and maybe are sexually active, but they might be the least likely to talk about it. I'm sure casual sex is happening." He paused to emphasize what he had to say next. "All I ask is that you make sure you have safe sex. Even if she says she's on birth control, use a condom." He held Carson's gaze. "Always."

The boy gulped.

"The other thing is…treat the girl decently. Don't make it about you scoring. Don't act as if she's less because she put out." The way Carson was staring, this was the most mesmerizing speech Ben had ever given. There was one more thing he knew he had to say. "And take care of her," he finished. "Make sure she's okay. Don't use her and leave her. You know?"

Carson wasn't looking at him anymore. His face worked, and he pushed away from the table. "I'm not hungry," he said. "I've got homework."

"What did I say?"

Ben was treated to a sullen stare. "Everything's not about what you say."

"No," he said slowly. "You're right. I'll do the cleanup. You go ahead."

The speed of the boy's retreat was a giveaway. No, everything wasn't always about what Ben had said—but this time, what he'd said had stung.

The part about using a condom? Ben hoped like hell that wasn't it. The idea of his kid, only sixteen, having to face up to the possibility of becoming a father... That would be bad.

But instinct said Carson hadn't reacted then. He'd even nodded, hadn't he? No, it was later.

When he'd said, *The other thing is...treat the girl decently. Don't make it about you scoring.*

Or was it the last thing Ben had said? The part about making sure the girl was okay? About not using her and leaving her?

Fear grabbed him, seeming to stop his heart.

Oh, crap. What if Carson had used her and left her...and she *wasn't* okay? What if, in fact, she was dead?

"Oh—forgot to tell you that Mr. Swenson says to talk to him again after the holidays," Olivia said.

Her mother set down the two cups of coffee she had just poured for them and resumed her seat. "That seems reasonable. They probably want to celebrate Christmas as if nothing has changed." She said that softly, her expression suddenly stricken.

She and Olivia hadn't even *talked* about Christmas. For them, there would be no denying that everything had changed.

And what she was about to say might end any possibility of their Christmas being even a faint shadow of the ones that could never be recaptured.

"Mom, there's something we have to talk about."

Her mother's expression smoothed out. Her "Oh?" was only inquiring, making Olivia realize she hadn't sounded even close to as grim as she felt.

"Last night, I found the card from Jessica Thomas, claiming Dad is her father."

Mom went completely still. Rigid.

"Dad must have hidden it."

"How…foolish of him." Icicles dripped from Mom's voice. "He wouldn't have wanted you to know."

"That's why you wouldn't tell me what was wrong." At least this was something she understood. "You didn't want me to think less of him."

"Are you rejoicing because you know the truth?" Acid had melted some of the ice.

"No." Olivia had a huge lump in her throat. "It makes me feel as if I never knew him."

"You didn't." Anguish briefly contorted her mother's face. "I didn't."

"You never suspected?"

Her mother's hair, the color of Olivia's, swung as she shook her head. "No."

"Did he...?" Oh, it was horrible even to ask this, but she had to. "Do you think there were other times?"

Those burning eyes met hers. "He said not, but how am I to know?"

There was no way, of course. Charles Bowen had died alone. No chance of any last confession, even if he'd been aware when death came for him.

"But he admitted to this...Joanna person."

"Yes."

Olivia swallowed. "Mom... Did he talk to her? Jessica?"

Not a muscle moved in her mother's face, and yet Olivia could have sworn a mask had closed over it. "I don't know."

"You must have asked!"

Mom's jaw set. "No." She sounded so hard now. "What difference did it make? He cheated. He had an illegitimate child. He had made our marriage a mockery. I didn't care if he wanted to embrace his newfound daughter or not."

Something else Olivia couldn't help understanding, even if she wished her mother had answers. She hadn't asked a single question about the girl Ben said he'd met, either. The one who took her place.

The memory stung. Yes, she'd only been sixteen, but she had been in love. Until she came home last winter and began seeing him regularly, she would have said she'd been over that first heartbreak entirely. Now she knew better. It wasn't like she'd lived for all those years with a constant ache of regret; in all honesty, she hadn't thought of him at all for months at a time. But she'd been left with a hollow place inside her, one no one else had ever filled.

She shook her head. What she needed to do now was think about the girl who might be—might *have been*—her sister. Not about herself.

"Mom, I think Jane Doe might be her. Jessica Thomas."

Horror filled her mother's face. "You can't say that to anyone. You can't!"

"You think she might be." Dismay had dropped Olivia's voice to a whisper. "Did you ask him? *Did you?*"

"No!" her mother yelled, pushing back her chair and rising to her feet. "I told you!"

"But you wondered."

Mom's mouth set in a thin, ugly line.

"You did." Dazed, Olivia shook her head in hopes of clearing it. Of making none of this ever have happened.

No answer.

"Mom… She might be my *sister*. Doesn't that mean anything to you?"

"She's dead. It doesn't matter anymore."

"It does. If it's her, she has a name. A grandmother somewhere, scared because she's disappeared. You must have seen the envelope. Do you remember the address? Or at least the postmark?"

"Don't do this." Angry and afraid, Mom looked... older. The lines in her face were more pronounced than they'd been even at the funeral. "If everyone knew, what do you think it would do to your father's reputation? Don't you care? And what about me? All I have left is my pride. If everyone finds out, I'd have to move away. I couldn't bear it."

"Is pride as important as finding out who that poor girl was?"

"She's dead!"

Olivia did not know this woman who now gripped the back of her chair as she glared. This couldn't be her mother.

"I don't know if I can pretend she doesn't have anything to do with me," she heard herself say.

"If you tell everyone," her mother's voice shook, as if it were a soaring Arctic iceberg cracking just before part of it crashed into the ocean, "I don't know if I can forgive you."

And she turned and walked out. A moment later, Olivia heard her footsteps on the stairs.

Her own legs felt too weak to hold her. Her heart sounded in her ears like a drumbeat.

Could she do that to her own mother?

If she didn't... Could she live with her own silence?

"SEE YOU IN the morning," Brenda Schultz said with a wave as she passed the open door of Olivia's office.

"Let's hope for no more snow tonight," Olivia responded, and she heard a fervent agreement as the young woman started down the stairs.

Their half-time bookkeeper, Brenda sometimes worked extra hours on the cash registers if they were especially busy. Olivia suspected she wouldn't want to be doing that in the future, as she was pregnant with her first baby. Whether she might be considering not coming back to work at all was a new worry…one Olivia tried to dismiss with the reminder that Brenda's husband, Dale, worked at the auto parts store and wasn't likely to be making a fantastic living.

Olivia sat without moving, listening to the light footsteps descending the stairs.

Finally, sure she was alone, she hefted her messenger bag up on the desk and unzipped the inside pocket where she had put the card this morning.

Last night, she'd had a burst of paranoia and locked it in her glove compartment instead. What if Mom went looking for it, intent on destroying it? Doing her best to make it never have existed?

Olivia shook her head. So what if she'd succeeded? The card presumably held fingerprints— hers, Dad's and likely Mom's as well as the girl's—but otherwise it offered no great clues. The fingerprints of a girl who'd never been arrested were no help whatsoever in identifying her. Without the envelope, there was no address or postmark. The note itself included no phone number, no hints.

Would anyone even believe Olivia's story without the card as evidence?

As for finding the girl...surely Jessica Thomas could be tracked by name alone, coupled with her mother's.

Olivia spread the card open atop the ancient scarred oak desk that had been her father's. Always before, sitting behind that desk was enough to stir warmth and grief in her, but now she tried to block every emotion connected to him. Eventually, she'd have to try to understand how the man she had known and loved and admired could have done something like this. And, for her own sake, she'd have to come to terms with him being the kind of man who would cheat on his wife. But... not yet. Just the thought of untangling what she did feel was too complicated and painful.

Instead she sat in Dad's big leather office chair, patched in a couple of places with duct tape, and stared at the girlish handwriting.

If only there was a phone number. She'd be able to find out in about one minute whether Jessica Thomas was alive and well or had mysteriously disappeared.

Yes, but even if she had the number, would she call? Whether that was the logical thing to do or not?

Oh, God, Olivia didn't know. Did she really want to hear Jessica's voice? Have to decide quickly whether to claim a misdialed number or identify herself, with all that would follow?

Olivia moaned and bent forward, closing her eyes. Panic suffused her, flooding her body with heat that made her skin prickle.

Whether Jessica was alive or dead, the real question was whether Olivia was willing to acknowledge her. To find out if they *were* half sisters. Did a biological relationship really mean that much, when this girl was so much younger and the product of Dad's affair? Wrenched by images she didn't want to imagine, Olivia dismissed the question, then tensed as she heard voices that seemed to be nearing the foot of the stairs. Lloyd on his way up? No, the voices faded as whoever was talking continued on.

What she groped desperately for was a way to determine whether this Jessica was still alive and well and home, safe wherever her home was. Preferably a way that didn't involve any direct contact, given Olivia's extremely mixed feelings and Mom's horror at the idea. She made a face. Yes, what she wanted was an easy out.

Call her a coward, but hiring a P.I. suddenly seemed appealing. Only…she had next to nothing to give an investigator to work with. It might be possible to find the list of attendees at that long-ago hardware show…but what if, instead of being an attendee, Joanna Thomas had worked for a vendor or been a waitress in a restaurant where

Charles Bowen had eaten? The possibilities were almost limitless.

Okay, what if she were to submit DNA to be compared with Jane Doe's? The medical examiner's office had allowed the unidentified girl to be buried only four weeks after her death rather than keeping the body indefinitely in cold storage the way they once would have done because DNA samples, dental X-rays and ample photographs should allow them to match her with a missing person's report if the right one came along. Olivia had a vague feeling that DNA testing was both expensive and slow, though, which meant Chief Weigand might want to try to locate this Jessica instead.

I could lie.

Tell him Dad had been approached by a girl who claimed to be his daughter, but that he hadn't shared her name or anything else he knew about her, not with Mom and not with Olivia. Definitely not with Mom. Olivia shuddered at picturing her mother's reaction to the police chief coming to ask her questions about her husband's possible illegitimate child.

Olivia had never been indecisive, but she was now. All she did was sit there, staring at the hated note, until a sound brought her head up.

Someone was coming upstairs. She recognized the pace, the tread. Lloyd. Hastily, she shoved the card back in the pocket in her bag and zipped it closed. Her hands, she was disconcerted to see, were shaking.

"Olivia, you up here?" he called, when he was still out of sight.

"I'm here," she answered, gratified to sound so much as usual.

"Got a call from Jim Dennison at Banner Plywood and wanted to see what you thought."

Olivia plunged with relief into a discussion about whether they might look for another supplier rather than agree to tighter terms. She was embarrassed at how glad she was to be able to put off making a decision about her maybe-sister.

CHAPTER SEVEN

"MOM THINKS THAT girl might have been *shot*."

About to step out of the copy room, Ben went absolutely still. The voice was a girl's, hushed and eager. *I know something no one else does,* it implied.

The buses had pulled out; the speaker and her friend must be walkers who'd either had an after-school meeting or had come back in to get something out of a locker. They were obviously unaware how well voices carried in an empty hall.

"How does she know?" asked the friend, clearly skeptical. Another girl. "Nobody said anything like that."

The two were almost on top of him. He'd already turned off the light in the room that held the copiers and paper supplies. Ben waited, the door cracked only a few inches, his hand still on the knob.

"No, but I bet the police wouldn't. Besides, why would she just have laid down and died if she wasn't hurt?"

Damn, all he could see was a quick flash of blond hair and a red book bag. Then the two were past.

"I don't know," the other girl said, still doubtful. "How come your Mom thinks that? About her being shot, I mean."

Yeah? How come?

Ben eased the door open and stepped into the hall, looking at their backs as they continued on. The skeptic he knew right away—Lina Ramirez, a smart, troubled kid who flaunted her sexuality in a way that worried him, given that she was only thirteen years old. The friend… He was silently swearing as he waited for her answer—and for her to turn her head so he could identify her.

"Mom thought she heard shots in the middle of the night. She says it had to be Mr. Ellison. You know, that old guy? He's, like, nuts. He shot at *Patrick* once, just 'cuz he was on his property." She sounded awed.

Lina pushed open the exit door, and the two went out, giving Ben what he'd been waiting for: a fleeting glimpse of another freshman girl. Mikayla…no, just Kayla. He relaxed. Kayla and Patrick Brown.

Deep in thought, Ben backtracked to his office, where he called up Kayla Brown's records. Yeah, the Browns did live just down the road from the old Connelly farm…and, if memory served him right, from the Ellison farm.

Bert Ellison was an old-timer. Ben had played sports with his grandson, Jay Ellison. He'd heard Jay was killed in a motorcycle accident a couple of years after graduating from Crescent Creek

High School. Hell, if Jay had been his only grand-child, maybe the poor old guy went out at night and took potshots at the moon on a regular basis! Who knew?

There'd been no hint that Jane Doe had *been* shot, either. Weigand wouldn't have lied about the medical examiner saying she'd frozen to death, would he?

The big question, though, had always been *why* a healthy girl would go out in the woods and let herself freeze to death. This wasn't the Alaskan backcountry. The mercury had dropped the night the girl died, but only into the twenties. There were half a dozen houses within a reasonable walk from where her body was found.

Given all that, Ben suspected the police chief and medical examiner both were keeping some secrets. If the girl had been bleeding from a bullet wound, that would explain why she might curl up out there in the woods and lose consciousness rather than seek shelter.

He groaned and scraped a hand over his face. He had no choice but to tell Chief Weigand what he'd heard. He could call now, or even run down to the police station. The roads were clear enough that Carson had ridden his bike today, and, despite the fact that dark was falling by the time he set out after practice, his son would get home fine. The new streetlights put up when the high school was built were bright enough to have garnered complaints from some home owners.

Decision made, he shut down his computer, stopped to ask one of his vice principals to stay to lock up and left.

The police station was downtown, not two blocks from Bowen's Hardware. As with a lot of towns, most of the businesses were situated on a main drag—in the case of Crescent Creek, it was the highway, known as Haley Road as it went through town. There wasn't a chain store in town, or in Miller Falls, for that matter. False-fronted buildings dated as far back as the 1920s. Newer constructions like the Chase Bank looked out of place.

The Downtown Merchants Association had done up the town for the holidays, with Christmas lights strung and giant glowing plastic candy canes and Santas festooning lampposts instead of the flowering baskets that were meticulously maintained from spring through fall. With dark having already descended at four o'clock, Haley Street looked bright and festive.

Even though on one level he knew when the holiday break was coming, Ben was still mildly startled to realize Christmas was two weeks from tomorrow. Maybe he'd suggest to Carson they go cut a tree Saturday.

The redbrick police station actually had its own small parking lot out back, and he was able to find an empty spot to leave his Jeep. He was lucky enough to find the chief in the premises, too.

Ben understood that Phil Weigand, about the age of Ben's dad, had grown up in the much more depressed mountain town of Darrington to the north. There were similarities between the two towns, even though Crescent Creek was more prosperous; the highway past Darrington also shut down every winter, and both towns had suffered from the downturn in logging.

Weigand had graying brown hair, shrewd brown eyes and a stocky build. Apparently an ardent fisherman and hunter, he'd been with the Snohomish County Sheriff's Department until he decided he wanted to live where he could all but cast a line off his back porch. Chief Weigand made his own deer jerky and was famous for pressing it on anyone he liked. The stuff was too pungent for Ben's taste.

"Ben," he said in surprise when he saw his visitor. "Come on in. Shut the door."

Aware of curious glances as he'd passed through the station, Ben complied. "I don't have anything big to report. Just heard some kids talking and thought I'd pass on what was said."

"This about our Jane Doe?"

"Yes. Maybe nothing new to you." Ben told him what he'd heard.

Frowning, the chief listened in silence. "I talked to Bert Ellison that day. He said he slept the night through, didn't hear a thing."

"Then this may be nonsense."

"It may." But he was still frowning. "Don't think it was Mrs. Brown I spoke to, though. Seems to me it was her husband who came to the door."

And the guy had probably claimed to sleep like a baby, too.

"If the girl wasn't shot, this story doesn't mean much," Ben remarked, not necessarily expecting an answer but hoping for one.

Weigand studied him. "No gunshot wounds," he said after a minute. "But I'd sure like to be able to trace her steps the previous day and evening. What if she *was* looking for shelter, and Mr. Ellison ran her off?"

With a chill, Ben pictured the landscape out there, east of town, nearing the place where the highway was barricaded from the first serious snowfall until late spring. Houses were far apart, most on what had once been working farms. The Connelly place had been a dairy farm in its day, as had been… He had to think. The Hansens operated the other dairy farm. The daughter, a year or two younger than him, had been the local dairy princess competing for the state honor. Hallie, he remembered. Hallie Hansen. Pretty, but not in Olivia's class.

Neither farm had been large enough to hold on long-term. The fields were now shaggy and increasingly overrun with blackberries, the silos and barns empty in the way that conjured ghosts. Marsha Connelly's husband Gene had died eight or ten years ago. She was known to be deaf and likely went to bed early. A kid who'd run in panic from the Ellisons' might not have known there *was* another house close by, not if Marsha had already turned out the lights. The girl could have gone the wrong way. Stumbled and fallen.

"Was she injured at all?" he asked abruptly.

The chief stirred in his chair. "I'll ask you to keep this to yourself."

"I can do that."

"She had bruises. Hard to say from what. If she was running through the woods, fell a few times, crashed into a tree..." He shrugged. "That could be enough. But she could have been assaulted, too. We just don't know."

They stared at each other.

"She wasn't raped?" Ben asked hoarsely.

Thank God, the chief was shaking his head. "If she had sex, it was likely consensual."

Ben nodded, relieved and yet...not. The sex could have started consensual, but that didn't mean someone hadn't gotten rough with her. Scared her enough she ran away from the kegger to hide in the woods?

Ben wouldn't believe Carson would ever hurt a girl. Not knowingly.

But he knew something. Felt guilty about something.

Ben stood abruptly. "Well, you know what I know now."

"I'll be talking to Mrs. Brown and Mr. Ellison tomorrow," the chief said, rising with him. "I'll let you know if anything comes of it. I appreciate the information, Ben." Walking him out, he added, "Keep your ear out. For all that I was ten years a detective, I don't much like mysteries."

"Can't say I love them myself," Ben agreed and went on his way feeling more disturbed than when he'd come in, not less.

PHIL WAS THINKING hard as he watched Ben Hovik depart. He liked what he'd seen of the high school principal, although every time he saw Hovik he was surprised anew at how damn young he was. Couldn't be over mid-thirties. He wasn't even as old as most of the parents of his students!

To give him some credit, though, he'd been impressive handling the assembly after the girl was found dead, and Phil hadn't had any complaints in their few interactions involving students who'd committed crimes. He did wonder, though, at Hovik's continuing fixation on their Jane Doe. Yes, he did.

The young principal claimed to think something was going on with the kids, thus his concern. Maybe that's all there was to it. Might be, too, that he'd taken seriously his insistence that this town treat that girl like one of their own until someone claimed her. Hovik probably saw every other high school–aged kid in town as "his," in a manner of speaking, and had taken to including the girl, too. Still, she'd been dead for almost eight weeks now, and Hovik's determination to find answers hadn't faltered at all.

Phil hadn't lied; he didn't like unsolved mysteries. He wanted answers, too, but finding them was his job. It wasn't Ben Hovik's. What he found himself contemplating was whether the guy might have some other worry riding him. Could be he had a suspicion of why she'd died and was desperate for an answer that would prove him wrong. Or he might have a suspicion of *who* she was, instead, and hoped she wasn't.

Phil sighed and decided he could go talk to Paula Brown this evening rather than waiting until morning, when he'd have to corner her at Crescent Valley Towing where she worked dispatch. He intended to put her on the spot, but didn't want to embarrass her in front of coworkers.

As he donned his sheepskin-lined coat, checked his weapon and turned out the lights in his office, he found himself hoping there was nothing to this latest story. If it turned out Bert Ellison had used his shotgun to chase some scared, innocent girl out into the woods where she died and then clamped his mouth shut out of shame or guilt…well, damn, that was just *ugly*.

"OKAY, GOOD PRACTICE today," Coach called.

Carson bounced the ball high, then on impulse

dribbled fast toward the nearest basket, leaped high
and slammed it through the hoop.

Man, I can fly, he thought in exultation.

Earthbound again, he snagged the ball and tossed
it to McGarvie, who dropped it in the rack with
the others.

A few minutes later, he turned the shower on hot
and stood under it with his eyes closed, letting the
water pound down on his head and back. Something had happened today, he didn't know what,
but it was like everything had come together. He'd
played like he had last year. No, better.

He let himself dream. In the fantasy, he wore
the Trail Blazers' colors—although wouldn't it be
cool if that Hansen guy actually fired up a Seattle
team again? Yeah, well, right now he'd go with the
Trail Blazers, he decided, seeing himself bumping
a defender hard, twirling, putting himself in perfect position. The point guard shot a pass at him.
He dribbled once, pivoted again and put it up. Perfect arc. The roar of the crowd rose. Buzzer went
off. End of the game, only chance of a win was his
shot, floating toward the basket—

"Eight o'clock, Saturday night," a voice said.

Jolted from his daydream, he shook his head,
spat out a mouthful of water and muttered, "What?"

Naked, Zurenko was toweling his hair dry. "You
heard me. Ronnie G's."

Carson shut off his own shower. "Do I get a daily
reminder?"

"Just making sure," Zurenko said, slinging the towel around his neck.

"What is it with you, anyway? Why do you care whether I show?"

The friendly expression suddenly wasn't so friendly. "You're not that stupid." He walked away, shaking his head.

For a minute, Carson stood where he was. One shower still ran behind him. Guzman, he saw, turning his head. Didn't look like he'd heard.

No, Carson thought, he wasn't that stupid. The pressure was still on. It was just taking a different form.

Still, he hadn't moved. The shower went off; Guzman grabbed his own towel from where it hung over the tiled half wall and disappeared toward his locker.

Yeah, maybe I have *been that stupid.* The thought felt like a revelation. No, revolutionary. That was different.

They were bullies, that's all. They liked to intimidate, and he'd let them intimidate him. He was mad, when he thought of how little it had taken. A few bumps, a foot stuck out to trip him. That's all, and he'd quailed like a little girl who somebody was mean to.

He needed to make a statement. Something that said, *In your face, sucka.* This *is what happens when you mess with me.*

Carson began drying himself as he went to his

locker. He didn't even hear the voices around him, the clang of metal, the hoots of laughter.

If he could play Friday night the way he had today in practice, he knew exactly how to make his point. Pulling on his briefs and jeans, he thought, *I can do this*.

There was more than one way to decline an invitation.

BEN'S ROUTE AFTER leaving the parking lot took him right past the hardware store. With Olivia never far from his mind, he wondered if she was still there. At four-thirty…probably. Bowen's stayed open until six o'clock except for shorter hours on Sundays. For all he knew, she came in first thing in the morning and stayed until late at night.

The impulse that had him stopping and backing into a parking space was familiar. She'd been friendly enough when they'd gone sledding, so this might be the time to ask her out to dinner. Maybe Friday night, and then she might like to go to the basketball game with him. At the very least, he could pretend he needed something at the hardware store and stop to talk if she wasn't tied up.

The first person he spotted when he went inside was Stuart Dodd, who had a daughter at the high school. Charlotte Dodd played the French horn in the orchestra. Another Dodd kid had graduated last year…Chase. Played football, middle of the pack scholastically. Ben hadn't heard what he was doing now.

Ben held out a hand. "Stuart. Good to see you."

As they shook, the other man said, "Tell me you're not looking for me."

Ben laughed. "Now come on—has Charlotte ever been in trouble?"

Stuart grinned ruefully. "There's always a first time."

"I was actually hoping to talk to Olivia."

"She's gone for the day. Just left, in fact. You might catch her out in the alley if it's urgent."

Too many people would notice if he tore out there after her. Ben said no, it wasn't anything that couldn't wait, and strolled out, more disappointed than he wanted to admit. *Hell.* Maybe he should take the opportunity to pick up some groceries. The milk was getting low.

He waited for an opening in traffic, then pulled out, almost immediately getting held up when the light at the corner turned red. Right there in front of him, Olivia's little compact took a right turn from the cross street. *To my wondering eyes what should appear,* he thought frivolously, intrigued because she wasn't taking the usual way home. Could she be planning to grocery shop, too?

Once his light turned, he hung a couple of cars back. He could waylay her in the aisles at Safeway. But she continued past the store and all the other outlying businesses, and so did he, feeling unpleasantly like a stalker but unable to resist finding out where she was going.

There was still one other vehicle between them as they reached the outskirts. Going this way, eventually they'd reach the Connelly farm where Jane Doe had been found, but why would Olivia be heading there?

He was momentarily distracted when the car in front of him put on a turn signal and cautiously entered a long, dark driveway. His headlights picked out Olivia's car ahead just as she turned off, too.

Into the cemetery, he saw, with less surprise than he should have felt.

ALARMED WHEN AN SUV pulled in right next to her, Olivia left her engine running and kept her hand on the gearshift. It was awfully dark and lonely out here. Probably it had been dumb to come alone, even if it wasn't even five o'clock yet. But then the driver side door of the SUV opened and, with the dome light on, she saw Ben getting out. The jolt of alarm became something else as disturbing. Her heart jumped every time she saw him, no matter how determined she was not to let herself get involved with him again.

If only he wasn't so damn sexy. And if she didn't have the uncomfortable feeling he saw right through her facade of indifference.

She turned off the ignition and got out, too. "You

followed me," she accused him over the roof of her Civic.

"I did. I'm sorry if I scared you. I didn't think."

One sodium lamp illuminated the parking lot and cast shadows in the graveyard. He stayed where he was.

"Why did you follow me?"

"I was on my way to the grocery store when I saw you up ahead. You kept going and…" He hesitated. "I'm being nosy."

"I shouldn't have come out here." She turned her head to look toward the cemetery grounds, headstones dark above the snowy landscape. "I'll freeze."

Still he didn't move. "You want me to leave? Or sit here while you visit your dad's grave?"

Heaven help her, he was here. At the back of her mind all day had been the thought of calling him. The temptation had been huge. He was the only person she could think of who could help her untangle her confusion and decide right from wrong. Every time she closed her eyes, she could hear his voice, deep and slow and somehow tender.

And then she'd think, *What kind of idiot am I?* Right. Of course she could trust this man just because he'd been her high school boyfriend *sixteen years ago*. And ditched her and probably cheated on her.

She hated being so drawn to him—iron filings to a magnet—when the truth was she didn't know him at all anymore, and maybe never had, or he wouldn't have gone off to college and promptly put her out of his mind, would he? Which part of that proved him to be trustworthy?

And yet…he was here. He'd followed her… Why? Because he was interested in starting something with her again?

As if he'd read her mind, he spoke again, his voice quiet. "I was worried about you."

And, oh God, she believed him. Tears suddenly burned in her eyes. Tears she hoped he couldn't see. After a minute she nodded. "I…found something out."

Am I really going to tell him?

Half horrified, half feeling a sense of inevitability, she knew. *Yes.*

"About your dad? Or our Jane Doe?"

"Both." Her voice cracked. "Maybe both."

His expression changed, and he abruptly slammed his door and circled around the back of her car to come to her. "Olivia?"

She produced a sort of twisted smile. "I've been engaged in high drama the past couple days." She was going to make a joke out of it, but instead she heard herself say, "I hate it."

His big hands clasped her upper arms, and he bent his head to look down at her. "Do you want to talk about it?"

She stared fixedly at his broad chest, covered by a sweater she thought might be cashmere. Unlike her, he wasn't wearing a parka, so he *would* be freezing in no time.

"If you've got a few minutes. And can keep what I say to yourself."

"Of course I can. And will." One cheek creased, as if he smiled. "Do we go sit by the grave, or do you want to get in my Cherokee?"

"We could get in my car…"

"I'd have to fold up like an accordion."

Despite the prickle of tears, he'd made her smile. "I guess you are a little oversized for my car, aren't you?" She closed the door, keys clutched in her hand. "I don't know why I came out here anyway. It's not like I think either of them are hanging around their graves. Dad is gone. I know that. And Je…Jane, too." She'd caught herself so fast, she wasn't sure he'd noticed. *I'm going to tell him anyway, aren't I?* But maybe not names.

Ben kept one hand on her as he steered her to his Cherokee. His care almost made her smile again, considering *she* wore work boots with excellent traction while he had on dress shoes with smooth soles.

Once again, she found herself settled on the passenger side with him behind the wheel. He turned on the engine, and heat immediately seeped out of the vents. Glad he hadn't also turned on the dome light, Olivia gazed ahead at the cemetery, although from here she couldn't pick out which gravestones belonged to her father and to Jane Doe.

Ben waited in silence.

"I told you about Mom and Dad," she said finally. "How something was wrong between them."

"Yes."

She squeezed her hands together. "I started cleaning out their bedroom. Mom asked if I'd do it. I mean, Dad's stuff, not hers." She stole a look, to see him watching her.

"I found something," she said abruptly.

"Something?"

"A notecard, hidden at the bottom of a drawer of clothes he hardly ever wore."

"He'd hidden it."

"Yes." Then she told him about the sixteen-year-old girl who believed Charles Bowen was her father. "I don't know what happened to the envelope. With no address or phone number, I can't just call her."

"Call her?" Even in the darkness, she saw his eyebrows draw together. "You aren't seriously thinking she *is* his kid?"

"He admitted to Mom that she could be." Oh, how she hated saying that! *My dad, the scumbag.*

Ben fell silent, the frown lingering. "Did he get in touch with the girl? Or the other way around?"

"Mom claims not to know."

"Oh, hell! You think she might be Jane Doe."

Of course he got it right away. Ben always had been quick. And, well, she'd hinted.

"Isn't it possible?" Olivia gripped her hands

together, feeling the bite of her fingernails. "What if she came to town to see him? She'd be the right age, and isn't one of the biggest questions why this girl who no one recognizes was here in Crescent Creek at all?"

"Yes." He was mulling over what she'd said even as he slowly agreed. "Damn, Olivia."

This might be the hardest part to say. "Mom blew up when I said we needed to find out if Jane Doe could be my half sister. Mom insisted Dad didn't want me to know, that he'd never have told me. She said I'd destroy his reputation, and she wouldn't be able to hold her head up in town if everyone knew he'd cheated on her. She said if I tell anyone, she didn't know if she could forgive me."

"Oh, damn," Ben said again, but softly this time. He reached out and covered her now writhing fingers with his much larger hand. "Way to put the pressure on you."

Olivia half laughed even though she felt like crying, too. "That was the point."

Her hands had gone still under his warm grip, which both comforted her and stirred her. Maybe because here they were, again, *parking*. Funny how Ben was the only person she seemed to end up sitting in a parked car with and always in a lonely spot.

"I'm sorry," he said simply. "Have you decided what to do?"

She nodded. Shook her head. Nodded again and

realized in complete humiliation that tears were dripping down her cheeks.

Next thing she knew, he'd gathered her into his arms and she was crying against his very solid chest.

CHAPTER EIGHT

THE SIGHT OF Olivia's tears shocked Ben. He'd never seen her cry, not even at her father's funeral, where her face had been white and set. Not even when he'd broken up with her all those years ago, and hurt had darkened her eyes and curled her fingers into fists. Probably she'd cried after he'd dropped her off that night, and when her dad died, too, but privately.

"It's okay, sweetheart—let it out," he murmured, laying his cheek against her head. Closing his eyes and breathing her in. She didn't use the same shampoo she had as a girl, which had been too flowery for her. This was something tangy. He moved one of his hands in soothing circles on her back, although with the way she was sobbing, she might even be unaware of it. For all her height, she was finely built, long and slim. Her shoulder blades and the bumps of vertebrae felt fragile. "We'll get through this," he told her. "You know your mother didn't mean it."

She suddenly went so completely still, he knew it had to be what he'd said. Up until then, he'd been generically soothing. The mention of her mother had been a mistake.

Too late. Olivia retreated to her side of the front seat, already swiping at her tears and mumbling, "I can't believe I'm crying. There's nothing to cry about!"

"Of course there is," he said brusquely, startling her into looking at him. He reached past her and opened the glove compartment where he kept a box of tissues. "Here."

She took one, wiped her cheeks and blew her nose with a defiant honk before giving him a puffy-eyed look. "What do you mean?"

"For God's sake, Olivia!" She couldn't possibly be serious. "Your whole world has been undermined. None of you knew there was anything wrong with your father until he had that first heart attack, did you?"

Her gaze clinging to his face, she shook her head.

"Then the schism between your parents, not helped by the fact that neither would tell you what had happened. Made you wonder if you ever knew them, didn't it? And with them shutting you out, you had to feel like an outsider. As if you had no right to know." He released a breath. "Then your father dies, your mother doesn't act the way you'd expect, she announces she's selling the house as if you have no voice in it at all—"

"I don't," she said in a pained voice.

No, and her mother had slapped her in the face

with it, which she hadn't had to do. He almost stopped there. Wasn't that enough? But for Olivia, Charles Bowen's death was barely the beginning.

"In the back of your mind was some unease about the dead girl," Ben said, "because I think we all know someone in this town has been hiding something."

She nodded, but he also saw her chin wobble. She thought she knew who'd been hiding something. What she didn't know was that the man sitting here was hiding something, too.

It might be cruel to remind her of all her troubles, but Ben truly believed she needed to hear it all right here, right now. So he went on. "Now you know your father screwed up in a way that deepens your feeling you didn't know him the way you thought you did, and you face the possibility of having an unknown sister, one who might have died before you ever got the chance to meet her. And your mother lashes out at you, of all people. Put all that together, and you don't think it's worth a few tears?"

She gave a funny, broken laugh. "Okay. You've made your point."

They sat in silence for a minute, Ben watching her. He wanted to take her hand in his at the very least, but her body language told him she was working at regaining the self-control that was so important to her.

"Am I crazy?" she said finally in a small voice.

"Crazy?" It took him a second. "You mean, to suspect Jane Doe might be this girl who wrote your father?"

"Yes."

"Do you know when she wrote him?"

"August. No surprise, the date coincided with the deep freeze in our house."

He was still putting the pieces together, his mind making jumps that might be skipping a square. "You think that's why your father went to her funeral."

"Mom was furious, I thought at the time because he was risking his health. Now…" Olivia broke off, her shoulders jerking. "Well, when I called her on it, I could tell from her expression that she already suspected Jane Doe could be my sister."

There'd been a barely detectable hesitation before she said those last two words: *my sister.* Ben could only imagine how she must be feeling.

"Do you know why your parents didn't have any other kids?" he asked. Damn, he'd give a lot to be able to see her face better, rather than barely making out the broadest expressions and gestures in the yellowish light from the one sodium lamp on a pole twenty-five yards or so away.

"Yes. When I was an adult, Mom told me she'd had miscarriages. When I was little, I thought I'd like a baby sister or brother. You know…" Her forehead crinkled. "I must have asked this once. I remember Dad's face when he shook his head and said, 'We can't, honey. I'm sorry.' He looked so sad." She grimaced. "I was self-absorbed enough, I quit wondering. And probably spoiled, too. You know. Who needs competition?" She made a funny sound, a cross between a laugh and a sob.

That gave him an excuse to wrap an arm around her long enough to give a quick squeeze. "You were a kid. We all take our families for granted, whatever shape they come in."

He was close enough to see her bite her lip. "That's true, I guess." As he straightened, letting his arm fall away from her, she stole a glance at him. "Do you think your stepson does?"

"No. I guess he might be an exception." Ben thought about it. "Maybe that's part of what he and I are striving for. To be able to take for granted that we're family."

"That's nice. I mean, that you want to be his family."

He almost hoped she'd ask about his marriage and why he had ended up with Carson, but she didn't. Maybe thought she had no right. He hoped it was that and not lack of curiosity.

"Do you know what you're going to do?" he asked again after another lengthy silence.

"Part of me thinks I should respect Mom's wishes. I don't want to hurt her."

Now Olivia was staring straight ahead into the darkness. No—toward her father's grave. And the grave that might hold her sister. Ben didn't know if this was a good place to be talking or a really crummy one.

He took a chance and captured her hand in his. She grabbed on as if to be sure he didn't let go. Did she even know she'd done that? Although the tension in her fingers wasn't all to do with recent events. Olivia had never been given to stillness, and her mind was always working. She got restless if she wasn't in perpetual motion, too. In fact, he didn't remember her ever completely relaxing against him, or her hand lying lax in his... He tuned back in to catch up on what she was saying.

"But then I get this sick feeling of guilt. The girl—her name was Jessica, did I tell you that?— said her mother had died and she lived with her grandmother now. And I think, what if her grandmother is searching for her? If Jessica didn't say where she was going, the grandmother could think she's been abducted or murdered."

Instead of just dying for no apparent reason. Ben knew damn well they were both thinking the same thing.

"You don't know where she lives?"

Olivia shook her head. "Not a clue. I told you there was no envelope."

"If your mother saw it, she probably remembers at least a partial return address or postmark."

"I think it's safe to say she isn't going to tell me."

"She's never worked, has she? Out of the home, I mean."

Olivia looked at him, probably wondering where he was going with that question. "No," she said. "Well, she's always been active with her clubs."

"Garden club," he remembered.

"She's helped raise a lot of money for scholarships for local girls."

He nodded. The local chapter of the American Association of University Women was active enough to offer three scholarships every year, two to undergrads, one to a graduate student.

"More recently, she's giving time to the food bank," Olivia continued. "Since the mill went under, more people have needed help. I think she and Dad gave a lot of money, too."

"Your parents were both good people," he said gently.

Her tension didn't abate. "What are you suggesting? That if I wait, Mom will come around?"

"I don't know." Ben wished he did. "She's right that if word gets out, people will look at her differently. That can be hard to face. Pride counts. She already knows *you're* looking at her differently."

Olivia bent her head. Her hair slid forward, a thick curtain hiding her face. It was shiny enough to reflect even the limited light. "The worst part is that everything you said about me is true for her, too," she said in a low voice. "Even more. I mean, accepting that your parents aren't quite who you thought they were is disorienting, but to discover the man you loved and have spent your lifetime with had done something so…so *hurtful* and you never knew… I can hardly imagine."

He hoped like hell she wasn't drawing parallels with their own teenage romance. But why would she? He'd broken up with her pretty damn quick after leaving for college and what he was ashamed now to realize he'd seen as greener pastures. The only secret he'd kept was that, as Carson had put it, he'd jumped the gun. Olivia's coolness toward him these past three years suggested she did hold a grudge, but that might be in his head. Indifference was an alternate and entirely real possibility. "Yeah." He had to clear his throat. "You're right, of course."

"That's why you asked why I don't have siblings, isn't it? You were wondering if the sting was even greater if, say, Dad hadn't wanted any more kids and she had."

"That crossed my mind."

She gusted a sigh. "Not true, fortunately, but… See what I meant? High drama?"

He gave a low chuckle. "We all have stretches like that in our lives."

"I suppose you did with a divorce."

"Oh, yeah." So she was curious. "One of these days, I'll tell you about it."

"I should get home," she said quickly, as if alarmed by the idea that there'd be a future talk where they exchanged life stories. "And you still need to grocery shop, don't you?"

"We'll live without until tomorrow." They were still holding hands. It was a connection, a conduit. He didn't want to let go. "You've made up your mind, haven't you?"

Even with the poor lighting, he saw how startled her glance was. "You mean, about…? No, I *don't* know. I told you. Part of me thinks—" Her shoulders slumped, as if in defeat. "Yes. Yes, I have to know. I'll try to keep anyone else from finding out, but I can't let it go. I just can't, Ben."

He smiled faintly. "I didn't think you could. It would be one thing if this was only about you and your mother, but it isn't."

"No." A shiver traveled down to the hand he held. "It isn't."

Ben nodded, then kissed her cheek, causing her body to jerk. "I know you."

"You think so?" Her voice abruptly cooled. She disentangled her hand from his. "Thank you for listening, Ben. Another good deed." So lightly said, as if suddenly they were polite strangers.

Abruptly annoyed, he asked, "You think that's why I followed you? So I could nobly lend an ear?"

Already opening the door, Olivia looked over her shoulder. Her eyebrows arched. "Isn't it? You said you were worried."

"Yeah. About you. I've…been thinking a lot about you." Crappy timing, but he couldn't help himself. There might never be better.

She made a huffing sound as she slid out of the

front seat to the ground. "I guess you have to recycle when there aren't many single women in town," she said, then slammed the door.

Bristling, he got out to meet her at the back of the Jeep. "You know better than that."

Her chin jutted. "Do I?"

"I was an idiot, but as you pointed out, it was sixteen years ago. Are you saying you won't consider having dinner with me because of our history?"

"You haven't asked me to dinner."

"Well, I am now." He winced at how aggressive he sounded. "Friday night."

"Don't you have to go to the game?"

"That's part of the invitation."

"It's not a home game, is it?"

Okay, what was happening here? "Uh…no," he fumbled. "But my kid *is* on the team. Miller Falls isn't that far." With an effort, he softened his voice. "We can have dinner there. We might even go unrecognized. Italian, Mexican…I hear the Thai restaurant isn't bad, either. Whatever you want."

"All right," she said. "I suppose, um, you *have* been nice."

Damn. He was pissed again. The up and down was enough to give him a headache. "So dinner is payback?"

She snorted and spun away. "Forget about it."

Ben rotated on his heel as she made a wide circle around him. "Olivia."

At the bumper of her small car, she paused with her back to him.

"I'm sorry," he said gruffly. "I've been wanting to ask you for a long time, and now I'm doing a really lousy job of it."

"Yes, you are." Her tone was implacable, but another sigh drifted his way and she turned partway around. "I didn't mean it the way it sounded. About, well…"

"Suggesting I was asking for payback?"

"Yeah, that."

"Okay." He smiled. "Can you get away at five? The game starts at seven-thirty."

"Pick me up at home." Suddenly she was smiling, too. He'd have sworn she gave her hips a little extra swing as she went around to the driver's side. Her expression when she gave him a last look over the roof was completely serious, though, and her voice soft when she said, "I do mean the thank-you."

He didn't know if she heard his "You're welcome." He got back in his Jeep and waited until she'd backed in a wide circle, put her signal on, even though the highway was dark in both directions, and turned left toward town, after which he closed in behind her.

Only with reluctance did he turn off at his street and see her continue on. Damn it, he wanted to have dinner with her now. Plus, he didn't like knowing what the atmosphere must be like at her house. *God.* Would she tell her mother her decision tonight? And what did that decision involve? They hadn't gotten as far as talking about the nitty-gritty of how she intended to pursue the possibility that Jane Doe was her sister, Jessica. With no address, no phone number...

She had to have a last name, he realized, and probably mother's name, too. That was enough to start with.

And right now, he couldn't make himself care how Olivia would find this maybe-sister. He was too filled with the knowledge that she'd said yes. He hadn't felt this good in a long time. Maybe never.

He waited for his garage door to rise and pulled in, glad to see Carson's bike already leaning against the wall. He pushed the button on the remote even before he turned off the engine, then just sat there listening to the hum of the descending door, smiling foolishly despite the gravity of everything he and Olivia had talked about.

PHIL WEIGAND BEGAN to wonder if the doorbell didn't work. He couldn't hear a damn thing. Bert Ellison's ancient pickup truck was parked in the barn, which suggested he was around. Out back somewhere? Phil gave thought to circling the house to see, but he was reluctant to take by surprise a man with such a reckless reputation for using a shotgun. Phil hadn't had to kill anyone since he served in Vietnam, and he'd rather not change that today.

All right, damn it. He hammered on the door

and finally heard the deep-throated bay of a dog, accompanied by the clatter of claws. Ellison must move a whole lot slower than his dog, though, because it had to be another two or three minutes before the door swung open.

When Phil saw the old man, dismay grabbed him. He hadn't often seen such a drastic change in anyone, not so quickly.

Bert Ellison's cheeks were gaunt beneath several days of white stubble. Greasy, stringy strands of white hair hung uncombed. Blue eyes Phil remembered as sharp were dull. He stood staring at the man on his doorstep for the longest time, as if puzzling out why he'd opened the door at all. The dog was still howling, but the old man had blocked him as if an old habit was still operating.

Crap, Phil thought. Could he have had a stroke? Did he have any family around? Was there anybody to check on him regularly, make sure he was eating?

"What'd'ye want?" Ellison mumbled at last.

"I'm Police Chief Phil Weigand—"

"I know who you are."

"May I come in? I'd like to ask you a couple of questions."

"Shut up!" Ellison bellowed, and the dog fell silent. There was a discernible pause before he shrugged. "If'n you want."

To Phil's relief, the living room didn't look too bad. In fact, at a guess, someone had to be coming out to clean regularly. The old guy shuffled to a worn recliner and sank into it, leaving Phil to sit cautiously on a sofa with dangerously sunken cushions.

"Don't know what I can tell you," Ellison said after a minute.

"I spoke to you the day Mrs. Connelly found that dead girl out in the woods on her place." The last time Phil had seen Ellison.

No flicker of expression showed on a face that wouldn't have looked out of place on a slab in the morgue.

"I have reason to think you might not have been honest with me, Mr. Ellison." Phil made his voice hard. "I've since learned you were out in the middle of the night with your gun. Folks heard you take a couple of shots. I need you to tell me what you were shooting at."

What happened next was terrible to watch. First were some tears, trickling down over the bags, catching in deep creases, glistening on the white stubble. What he saw in that blue gaze wasn't emotion so much as a man who *wanted* to be dead.

"I guess you know then." He didn't seem to notice that he was crying. "I ran someone off. Swore I heard kids hooting and hollering off in the woods. Don't seem to bother none of them to trespass. Weren't the first time I run the damn kids off."

Oh, hell, Phil thought.

"Did you see anyone?" He kept his voice as gentle as he could make it. Whatever he'd expected to feel when he came out here, it wasn't pity.

The old man bent his head and stared down at the hound lying at his feet. "Yeah." His throat visibly worked. "Just a real pale shape. Almost ghostlike."

The dead girl had been found in faded jeans and a powder-pink sweatshirt that would have appeared colorless in the dark, with only a partial moon to add silver illumination. Her hair was pale, too, an almost blond, almost brown shade.

"I heard someone yell, 'Don't shoot me—don't shoot me.'" Every nerve in his face seem to be twitching now. The dog's skin shivered when tears dropped onto it. "The voice was…was a girl's. She ran for the woods. I heard crashing and then…nothing." He heaved a deep breath. "I went back to bed. Thought, *she* won't be coming back." He lifted his head with aching slowness, until wet blue eyes met Phil's. "Then I heard the next day. 'Bout that dead girl. And I knew it had to be her."

"You didn't shoot her, Mr. Ellison. She wasn't wounded."

Comprehension took some time to sink in. "It weren't me that killed her?"

Well, shit. How did he say, "Not directly, but she'd be alive if you'd let her shelter in your barn for the night?"

He couldn't, that's how. Bert Ellison knew already, and he was being destroyed by the knowledge.

"It wasn't your fault she was out here alone in the

middle of the night," Phil said, picking his words carefully. "She could've used some help, but you weren't to know."

The torment didn't ease any.

"I'd like you to give me that shotgun, though. I think we'd both be happier if you never fire it again."

The head bobbed after a minute. "You ain't gonna arrest me?"

"No, Mr. Ellison. You didn't kill her, assuming it was her at all."

"Who else could've it been?"

"I've heard rumors there might have been a kegger out here somewhere that night."

"I thought that's what woke me. Don't know why one lone girl would've— 'Cept..." He looked down. "Bucky here, he was carrying on. Wanted to tear after her. I wouldn't let him," he said with a faint hint of pride.

"Next time you hear teenagers out partying in your woods, you call nine-one-one and a police officer will come out. You hear me, Mr. Ellison?"

"I hear you."

He shuffled into the depths of the house, leaving Phil to wait for his return. When he did, the shotgun he held was an old-timer, a Mossberg twenty gauge that at Phil's guess dated from the 1950s. Still in good shape; Bert had kept it clean. Arthritic hands surrendered it reluctantly, as an old friend.

"I'll keep it safe," Phil said quietly. "Is there anybody you'd like me to call? Your son?"

"He checks in now and again. I take care of myself." He hesitated. "People gonna know? That I chased her away?"

"I don't see why it has to become common knowledge. Don't worry." Phil nodded. "Thank you for being honest. Good day, Mr. Ellison."

He opened the trunk of his car, ejected the shells and laid the Mossberg down, them slammed the trunk. The dog was back to baying away. For a minute, Phil gazed at the house, sagging at one corner, and shook his head.

Nothing he'd said was going to ease Bert Ellison's burden of guilt. Probably he shouldn't have even tried. Sure as hell, if the girl had taken refuge in his barn, she would have survived the night. If he hadn't chased her away. But the guy wasn't doing anything he hadn't done dozens of other times, from the sound of it. Unfortunately, the Connelly and Ellison acres were party central for Crescent Creek teenagers. They all knew the home owners were old and deaf, and they took advantage of it.

In this case…well, it was a tragedy, that's all. No real malice, but a very bad outcome.

Phil drove away, his mood somber.

OLIVIA HATED TO be a skeptic, but was it really possible to find good Thai food in small-town America? She'd opted for Mexican. Ben accused her of playing it safe, which she was.

Except, of course, for the fact that she was having dinner with him. Giving him another chance?

Am I really?

She didn't actually know the answer to that question. He'd been nice; he was someone she could talk to. Maybe they could be friends. Even lovers. Didn't mean she was even thinking about *really* letting him in.

She'd seen Ben's relief when they first arrived at the restaurant and he scanned the booths. "Don't know a soul," he'd murmured.

She didn't, either, which lightened her mood immeasurably. Wow, she'd needed to get away, even if she had discovered she loved her hometown and that her tolerance for its many eccentric citizens was greater than she'd known.

Now, as he scooped up salsa with a tortilla chip, Ben pinned her with a gaze. "So, did you tell your mom what you've decided?"

Olivia made a face. "No."

"You did decide."

"I not only decided—I talked to Chief Weigand today. He…swabbed my cheek."

His dark eyebrows rose. "That quick?"

"Apparently that's the only quick part."

"Yeah, I've read that. It can take months to a year to get DNA results."

"Unless you're willing to pay for a rush job." She hadn't even hesitated. "I'm paying."

"How long?"

"Maybe a few weeks," she replied.

"Ah."

"Not knowing eats at me."

Not taking those penetrating dark eyes from her, he took a long swallow of his beer. "I do understand."

"You heard anything else?" she asked. "About the kegger, I mean?"

He set the glass down more carefully than the small action deserved. Somehow she could tell Ben was thinking furiously. Which meant he knew something he hadn't decided whether he was going to tell her.

Her eyes narrowed to slits.

"I promised to keep this confidential."

"What? You're the repository of everybody's secrets?"

"Everybody's? No. That would be Chief Weigand."

Her anger deflated. "Are you going to tell me what you *do* know?"

"If you swear, cross your heart, not to tell one more person." There was no give in his voice. He was letting her know he meant it.

Olivia nodded. "There's no one I talk to." Except Ben, of course.

"You're spending some time with friends."

"Sure, but I realized right away that they've

become part of the local information network. I mean, I suppose they always were, but I probably was, too. Now…" She shrugged, although what she had almost said was, *I feel as though I'm standing apart.* She didn't want to sound pathetic, though, especially since he already knew these past months her parents had made her feel like a distant relative who was a guest in their home and not privileged to be part of the inner workings of the family.

The kindness in his eyes told her he'd heard what she hadn't said, which wasn't a surprise. Ben had always had a gift that way. "My hesitation is the possibility that Jane Doe will turn out to be your sister."

"And you think I don't want to know the worst."

"Something like that," he admitted.

"I've already imagined some truly horrible possibilities," Olivia said. "I think I'd rather *know,* no matter what. Accepting fact would be easier than constantly thinking, oh God, what if *that* happened?"

Ben grunted; then his gaze shifted past her shoulder. The approaching sizzle made his words unnecessary, but he said them anyway. "Our food's here."

They'd both opted for chicken fajitas. There was a pause in the conversation while they each constructed a first fajita. Olivia had to grab for a napkin as she took a bite and sour cream oozed out.

"It started with something I overheard," Ben said abruptly, then went on to tell her about two high school girls talking and him passing on what they had said to the police chief. "He called today to tell me he'd talked to the girl's mother and then, uh, a neighbor."

So he didn't plan to name names. She couldn't blame him, especially after she heard the rest of the story.

"Bert Ellison," she said flatly.

Ben just looked at her.

"Come on, how many cranky old men are there who live anywhere near the Connelly farm?"

The lines on Ben's face aged him. "I knew I shouldn't tell you."

Olivia examined how she felt about the story without coming to a conclusion. The knot in her chest was tangled too tightly. "No, I will keep it to myself."

His eyebrows slid up. "You promise?"

"Yes. Now spit it out."

"Phil said the old guy was pathetic. He thought all he was doing was running off the usual teenagers out partying. Apparently, someone tossed a cigarette and lit a fire in old straw a few years back. Burned an outbuilding to the ground. Kids have also spray-painted graffiti on the sides of his barn over and over, really obscene stuff."

She hadn't heard that, although it was common for graduating seniors to paint their class year on any large available surface. Local farmers must get really tired of it.

"He's been feeling guilty ever since. He was relieved to find out he hadn't shot her, at least."

"He thought he had?"

"When he heard a dead girl had been found, he put two and two together."

"But the answer wasn't four."

"No." He watched her steadily. "This is part of whatever the answer is, though."

Yes. And considering they were searching for the answer to a tragic death, no part of it would be good.

"Thank you for telling me," she said.

Ben nodded. "Eat your dinner."

"Right. We want good seats."

He only laughed. "Come on. This is the same gymnasium you and I played in. The nosebleed section isn't all that high off the court."

"They *still* haven't passed a bond issue to build a new high school?"

"Nope. They tried again as recently as last fall. Rumor says they're bitter that we did. It's made the rivalry even more intense."

That made her laugh. The league championship hadn't been nearly as sweet as beating the crap out of the Miller Falls girls. More intense? That she had to see.

CHAPTER NINE

THE CROWD ROARED. Unable to help himself, Ben leaped to his feet. "Pass," he said under his breath. "What are you *thinking?* Pass, pass, pass," he chanted. "Pass."

Ignoring his teammates, Carson powered toward the basket. He dribbled, spun past a defender...and slam-dunked the ball to the exultant screams of the Crescent Creek fans.

Ben laughed and swore at the same time. Coach McGarvie was going to be pissed, and rightfully so. Carson was playing selfish ball—but, oh damn, he was playing it well. The talent was back with a vengeance, and Ben was almost embarrassed by his exultation.

As one of the Miller Falls boys put the ball back into play and action moved down the court, Ben sank back to his seat on the bleacher and saw Olivia doing the same.

"He's good."

Ben's legs actually felt weak. "He's *great.*"

She was laughing at him. "You said he hasn't been playing well."

"Not all season. I don't know what happened."
Something had the past few days, though. Ben had
noticed without understanding. Carson had been
even quieter than usual, but somehow steely. Just
today, he'd said, "I'm starting tonight."

When Ben had asked if he'd been getting it together, Carson had shrugged. "I decided to quit
taking crap. That's all."

If Ben hadn't watched the one practice, he
wouldn't have had a clue. As it was…he still didn't,
although his confusion differed from what it otherwise would have been. Maybe tomorrow they
could talk.

"He's going to be taller than you," Olivia com-
mented, then shot to her feet and let out a pierc-
ing whistle when Carson deigned to rocket a pass
to the Russian kid, Vadim Bukin, who slid in the
neatest layup you could want. "Yes!"

Crescent Creek was running away with the game.
The Miller Falls fans had been stunned into near silence. The Crescent Creek contingent was making
more than enough noise for the small gymnasium.

Moving with lightning speed, Carson snatched
the ball out of an opponent's hands and they all tore
down the court again. This time, Ben made himself set aside his emotions and just watch. A great
chance to pass came and went, untaken, leaving
Dylan Zurenko, center, hovering uselessly under
the basket. Not until he circled away did Carson
throw up a…no, not a shot, a high lob to Bearden,

who slammed it down. The crowd yelled more approval. McGarvie dropped to his bleacher seat as if his legs had given out.

Ben mentally reran the game. Realization came slowly. Carson wasn't playing selfish ball. He was shutting down two of his teammates. Passing when he could to the others, while refusing when he could to let Zurenko or one of the guards, Dex Slagle, get their hands on the ball. Ben couldn't believe he hadn't figured it out sooner. He wondered if McGarvie had. He felt pretty damn sure Slagle and Zurenko had noticed.

The thing was, you didn't see something like this often, mainly because a player had to be exceptionally dominant to single-handedly manage the game while also ensuring his team didn't get their asses whupped because of his cold-shouldering two guys on his own side.

Ben surely did hope like hell Carson had thought out the consequences. And that he sat right up front on the team bus during the drive back to Crescent Creek.

Brooding, he missed the last plays. The buzzer startled him back to the present. That and the foot-stamping, screaming approval from this side of the gym. The team engulfed Carson, who exchanged a jubilant high five with Bukin. Two of the other boys swept Carson off his feet and lifted him head and shoulders above the rest. Only Slagle and Zurenko stalked away, grabbed towels and started for the locker room.

Impelled by sudden urgency, Ben grabbed Olivia's hand. He had to yell to be heard even with his mouth right at her ear. "Let's get out of here."

She looked startled but let him tow her down the bleachers, creaking and groaning beneath the happy crowd. People called congratulations, and Ben nodded and smiled without stopping.

His ears appreciated the relative silence once they escaped the gym. Engines were already starting and headlights coming on across the parking lot. Disappointed Miller Falls fans departing.

"Wait!" Olivia put on the brakes, dragging him to a stop. "Aren't we going to hang around until the boys come out?"

"No."

"But—"

He got her moving again. "I need time to take you home and kiss you good-night—"

"What?"

"And be waiting when that bus pulls in at the high school." He knew he sounded grim.

Olivia didn't say another word until they were on their way out of the parking lot, inching along in the line of other exiting vehicles.

"Okay, what's the deal?" she asked finally.

"The kissing part?"

"No." She sounded prim. "*That* I understand.

What I don't get is the life-or-death race to be at the high school before the bus gets there."

He tried to remember what she already knew and think of a way to explain without mentioning his suspicion that Carson held another piece of the puzzle of Jane Doe's death.

"Uh…" They moved forward another car length. "Something's going on with him. I told you about watching a practice."

She nodded.

"Two of his teammates were knocking him around. The coach said it was subtle enough he didn't feel like he could do anything about it, and Carson sure isn't telling me what it's all about, but I didn't like it." That was one way of putting it.

"You think that's why he hasn't been playing well."

He glanced at her. "Some of it, yeah."

Another car length opened ahead, but he decided to do the polite thing and let someone else in. "Tonight, he completely shut down those two teammates."

Out of the corner of his eye, Ben watched her play a rerun, the way he had earlier.

"The center," she said slowly. "I don't remember his name."

"Dylan Zurenko. It was him and one of the guards, Dex Slagle. They're both seniors, buddies."

"Slagle didn't score a single point, did he?"

"No. Zurenko did because others passed to him, but Carson didn't. Not once."

"While making the point that he didn't need them."

"Oh, yeah." Suddenly he was grinning again.

Olivia chuckled, a low, delicious sound. "And Dad enjoyed every minute of it."

"I cannot tell a lie." The words sobered him, though, because they weren't true. He *hadn't* lied to her, not exactly, but he hadn't been entirely honest, either.

"You want to be there waiting to pick him up so the two of them can't corner him in a dark parking lot."

"Yeah."

"If we're going to get anywhere, you're being too polite," she pointed out.

"Huh?" He focused ahead to see that he was about to lose a chance to make progress if he didn't move. His foot touched the accelerator lightly.

"So," she said. "You were going to tell me how you ended up with Carson. Where his father and mother are…?"

Ben guessed there'd never be a better time. They weren't getting anywhere very fast and still had the twenty-minute drive to Crescent Creek ahead besides. What he hadn't quite made up his mind was how much to tell her.

"He's never known his father. Melanie didn't put a father's name on his birth certificate. She told me about him, but…" Some of this complicated stew of emotions had to do with Carson, not himself, but he also didn't like remembering how thoroughly he'd been taken by her. It had been a couple of years after the wedding before he realized fully that Mel had played a role to land him, and he'd been stupid enough to fall for her act. "I've come to suspect she doesn't even know what man is his father," he said finally, his voice a little rougher.

Olivia was watching him, but he didn't turn his head. "Does Carson know that?"

"I don't think so." His mouth twisted. "I hope not. A lot of men don't want to take on another man's kids. Me, I fell for Carson as much as her. He was a great kid. He *is* a great kid," Ben corrected himself. "We bonded right away. Good thing, because a year or two into the marriage, I figured out she was using cocaine. Just for fun, she said, but it wasn't. She was an addict. She agreed to treatment, got out and lasted about this long." He snapped his fingers. "Sometimes I thought she was really trying. Whatever I felt for her died quicker than I want to admit, but…"

What was he waiting for? Did he expect Olivia to say, *You're the kind of guy who keeps his vows. Who digs in for the tough times.* He thought he really was. But why would she believe that?

When she didn't say anything, Ben continued. "She…had a lot of problems. Maybe all drugs, but I think she's mentally ill, too." There were other men, too, but he edited out that part of the confession. He was still humiliated to have been so blind. "It was really a mess. I stuck it out longer than I should have because of Carson. How could I leave him?"

Olivia laid a hand on his thigh and squeezed. His muscles tightened. She took her hand back, and he wished she hadn't. He liked the gesture of understanding, but he liked even better having her hand on him.

Finally, thank God, he was able to turn out of the parking lot. They were only a few blocks from the highway. Almost home free.

"Carson doesn't know how heavily I pressured her toward the end. I said our marriage was over and that, if she didn't surrender custody of Carson to me, I'd call in child protective services and she'd lose him anyway. The sad thing is, I think she really does love him. She signed."

"Does he see her at all?"

"We tried some visitation. I left him at the mall for a couple of hours with her, that kind of thing. But she kept derailing. Canceled, didn't show, was high when she did. So I cut it off." He gripped the steering wheel tighter. "Then she started calling him without my knowing, and he ran away once because he was convinced she needed him to take care of her. I caught up with them, and I could tell how glad he was. Even he could see that she was beyond his help."

"That must have been really hard for him." There was a small pause. "And you."

The interior of the car had gotten even darker since they'd left the well-lit parking lot behind. With a green light, he turned east on the highway and night closed in. Only dashboard lights and headlights well behind them offered any illumination. Ben was glad. He knew she was watching him. Telling her about his marriage in the baldest of terms was one thing; letting her see the devastation Melanie had wrought was another altogether.

"Me?" He heard how harsh he sounded. "By then I mostly felt like an idiot. I figured out early on that the only sincere part of our romance was her wanting me to marry her. Otherwise, it was all pretense. One thing Melanie is good at is reading other people, figuring out what they want."

"She's a con artist."

"In her way," he agreed. "Her big incentive is finding enough money to pay for her addiction. I'm not sure if she actually likes having a man in her life—" he grunted "—or whether it's all about having someone to take care of her."

"It's probably lucky you didn't have kids with her."

"Not luck. I was damn careful not to get her pregnant. At first I was in grad school and working an insane amount of hours besides. By the time I finished my dissertation, I knew I'd made a mistake."

"But there was Carson."

"Yeah." Remembering his own naivety made him shake his head. "And I kept thinking if she could kick the addiction, maybe she'd be the person I remembered."

"Where's she live?"

"Bay area. Actually, I think she's in Sacramento now. Sounds like there's a new guy. Or was," he corrected himself. "Last time Carson talked to her was August."

"He seems amazingly together given all that."

"He is." Ben grunted. "Most of the time."

Olivia touched his thigh again, more tentatively this time. "He's a teenager. They're all up and down. You know that."

Probably, he should be amused. With a career in secondary education, he was supposed to know teenagers. Your own kid, though, that was different.

"Thank you for telling me," she said after a minute, voice soft.

"You've told me plenty."

"Yes, but…"

When she didn't finish, he cut a look at her. "But?"

"I told you about my parents' marriage going bad. Your own, that's more personal."

"You haven't had a marriage that could blow up."

"Nice imagery."

"You must have had serious relationships."

An oncoming car momentarily lit the interior of his with bright white light. Blinking in the afterglow, he tried to analyze the odd expression he'd seen on Olivia's face. And failed. He couldn't tell what she was thinking.

"Not that serious," she said finally. "I've never lived with a guy or considered saying 'I do.'"

Ben was suddenly, fiercely glad. So glad, he shocked himself. He was getting ahead of himself here. Olivia wasn't the girl he'd known, any more than he was the boy who had dumped her. Falling in love because of a memory was a very bad idea. Wait and see.

"Maybe you were smarter than I was," he heard himself say.

She made a huffing sound. "Yeah, my faith in 'happily ever after' is flagging right about now, I've got to tell you."

"My parents are still happy," he was startled to hear himself say.

"Are you so sure?" she asked, with such deep cynicism he was reminded again that she'd changed.

"Yeah." He'd come out of the bathroom and caught them kissing the last time he was at the house. Embarrassed himself more than them. His father had just laughed. The thing was, the tenderness and lust had been palpable. He hadn't been able to help feeling a spurt of envy. Because of his parents, he'd gone into marriage assuming that kind of closeness and longevity was possible. "Yeah," he said again. "I've always figured I'd find what they have."

"I thought I'd find what my parents had, too," Olivia said, so sad he reached out for her hand. He fumbled for a second but found it. Having her hold on the way she had the other time sent a jolt through him. There it was again—the sense that he could feel her emotions through the physical contact and maybe send his zinging back to her, too.

He had to reclaim his hand when it came time to turn off the highway. They didn't talk for the last five minutes of the drive. Ben wasn't looking forward to leaving her.

"You working tomorrow?" he asked, as he slowed for her driveway.

"I don't know. Maybe part of the day. Mom and I haven't gotten very far on the house."

"Is there any hurry?"

Her shoulders moved. "I keep feeling like there is. I don't know if she's signed papers yet or not. Our conversations are really careful. I definitely got the feeling she was in a hurry. And…" Her voice was faltering. "I guess now that I've started, I want to get it over with. You know?"

"I can imagine." He came to a stop, putting the gearshift into Park, aware the stomach-tightening sense of urgency hadn't left him once during the drive. It had taken them a hell of a long time to get out of the parking lot back in Miller Falls. The bus, able to use a different exit, might not be that far behind.

Not until he unfastened his seat belt and then

Olivia's did he discover that a whole lot of that urgency was focused on her. Yeah, there was a hum in the background that had to do with Carson, but right now... Damn, he wanted to kiss her. Even more, he wanted her to kiss him back, to respond with something close to the passion she'd once given him.

"You okay with the kissing good-night part of this program?" he asked, his voice a notch huskier than usual.

"It seems only polite."

"Polite?" He stiffened.

Her eyes were wide. "I was...teasing. I'm sorry. I guess I'm, um, a little nervous."

"Okay." His throat felt as if he had gravel in it. He was nervous, too. This kiss meant too much.

He slid his fingers into the thick silk of her hair to cup the back of her head. She tilted her head, just a little, as if savoring his touch. He bent, determined to take this slow even as his heartbeat jumped. Her lips were so soft; he groaned as he gently rubbed his against them. Hers quivered; he nibbled until she let him in and he was able to touch her tongue with his. The damp contact felt incredibly erotic to him. *It's deprivation,* he thought desperately, even as he knew better. *It's her. Olivia.* His first love.

That was his last coherent thought.

So much for slow. He kissed her like a starving man, his tongue plunging, stroking hers. Somehow he'd come to be gripping her waist with his free hand. He wanted her closer, but the bucket seats and confines of his Jeep frustrated him. Once he had to tear his mouth from hers so they could both suck in air. His brain had hazed over, but a dim thought edged in. She *was* kissing him back, wasn't she? *God, don't let this be one-sided.* Even the prayer disappeared when she moaned and lifted her mouth to his. One of her hands pressed his chest right over the hammer beat of his heart, while the other gripped his nape. *Yes.*

Something buzzed at his hip. Olivia tried to retreat. He captured her mouth in another kiss. The vibration continued.

"Your phone," she whispered against his cheek.

He swore. "Don't care."

"What if it's Carson?"

Ben went still. He closed his eyes and struggled to center himself. Damn, he'd lost it.

Carson.

He fumbled for the phone and discovered he'd missed the call. Apparently he could take everything slow but Olivia. Reluctantly, he separated himself from her enough to go to missed calls. Carson. *Send.*

"Dad?"

"You called." His voice was so hoarse as to be unrecognizable.

"Uh…" There was a pause. "Are you going to be

there? I mean, at the high school?" Carson was almost whispering. He didn't want someone to hear.

His brain was coming back online. He didn't look away from Olivia as he talked, though. "Yeah. You getting close?"

"Like, five minutes?"

Shit. "Okay," he said. He cleared his throat. "I'll be there."

"Thanks."

The phone went dead.

Ben hooked it back on his belt. "I'm sorry."

"Because you have to go?" She finger-combed her hair. "That's…probably just as well."

"Because I fell on you like a ravening beast?"

"Because we were getting carried away, and I don't know if I'm ready to go there. It's…awfully fast."

The go-slow instinct had been right on. However, Ben had a bad feeling the next time he touched her, it would be obliterated again. "We seem to be combustible."

Olivia gave up on her hair. "We always were. I'm not sure…"

I want to be again.

He heard the unspoken part. He just didn't like it.

"We'll go at your speed, Olivia." He sounded almost gentle. "At least, I'll try."

"Okay."

He cupped her cheek and felt her heat. She was blushing, had to be. "I'll walk you to the door."

"You don't want to be late."

"I can take a minute." He smiled. "Got to prove I can be a gentleman."

He caught her rolling her eyes as she opened the door. "Right."

He loved walking next to her, always had. With her height and long, leggy stride, he didn't have to shorten his own. She didn't object to the hand he splayed on her lower back, either, which meant he could enjoy the subtle play of muscles.

At the front door, he waited until she unlocked, then bent to kiss her lightly on the mouth. He didn't dare let himself linger. *Carson,* he reminded himself desperately.

"Good night, Ben," she said, voice throaty, and gave him a slight push.

She slipped inside and he went, hoping his raging hard-on subsided before he got to the high school.

OLIVIA'S RESOLVE DID battle with her cowardice as she started down the stairs the next morning. She did not want to tell her mother what she'd done, but she couldn't keep living in her house and *not* tell her.

Mom had beaten her downstairs, as she seemed to every morning. Olivia wasn't an early riser by nature, but Mom must be. Or else she'd spent so many years making Dad's breakfast and seeing him off to work, she'd never learned to sleep in.

Remembering their closeness and her mother's

devotion, Olivia was hit by a tidal wave of anger. How could he *do* that? She would have sworn he wasn't that kind of man. But could you ever really know anyone? She'd once believed so.

"Good morning," her mother said. "I was going to poach a couple of eggs. Would you like some?"

"Sure. That sounds good."

Oh, sure. Let her make me breakfast before I give her the bad news.

Marian made the toast, poured them both juice and brought raspberry jam to the table.

"Did you have a good time last night?" her mother asked as Olivia buttered toast. "Who won?" She'd already been upstairs and behind her closed bedroom door when Olivia got home. Asleep, or not wanting to talk, at least.

"Crescent Creek kicked ass," she said with a grin at her mother's disapproving expression. "Ben's stepson was a star. He was amazing. His teammates were about ready to fit him for a laurel wreath." Well, except for the two who wanted to kick *his* ass.

As they ate, she passed on bits of local gossip Ben had shared over dinner and the names of people she'd seen at the game. "I'll bet you don't miss having to sit through so many sporting events, do you?"

"Oh, I didn't mind the basketball. I could never work up much enthusiasm for softball, though."

Olivia smiled at her. "I remember." Olivia had played for five seasons, and her mother had faithfully driven her to practices and cheered for her at every game while not-quite-successfully hiding her complete boredom.

Her mother laughed. "I tried."

Olivia's heart squeezed at the sound she hadn't heard much in a long time. It didn't make what she had to say any easier.

She pushed her plate away. "Mom."

Her mother's head came up, alarm sharp on her face.

"I talked to Chief Weigand the other day."

"Talked to him about what?"

"I told him I wanted a DNA comparison test."

Her mother's eyes burned. "You *what?*"

"Nobody else needs to know. Unless..." Her throat clogged. She couldn't even say it. *Unless there's a familial match.*

Mom jumped to her feet, knocking over her juice. She didn't even seem to notice, although it ran over the table edge and dripped to the floor. "*Nothing* in this town stays secret. You know that."

Olivia stayed sitting, giving her mother the high ground. "He...took the sample himself." She hated to hear her voice shake. "He was going to send it off right away. Nobody else was involved."

"I asked you. I begged you."

Olivia didn't let herself look away from her mother, however much it hurt to see her shattered expression. "I had to find out," she tried to explain. "I'm sorry if that hurts you, Mom."

"Within twenty-four hours, everyone will be talking." Spots of color burned on cheeks that had blanched too pale. "And what if you *are* a match? Will you feel virtuous because you can put your sister's name on her headstone? With no thought for what you've done to me?"

Doubt cut deep, a scalpel slice. What *was* she hoping to accomplish? Had she been self-righteous? She didn't even know if she wanted to stay in Crescent Creek, but this was her mother's home. Olivia was suddenly burning with shame and fear that she'd done the wrong thing. She wasn't sure she could stand.

"Do you want me to move out?" she asked, with as much dignity as she could muster.

"And then what would people think?" her mother spat.

The shame iced over. "Is that all you can think about?" she asked, with some incredulity.

Her mother gave her a last look that was both scathing and hurt, and hurried from the room. Stunned although she didn't know why, Olivia sat listening to the flurry of footsteps on the stairs.

CHAPTER TEN

THE DAY WAS mild enough that Carson was out in the driveway hosing down Ben's Jeep Cherokee when Olivia arrived to have Sunday dinner with the two of them. It was early afternoon, which meant taking a break from packing, but she'd been glad to do that. She parked at the curb instead of behind the Jeep so her car didn't get splashed. When she got out and started up the driveway, the lanky boy said, "Hey."

She grinned at him. "Slave labor."

An answering grin played on his mouth. "Ya think? He says if I want to drive, I've got to pay the price."

She commiserated, then said, "He could have made you cook."

"Yeah, not when a pretty lady is coming over. He wouldn't want to be embarrassed."

"That bad, huh?"

"It's not good."

Olivia laughed and kept going, then turned before she reached the porch. "Great game."

"Thanks." He waved, unfortunately with the

hand holding the hose. The stream ricocheted off the side of the Jeep and splattered him. He was swearing when she rang the doorbell.

Letting her in, Ben looked past her. "Cold out there to be letting himself get wet," he observed.

On the way to the kitchen, Olivia had to explain why she thought that was so funny.

"I love your house," she said, peeking into the high-ceilinged living room with hardwood floors and beautiful molding. "Wasn't this the Langworths'?"

"Yes, but there was another owner in between," Ben said over his shoulder. "Mom says the Langworths moved to Wichita. Job," he added, and she nodded. Mr. Langworth had worked for Boeing, and transfers to Wichita happened.

She'd forgotten what it was like, living somewhere you always knew your neighbors, who knew their neighbors, who knew... Everybody's lives woven together. People here had a sense of context.

"The couple I bought from had already moved out," Ben was saying. "I never met them."

Olivia leaned a hip against the counter. "But I'll bet your mother told you their life story."

Amusement in his dark eyes, Ben said, "Oh, yeah. Mom knows all."

She hoped not *all*.

She only half listened to what he said about the previous owners. Instead, she surveyed the kitchen, which seemed to be a work in progress. Dated cabinets, but the bay window bump-out was obviously new, creating space for an eating area. The floor was still plywood up to the edge of the really ugly orange-and-yellow linoleum.

Ben saw the direction of her attention. "I'll have you know Dad, Carson and I built that on our own."

"Really? I didn't know either of you had ever done any construction."

"Dad worked construction summers through college. I guess enough of what he learned stuck. You didn't notice we were in and out of Bowen's this summer?"

"Well...I noticed you," she admitted, feeling a brief attack of shyness. At the time, she'd pretended for all she was worth that she *wasn't* noticing. "I'm grateful you shopped local."

He swept the rest of the kitchen with an assessing glance. "Can't do much else until I replace the cabinets."

"You plan to install them yourself?"

"Probably." He grimaced. "My original goal was over Christmas break. Now— Hell, maybe spring."

"You're buying ready-made?"

"Yeah, there's some nice ones out there."

Not at Bowen's, unfortunately. He'd need to go to Home Depot or Lowe's for those. Even in her dreams, Olivia didn't imagine having enough floor space to display anything like cabinets.

Bathroom vanities, maybe, she amended.

"Smells great," she said, watching as he added

a dash of wine to the spaghetti sauce. A loaf of French bread lay on the counter waiting to be sliced.

"I might go for the basics, but I do them well." Instead of smiling, he only looked at her, heat in his eyes.

Heat that transferred to low in her belly. Olivia fidgeted, resisting the urge to press her thighs together.

She couldn't believe she was here. Dinner out and a high school ball game was one thing, but now she was at his house? About to partake in a home-cooked meal? Big jump. He had a kid, for God's sake! Making her part of his kid's life, too, sent a signal that scared her.

Not, however, enough that she'd said no. Her intense desire to escape her own house—and Mom— had given her adequate justification for accepting his dinner invitation, she'd decided. She was less sure now, when she thought about it, but...she liked being here with Ben. Liked it too much.

And that scared her, too.

"Things with your mom ease at all today?" he asked, as if reading her mind.

He'd called last night, and next thing she knew, she was telling him all about the latest confrontation with her mother. Either to provide balance or because he needed someone to talk to, as well, he worried aloud about Carson, who'd blown him off when he'd asked about the tension between him and the two seniors on the basketball team. At the end, when Ben asked her to Sunday dinner, she'd said yes before she had a chance to think, *No, wait*.

The front door opened and slammed. Carson called, "I am so freaking *cold*," after which he thundered upstairs.

Ben turned on the burner to boil water for the spaghetti, then stepped over to her. He framed her face with his big hands, one thumb rubbing lightly over her lips. "I give us five minutes before he's back down here." His voice came out husky.

"Better grab the time we have then." Olivia hadn't known she could sound sultry.

He bent his head and pressed a kiss to her forehead before his lips traveled softly to the bridge of her nose, over her closed eyelids, her temple, her cheek. She waited, suspended, not even breathing, until he nuzzled her nose with his, then smiled against her mouth. *Then* she sucked in a breath.

"Ready?" he murmured, humor an undertone beneath the gravel she recognized as desire.

So ready. In answer, she sought his mouth, and the next moment they were kissing. Deeply, passionately, their tongues tangling, their bodies straining together. She wrapped her arms around his neck so she could hold him closer. His hips rocked, and hers rocked, too. He cupped the back of her head to control the kiss, and now his free hand gripped her buttock to time her involuntary movements.

She had never felt anything like this. Not when they were so ridiculously young, and not with any other man. It was as if her mind had shut down. She was all sensation. All awareness. The flex of the muscles in his neck and shoulders, the cool, thick texture of his hair, the hard wall of his chest, the rigid bar of his erection. The ache between her legs.

He lifted his mouth from hers and a groan tore its way out of his throat. Confused, Olivia pushed up on tiptoe to reconnect.

He nipped at her lower lip, then sucked briefly. "Our five minutes are up," he said, sounding tortured.

"Five minutes."

"I have a teenage son. Remember?"

She whimpered, then flushed in embarrassment. And…five minutes? The kiss had gone on that long?

Probably. *Oh, lord.* As far as she was concerned, he could have peeled her jeans off, lifted her to the countertop and had her, here and now.

"I have my occasional regrets," Ben growled in her ear before he backed away. Now the deep brown of his eyes all but crackled with the intensity of his hunger for her.

Regrets? What was he talking about? She had to lock her knees to keep from slithering to the floor.

Oh. Regrets. About having taken on Carson…

"Don't believe you."

"Shit," he muttered, and she heard it, too. This time, the thunder descended. Carson would be with them momentarily.

Her gaze dropped to Ben's very obvious erection.

He looked down at himself, swore again and turned to the stove, presenting his back to the kitchen doorway where Carson appeared about thirty seconds later.

"I'm starved," he declared, and Ben's laugh sounded almost natural.

"You're always starved. Pour us drinks, will you?"

Just as well they'd been interrupted, Olivia tried to convince herself.

Unfortunately, her body did not agree, and neither did Ben's, from the one desperate glance he cast over his shoulder.

CARSON WAS PRETTY sure Zurenko and Slagle weren't surprised when he didn't appear at Ronnie G's Saturday night. In fact, he kind of doubted he would have been welcome.

From the minute he chained his bike Monday morning and sauntered into the school, students he didn't even know were slapping his back or calling, "Man, that was something!"

Hey, this works, he thought. His star status would give him some protection. Practice, now, he was a little bit nervous about. McGarvie liked winning, but he wasn't going to like the way Carson had done it.

He'd almost reached the door to his first class

when he saw Zurenko down the hall. Their eyes met over the heads of everyone else, and fear jolted through Carson. It was all he could do not to let it show.

They were bullies, remember? He wasn't going to let one seriously hostile look scare him.

Carson seemed to be in a crowd everywhere he went for the rest of the day. He had precalculus with Slagle, but they never sat near each other anyway. Slagle wasn't as good with the "I will kill you" look, but he tried. Mr. P. noticed and actually paused in his discussion of a logarithm briefly until Slagle bent his head. After the bell rang, Carson swaggered out the door ahead of him.

After the last class, he did a little lurking until he saw John Finkel and Vadim Bukin coming because—okay, admit it—he didn't want to chance being alone in the locker room with the assholes.

Finkel spotted him and said, "Man, you're on Zurenko's shit list. He's talking real ugly."

Carson shrugged.

Vadim's locker was closest to Carson's. Not until they were changing did he say in a low voice, "Do you know what you're doing?"

Carson pulled the jersey over his head. He could tell from the clang of lockers and yells that most of the guys were here. "What were my choices? Keep eating shit?"

"They were backing off." Vadim shoved his shoes

into the locker on top of his backpack and tried to slam the locker door fast, then muttered something under his breath as he had to restow his crap.

Carson shrugged. Vadim wasn't there that night. He didn't know what started this.

He was smart.

Vadim sat and tied his shoes. Then he looked up and said simply, "I'm with you."

Carson had to swallow before he could answer. "Thanks. But I don't want you getting hurt."

"We're friends, right?" Once in a while, Vadim's usually faint accent thickened. This was one of those times.

"Yeah." Carson worked up a weak-ass grin. "Sure we are."

"Good, then."

They were walking toward the gym when Coach stepped out of his office, timing it just right. "Caldwell."

Carson stopped. Vadim gave him a speaking look and kept going.

Coach jerked his head toward the office. Carson went in, and McGarvie shut the door.

"You going to tell me what you were trying to pull?"

"I was trying to win the game. And we did, didn't we?"

"*We?* You remember that word?"

He went for bravado. "I made some awesome passes."

"And you did one hell of a lot of hotdogging."

Um…yeah? Carson went with not saying anything.

"You've had provocation," the coach said unexpectedly. "I don't like the way you chose to retaliate, but I can't entirely blame you."

"Uh…"

"You want to tell me what those two have against you?"

Carson shook his head emphatically.

"The thing is, son, whatever they *had* against you doesn't much matter now." He paused, waiting until Carson reluctantly met his gaze. "Because now they have a new grudge. You made them look bad in front of the whole school. The whole damn *town*."

Feeling a chill, Carson wrenched his gaze away and stared at a bulletin board hung with schedules and diagrams of plays.

"That what you had in mind?"

"Uh…kind of?" He cringed at his voice coming out so small and uncertain.

"Guess it doesn't matter what you had in mind." Coach sounded thoughtful now. "You may not want a suggestion, but I'm going to make one anyway."

Carson had to look at him again.

"Mend fences. You made your point. Mess with me and I'll mess with you. Now you need to let them know you can also be a hell of a good teammate. You get what I'm saying?"

Carson nodded.

"Then let's get out there and play."

They were the last two on the court. Just as they entered the gym, Zurenko smashed in a dunk like he was flattening a bug. The guys all hooted approval.

Carson was pissed to discover he was scared again. Maybe it would have been smart to make his point in practice rather than in front of "the whole damn town," as Coach put it.

Yeah, but now he was a star. They'd have to leave him alone in front of everyone else, right? He'd just be careful not to be caught alone, that's all.

He jogged onto the floor, and Bearden bounced a ball to him. Carson dribbled a few times, flexed his knees and launched a shot from half-court. It dropped through the net.

"Sweet!" Chris Neff called.

Carson didn't look at Slagle or Zurenko. *Take that, assholes.*

OLIVIA SPENT LUNCHTIME Monday checking out rentals on the local newspaper's online classifieds and on Craigslist. Her mother still hadn't said, "Yes, I want you to move out," but the atmosphere at home was so awful, Olivia didn't know if she could stand it. They either didn't speak at all or maintained a state of freezing civility. She'd have to keep helping sort and pack—but maybe they'd both be happier if they didn't have to face each other every morning and at bedtime, too.

She was frowning at a listing for an above-a-garage studio when a throat was cleared close enough to make her jump. Stuart Dodd hovered in her doorway. She couldn't believe she hadn't at least heard him coming.

"Stu. What's up?"

He made that same rumbly sound, which sounded like nerves in action. "Ah...I heard a rumor."

Her heart sank. Out of the myriad possibilities that sprang to mind, none were good. "About?" she asked pleasantly. "Hey, have a seat."

He stepped into the office with apparent reluctance, perching on the edge of an old oak armchair.

"I thought you should know people are talking."

Please let this be about the store and whether we'll be selling it.

"About?" she repeated.

"The girl. That you think you might be related to her."

Oh, God. Her mother was right.

And yet, in the middle of a panic attack, she was caught by a fleeting expression on his face. Not uncomfortable. *Frightened* came closer.

Back to the panic.

"And why do people think this?"

"They say you gave a DNA sample."

Olivia sat very, very still and tried desperately to marshal her thoughts. Could she be honest with Stu, ask that he keep what she told him confidential?

But she hadn't known him well until this past

year, and she still wasn't sure she did. Yes, he was a good employee, but… What did that oddly tense expression mean?

She let herself get mad. So much for confidentiality. "Who are 'they'?" she asked coldly.

He flinched. "Ah, I think it's going around pretty generally."

"I'm going to say it's none of *their* business what I did or didn't do." Or his. But that might not be fair. He could be here with the best intentions. With a lot of effort, she reined in the anger. "And thank you for letting me know. In case Chief Weigand hasn't heard the latest, I'll be calling and telling him."

Stu Dodd shot to his feet. "Okay. Well. I just wanted you to know."

"Thank you," she repeated, without meaning it. No, she didn't believe he had been kindly passing on a rumor out of the goodness of his heart. For whatever reason, this rumor worried *him*.

Watching him retreat faster than he'd come in and listening as his footsteps receded down the stairs, Olivia tried to imagine why he of all people would care.

She snorted. *Of all people?* What did that mean? Bert Ellison was an unlikely soul to have been involved in Jane Doe's final hours, but there he was, playing his part. Who would have guessed Charles Bowen, well-liked businessman and devoted husband, might have fathered a girl he hadn't known existed?

Oh, and it was important to remember some-body had given that girl a ride to Crescent Creek. Dropped her off on the far side of town, beyond the cemetery, on a dark stretch between farms. That could even have been a *second* somebody.

And…what if Olivia wasn't the only one who feared Jane could have something to do with her family? Stuart was of an age—she could be his daughter. Or a friend of his son? Theo was…fif-teen, she thought. What if Stuart had reason to fear she had been to his house to see his boy?

Olivia had sat unmoving the whole while she speculated, knowing as she did that she was prac-ticing avoidance. Facing the fact that her mother and father's secret wasn't secret anymore. That ev-erything her mother had dreaded would come to pass.

Because I was so sure I knew right from wrong.

She felt as if a block of concrete were hardening inside her chest.

After a long time, she picked up her phone. Prob-ably no one would have had the audacity to call Marian Bowen and ask whether her husband might have had an affair. But Mom would hear, sooner or later, and she deserved a warning.

PHIL FELT AS if his head were going to explode when he hung up from talking to Olivia Bowen Monday afternoon. Wanting to dent a wall with his fist or kick his wastebasket across the room, he didn't let himself move from behind his desk. *Goddamn it!* he told himself. *Think this through.*

What were the odds the lab that had the sample employed an indiscreet tech or clerk who by happenstance lived in Crescent Creek or was gossip buddies with someone who did? *No.* The anger and regret churning in his gut was answer enough. He knew who had flapping lips. He'd had a careless moment when he was filling out the paperwork and been unaware until too late that Nancy Tulluck, the department's receptionist slash dispatcher, had gotten close enough to be avidly trying to read the form. Upside down, but he was willing to bet now that was one of her undisclosed talents.

He'd seen her as a mixed blessing since he took the job. A long-timer with the department, Nancy had lived her entire life in the area and was related by blood or marriage to what seemed like half the folks in town. All he had to do was ask when he wanted to hear the faintest whisper of gossip. Trouble was, he'd long had a suspicion the flow went both ways, and he had talked to her a couple of times about that.

He'd said as plainly as he could, "You can't share anything you learn on this job. Do you understand that?" She'd managed to look offended that he would believe he had to say anything. Despite his lingering suspicion, he had continued to weigh the positives against the negatives where she was concerned.

The balance had just sunk hard on the negative side.

Swearing under his breath, he went to the door. "Nancy? Can I have a word?"

Fifty-five years old, she dyed her hair an improbable shade of red and wore too much makeup. Even so, she had a motherly air that calmed distraught citizens. Either that, he thought grimly, or they'd known full well that everything they did or said would become common knowledge, so they'd behaved in front of Nancy.

She zigzagged past the several desks that qualified as a bull pen in this town and joined him in the office. "Chief?"

Feeling older than his years, he closed the door and sat behind his desk. He didn't invite her to take a seat. "You saw me filling out a DNA request last week."

She didn't widen her eyes in innocent inquiry quite fast enough. The flicker of guilt was all the confirmation he needed.

"You are the only person besides me who knew about it," he said heavily.

"I didn't see that much," she protested.

"You saw enough." He shook his head. "I have to let you go, Nancy."

"What?" Her shock was real.

"People need to be able to trust that we keep

what we know to ourselves. I've had my suspicions before that you weren't doing that. This time, the talk you started is going to hurt some people. I can't let that pass. Please clear out your desk."

"But—" Her mouth formed into a circle. "You can't."

"I can." He rested a cynical, weary gaze on her. "Unlike you, I'll keep my mouth shut. You can tell people you resigned if you want, or complain about me firing you. I don't care. But if I can't trust you, I won't have you working for me."

Aghast morphed into open rage. "You have no proof!"

"I do," he said. "You are the one and only possible source for the rumor making its way around town. That's good enough for me."

"If it's about the Bowens, well, they always have been snobs," she said nastily. "I'm not going to feel sorry for them."

Phil rose to his feet. "Collect your things." He made his voice hard. "I'm walking you out."

"You're an outsider. Nobody respects you. They listen to me."

To think he'd wasted even that fleeting moment on regret.

"Now," he said, and rested a hand on the butt of his weapon.

He didn't like himself for scaring her into scuttling backward as if she thought he'd pull the goddamn Ruger, but he was just angry enough not to care as much as maybe he should have.

The only officer present, Jeff Mullen, stared openmouthed as Phil stood over Nancy while she snatched her purse from the drawer and shoved a couple of framed photos and a few doodads she'd decorated her space with into it, after which he walked right behind her to the back door.

She stopped suddenly. "My mug."

"Jeff," Phil said.

Mullen, twenty-three years old and fresh from the academy, hustled into the tiny break room and returned with the ceramic mug that said "Queen Nancy" on the side. She grabbed it from him as if it was her most precious possession and then marched out. She'd never had a key to the station, thank God, so Phil didn't have to worry about that. All he did have to worry about was how to explain all this to Mullen and not break his word to Nancy.

After watching her burn rubber accelerating out of the parking lot, he stood there for a long time. His wife had been pushing the idea of early retirement, maybe wintering in Arizona. The idea had never held as much appeal as it did right this minute.

BEN WAS HALFWAY out of his office when he heard women's voices, low enough he caught only a couple of snippets.

"DNA testing…Olivia Bowen… If she thinks that girl is related to her…"

Son of a bitch. He knew who the speakers were. The school secretary and the nurse, neither of whom were usually on the cutting edge of local gossip. Which meant this had already been spread far and wide.

It was bad enough that Olivia was suffering from guilt over the pain she'd caused her mother. But having this get out… It might be the last straw for their relationship. And hell. What if Mrs. Bowen fired Olivia and put the store up for sale? Olivia wouldn't have any reason to stay in town. In fact, she'd about have to leave.

And he was a selfish bastard to be thinking about his own hopes.

Did she know people were talking? They might not want to say anything in front of her.

His instinct was to leave early and drive straight to the hardware store, but he was held in place by his worry about Carson. Normally the bike ride was safe enough, but given the firestorm he'd ignited Friday night, Ben couldn't chance him getting cornered. His office looked out toward the gymnasium, and he'd planned to casually leave just as practice let out. Carson could toss the bike in the back of the Jeep.

Ben pictured Olivia helping customers at the store right this minute, teasing people she'd known for a lifetime, laughing. Wishing them a merry

Christmas. Maybe ignorance was bliss… No, he knew better than that.

Not liking the idea of being the bearer of bad tidings, he closed his office door and called her.

She answered, and interrupted when he was still fumbling his way through an explanation. "I already heard," she said tersely. "Stu Dodd thought I needed to know."

"You tell your mom?"

"Yes." Pause. "She hung up on me."

"Damn, Livy."

There was another brief silence. "You haven't called me that in a long time."

"Don't most people?"

"Mostly Mom. I…usually nip it in the bud."

He used the heel of his hand to ease the ache beneath his breastbone. "Would you rather I didn't?"

"No, it's okay. It sounds sort of right when you say it." She sighed. "I rented an apartment."

He sat forward abruptly, caught between exhilaration—they'd have a place to be alone!—and dismay that she felt unwelcome enough in her own home she'd thought she had to do this. "You what?"

"I was thinking about it anyway. Mom and I were hardly talking. Now I can't imagine—"

"Where?" he asked.

"Actually, I got lucky. It's the one above Finders Keepers." The store, in the next block from Bowen's, sold antiques, collectibles and secondhand items that didn't qualify as either. Most of the old

buildings along the main street were two stories
and had either offices or apartments upstairs, as
did Bowen's. "I'll be able to walk to work."

"You told your mother yet?"

"No, I'll do that when I get home. She might
have made dinner."

"You want help hauling stuff?" he asked, gen-
tling his voice.

"I...maybe. The place is furnished, but mini-
mally. Let me find out what Mom has to say first.
If she's mad enough to fire me, well, I won't need
the apartment after all."

"She loves you, Livy."

"Does she?" She sounded so bleak, the ache in
his chest felt like a spreading purple bruise.

"In our own turmoil, we hurt the people we love
sometimes."

Another of those silences felt...he didn't know.
"I guess I just hurt her," she said.

"On some level, she has to understand."

"There's no rule that says people have to see both
sides." Now she was brisk. "Listen, I've got to run."

"Are you moving in tonight?"

"Probably not. The apartment's cold, and I'll at
least have to grab bedding, towels, some kitchen
basics. You know."

"You must have your own stuff somewhere," he
realized.

"Yeah, in a storage unit in Portland. If it looks
like I'm going to stay for any length of time, I'll

drive down and root through for the things I really want."

"Like a coffeemaker," he said, figuring a note of humor wouldn't hurt.

"Definitely a coffeemaker."

"Will you call me later?" he asked. "Let me know how it goes?"

"You really want to know?" The vulnerability she usually hid so well infused her voice.

"I really do."

She made a tiny sound. A swallow? A hitch of breath? God, not the beginning of a sob. "Okay," she said softly. "Thank you for listening, Ben."

And she was gone, saving him from saying words she wouldn't want to hear and wouldn't believe.

Words he wasn't even sure *he* believed, except why else did he hurt so damn much for her?

He made a strangled sound and thrust his fingers into his hair to give a good, hard yank.

CHAPTER ELEVEN

BEN SLAMMED THE rear door of his Jeep. "This the last of it?"

"Yes, thank God." Olivia stole a look back at the front window of her childhood home, thinking…oh, silly things. That Mom would be standing there, wistfully watching her go. Instead, the window showed only a faint glow from deeper in the house. If Ben and Carson weren't there, Mom probably would have turned out the porch light before Olivia so much as got in her car.

Truth was, she hadn't the slightest idea how her mother felt about her decision to move out. When Olivia had told her the evening before, Mom had only nodded once and said, "If that's what you want to do." Not so much as a crack showed in her marble-hard impassivity.

Now it was Tuesday evening, and the big move was taking place. This was the third and final load. Ben and Carson hopped into the Jeep, waiting politely until she'd backed out of the driveway and started toward town before doing the same and then falling in behind her. Combating her desolation, Olivia reminded herself she'd be back. After all, she'd promised to continue to help packing up the contents of the house and had received an emotionless "Thank you" in response.

Seeing the headlights right behind hers during the short drive was a comfort. Once both were parked in the alley behind her new apartment, she carried up a box while Ben and Carson wrestled her dresser up the stairs, followed by a bookcase. Once everything was in, Carson helped her make her bed, while Ben set up the television and DVD player that had been in her father's bedroom. Then they both insisted on crowding into the tiny kitchen with her to put dishes, pans and utensils in drawers and cupboards.

"Now all I have to do is grocery shop," she said with a sigh. "Tomorrow."

Carson burst into song. Amused, Olivia recognized "Tomorrow" from the musical *Annie.*

"How did you know that?" she asked.

Smiling, Ben leaned back against the cupboard and crossed his arms.

"I played Daddy Warbucks in the school production two years ago. I was awesome," his son assured her, not so modestly.

Olivia laughed. "What did they do for an Annie?"

"We got this sixth grader. Really short little thing." He held up a hand about chest high.

"One of the Deaton kids," Ben contributed. "You know they're all freckled and redheaded. This one's hair is curly besides. She even let them cut it so she'd look the part. Fortunately, she could sing, too."

"Is this the next generation?"

Ben grinned. "Nope. Mom says Tisha was an 'oops' kid. I think the next youngest is something like twenty-two."

"But…oh my God. Hasn't Mrs. Deaton gone through menopause *yet?*" The words having burst out of her before she thought, she glanced at Carson to see if she'd embarrassed him.

He was laughing as hard as his dad, who finally got it together enough to say, "By now, probably. The girl is…what now? Thirteen?"

"And her mom must be, like, sixty-five," Olivia muttered. She was pretty sure the oldest Deaton was a contemporary of Ben's. Or even a couple of years ahead of him? She wondered what *he'd* thought when he saw his probably graying mother pregnant.

Olivia was surprised to hear footsteps on the staircase at the back of the building.

"I ordered pizza," Ben said. "Thought we'd have a housewarming."

"We'll be drinking water," she warned, but he shook his head.

"Nope. I asked for a couple of liters of pop, too."

Sure enough, he accepted delivery of two boxes and two bottles of soda. The smaller box turned out to have a cinnamon dessert pizza, the leftovers of which, he told her, could be her breakfast.

His kindness had her blinking back a sting in her eyes.

As they ate, she found herself enjoying Carson's company almost as much as Ben's. Occasionally she was startled when he said something typically teenage-boy dumb, because most of the time he was so mature sounding. He was cocky but also self-deprecating and funny. He didn't hesitate to tease her, and he didn't seem to mind being teased in his turn.

Olivia hated it when they finally said good-night.

Carson bounded at reckless speed down the somewhat rickety stairs, barely skimming a hand along the rail. Ben hovered at the door.

"You okay, sweetheart?"

Sweetheart. Nobody had called her that in…sixteen years, of course. Looking at the concern on his face, she wasn't sure he realized he had used an endearment instead of her name.

Don't make an issue of it, she decided.

"Sure." She attempted a smile. "Better than I would have been without you two."

"The Hovik-Caldwell Moving Service is available whenever you need us."

Now. I need you now. Forever.

No…she knew better.

"Thanks," she said again.

He didn't oblige by leaving. Instead, he frowned down at her. "Your mother was…really repressed."

Past a lump in her throat, Olivia said, "You could say that. I don't know if she's mad or relieved." She pulled a face. "Probably relieved. You could have cut the tension between us with a knife."

"No idea what she wants to do about the store?"

She shook her head. "We *really* haven't been talking."

"Okay." His voice was suddenly low and tender. "You look exhausted. Good night, Livy." He kissed her, the merest brush of his mouth against hers, the warmth of his breath, a nuzzle, and he left her, his descent only a little slower than Carson's.

Olivia didn't let herself watch them go. Instead she closed the door and locked it, then looked around her new home away from home.

It was…not very inspiring. The sofa was like something vaguely remembered from her grandparents' house, the fabric scratchy and durable. Cabinets were newer but basic. The kitchen and bathroom windows looked over the alley, the living room and bedroom windows at the street. She crossed the living room to gaze out from this new perspective. Instead of cheering her, the Christmas lights shining in the darkness made her feel hollow inside.

She and Mom hadn't put up a tree or talked about exchanging gifts. For Olivia, the idea of celebrating so soon after Dad's death had felt wrong. Even so...she couldn't leave Mom sitting alone in the big, empty house over the holidays. With a small panic, she thought, *Then what? Squeeze a skinny tree in here? Suggest we go out Christmas Eve to a restaurant?* And...what did you buy a woman who was trying to get rid of half of what she owned so she could move into a smaller place?

That hollow feeling expanded.

After a night spent tossing and turning, she hustled down a slushy alley to let herself into Bowen's. As was so often the case, Lloyd was ahead of her. Olivia prayed he'd put on the coffee. By the time she started upstairs, she smelled it.

The carafe was only half-full, but she hijacked most of a mugful anyway, only then looking up to see Lloyd leaning against the frame of his door, watching her.

"Bad night?"

"Not great." She hesitated. "I moved yesterday. Rented the apartment above Finders Keepers."

He didn't look surprised. "Is there any truth to what I'm hearing?"

"Let's see." She could fake humor, couldn't she? "Did I have a baby when I was twelve? Or did I make it to fourteen?"

He didn't laugh. "Well, one version says you had Ben Hovik's baby and gave it away."

Olivia's mouth fell open. "But that's—"

He shook his head. "No need to tell me it's nonsense. Slim as you are, you couldn't have hidden a pregnancy."

"Oh, God. I never dreamed people would think—" Her throat closed up.

"I'm guessing you have some reason to suspect that girl might be your father's," he said sympathetically. "You don't have any other family around, do you? Didn't Charles say your mom has a sister back east somewhere?"

"Pennsylvania. I guess I have some cousins there, too. Mom and Aunt Roxanne exchange Christmas cards. That's about it."

He nodded and didn't say anything else. If she didn't, either, she knew he'd accept her silence. But any possibility of keeping the whole thing between her and Mom was lost now. And…she thought she really could trust Lloyd anyway.

"Yes," she said. "Apparently Dad had an affair. He was approached a few months back by a girl who said she thought he was her father."

"Your mom found out."

"Yes. She says Dad admitted it."

He nodded again. "You know I visited your dad regularly. I could tell something was wrong between them."

"Very wrong. It's been—" She looked away. So far, Ben was the only person who'd made her want to cry, but the kindness in Lloyd's eyes was having the same effect.

"You have any reason to think the girl who wrote that note could be our Jane Doe?"

"Only the coincidence of timing. And..." She shrugged. "Coloring. She was tall, too. Like Dad."

Lloyd didn't say, *And you,* but she could tell he was thinking it.

"Rumor has it Phil Weigand fired Nancy Tulluck yesterday."

"I heard she told everyone she'd quit."

"One of my nephews is an officer, you know. He saw enough."

After a moment, Olivia nodded. "Phil said it was her."

"She's one of the worst gossips around. I'm sorry."

"Thanks." She gave a wry but more genuine smile. "Anything business related I should know?"

"Nope."

They parted to start their days, Olivia thinking how very lucky she was to have Lloyd.

WEDNESDAY NIGHT'S GAME was to be in Sultan, a fair drive. Ben went to most games, but he decided to give this one a miss. He did hear the hint of anxiety in Carson's voice when he said, "You'll meet the bus though, right?"

"You bet. Call me when you leave Sultan and then again when you're ten minutes or so out, okay?" He'd already pulled into his reserved slot at the high school, where they sat talking.

"Deal." Carson jumped out and slung his pack over his shoulder.

Ben got out, too, and looked at him over the roof. "Try to make your game a little less spectacular than Friday night's, okay?"

He was rewarded with a huge grin.

"Yeah, Coach had that talk with me already. They play fair—I'll play fair."

"Good enough."

Carson jogged off while Ben reached in back for his briefcase. As he locked up and walked toward the front entrance, his thoughts were stuck on that last exchange. What were the odds *they* would play fair?

Carson had remained cheerful since Friday night, though, which meant that either he'd dodged any confrontation—or they'd talked and agreed on a standoff.

No. Ben was shaking his head even before he finished the thought. Ben didn't picture Zurenko in particular as being able to swallow Friday night's humiliation and move on. No, he was still seething; Ben didn't doubt it for a second. The big question was: How far would he take it? Ben didn't know him well enough to guess.

By the time he greeted Marco Serrano, his vice principal, as well as the secretary and school counselor, and let himself into his office, his mind had turned with embarrassing eagerness to his plan to call Olivia and hope she'd let him take her to dinner tonight. Unfortunately, it was too early. The high school started the day at seven-fifty in the morning, and it wasn't first bell yet. She was probably awake, but he'd give her another hour anyway.

In the meantime, he reviewed the school's next couple daily bulletins, both checking for errors and keeping himself apprised of the extracurricular club schedule. Then he looked over plans for upcoming events for seniors, including their opportunities to order caps and gowns, and made a note to himself to sit down with Jen Pearson, the counselor, to find out which local businesses had kicked in for scholarships. There was some fluctuation year to year. He guessed Swenson's wouldn't be giving, for example, and, damn it, he could think of two others that had gone out of business.

Shortly thereafter, he ended up hearing about three boys caught smoking weed behind the gym before school started, and he wasn't able to try Olivia until after nine, when Bowen's opened. He had to leave a message, but she called him back fifteen minutes later.

"Dinner sounds great. Does this include Carson, too? I could cook for you instead of us going out."

His heart kicked up a gear at the idea of the two of them alone. "No Carson. He has a game tonight."

There was a tiny pause. "Oh. I should have realized. You don't always go?"

"This one is in Sultan. It's not only a long drive—Crescent Creek should win easily."

"I see. What would you prefer? Dinner at my oh-so-elegant new home or go out?"

"You won't be too tired to cook?"

"Oh, I was thinking something easy. Chicken tacos, maybe."

"Then you're on," he said promptly.

They ended the call, and he had a pleasant buzz of anticipation to carry him until the agreed-upon six o'clock.

Feeling restless, he stuck around after school let out at two-thirty and dropped in on two of the club meetings. Math club was poorly attended, he was sorry but not surprised to see—this one always had been geek central, and these days most of the geeks belonged to the computer club, too, or instead. The Japanese club had attracted twelve students. Small as the high school was, they'd added Japanese to the usual German, French and Spanish classes three years ago. It was proving popular, while French and German both had slipped. He was giving thought to dropping one or the other in favor of Arabic but was meeting resistance from some school board members who were traditionalists.

Nobody seemed to mind him sitting in on the meetings, and he enjoyed the enthusiasm.

Somehow he ended up on Olivia's doorstep ten minutes early. Her face brightened at the sight of him. "You can slice and dice," she told him, leading the way—all of four steps for him—to the kitchen. He didn't like noticing that she had lost weight recently, but he loved looking at her anyway. From the time he'd really noticed her in high school, he'd always found her beautiful, with delicately formed cheekbones and nose, and lips plump enough to give him lustful thoughts. Then there was that tall, supple body, endless legs and breasts—a little more generous than you'd expect with her long and lanky build.

He'd met plenty of women who could be called beautiful, though, many of whom didn't attract him at all. It was amazing how much less appealing Melanie had become physically the more of her real nature she revealed.

No, Ben thought he was mostly captivated by Olivia's more indefinable qualities. When he saw her, it was those inner qualities that drew him: the sometimes too-serious woman he'd seen wrestling with ethical decisions, the confident woman who had not only stepped in effortlessly to run a business geared principally to men but was making a greater success of it than her father had. The woman who had slugged him when he dumped her in a snowbank, who was sometimes so shy with him he couldn't help wondering about her sexual experience in the years since they'd parted ways.

Hoping she hadn't noticed he was already aroused, he chopped first onions then cilantro per her specs while she browned chicken she must have rolled in some powerful spices. "Pico de gallo out of the jar," she told him, plunking said jar onto the counter, then asking him to tell her about his day.

He did, watching while she warmed tortillas and put ingredients in serving bowls that she set out on the gateleg table he'd moved from her parents' house last night. She had to unfold it to seat even three, as she had when Carson was with him, which had made opening the refrigerator a challenge. Two was better, in more ways than one.

Once they were seated and he was assembling his first taco, she snorted when he mentioned the resistance to teaching Arabic at the high school, and of course knew all three school board members who were being particularly stubborn.

"Did you know Sam Pruitt's daughter dated an Iranian exchange student when she was in college? From what I hear, Sam about blew a gasket," she said with satisfaction. "I have no doubt he's convinced if you once open the doors, we'd have a mosque in town before we knew it and probably a terrorist cell. He's a dinosaur and an idiot."

"That part, I knew." Ben's mouth turned up. "Cynthia Pruitt actually went to college? Now that, I didn't know."

"Eastern. Heaven knows what she majored in. I, for one, applaud her courage in defying Dad however briefly. I'm sure it goes without saying that she came home and married someone Daddy approved. I think she lives in Marysville now."

"Huh." Ben took a swig of beer. "Always good to know the background."

"I'm surprised your mother didn't fill you in."

"I didn't think to ask."

Her eyes met his. "Has she said anything about the DNA fiasco?"

"Yeah." He hated to admit it. "She asked delicately if I knew a rumor was making the rounds. I said yes, and she dropped it."

She looked away for a moment, then back at him. "Does she know we've been seeing each other?"

"Yeah. She approves."

"Does she? I'm surprised. I've always had the impression she and Mom didn't much like each other."

"I wouldn't have put it that strongly." Diplomacy in action, although it was also truth, as far as he knew. "Your mother's a very reserved woman. Mine isn't."

Her smile showed more pain than he knew she wanted to reveal. "That's true. I do love my mother, but…"

"But?" Ben prompted when she trailed off. He reached across the small table to cover her hand with his. It hadn't quite formed a fist, but close. He found himself thinking of high-tension wires.

"Oh…I've had good friends talk about how close they are with their mothers. For me, it was always Dad." Those haunting eyes met his again. "I said that, didn't I? It's just hit me lately how hurtful that must have been for Mom, especially given that I was an only child. *And* a girl."

"Are you so sure she knew?"

"How could she not? When was I ever interested in anything girlie?"

He shook his head in disbelief. "You don't think you're feminine?"

She looked at him like he was crazy. "Um, gee. No. That's not exactly a word that leaps to mind to describe me."

"You're wrong." She'd said things before about seeing herself as a tomboy, but he hadn't realized that translated to unwomanly in her eyes. "Don't you know that the way you move, gesture, gets to me? Do you still paint your toenails?" She flushed, telling him the answer and jolting him with a new source of arousal. What color were they right now? Soft pink? Lurid red? He cleared his throat. "And there was your underwear." *God.* He tried not to think about the delicate lacy panties and bras she used to wear.

Her blush deepened. "Okay, so I like knowing I'm female underneath the denim and flannel. That doesn't make me anything like my mother. I swear, she defines the word *feminine*."

Lightbulb moment. "You mean, she does for *you*."

Olivia's gaze went unfocused. "Wow," she said at last, blinking. "I get what you're saying. I compared myself to her and came up short."

"I'm saying there are a lot of different definitions of femininity, just as there are of masculinity. Some cultural, some personal." Okay, now he sounded like he was in front of a classroom. He shrugged and went for simpler. "Ask a bunch of men what pushes their buttons, and you'll get a thousand different answers."

"You mean, they're not all fixated on tits?"

He chuckled, unable to resist letting his gaze lower to hers. "No, although you have very nice ones."

Olivia blushed. That she still could amused him and, yeah, turned him on, too.

"Okay, for some it's legs—"

"And yours are amazing," he assured her.

She gave a huff of displeasure belied by those fiery cheeks. "I'm saying men react to *looks*."

"Don't women, too, at least initially?" He shook his head. "You're straying from the point. "Some guys like dainty china dolls, some—"

"Like Amazons?"

Ben grinned. She was determined to be offended by whatever he said. "If you want to put it that way."

"I'm glad you're one of those, okay?" It came out gruffly, although suddenly she frowned. "Have you always?"

He shrugged. "Sure, tall women tend to appeal to me. Why get a bad back stooping?" When she just kept looking at him, he sighed. "If you're asking about Melanie, yeah, she was, I don't know, five-eight or so, but I think we've wandered off topic," he said. "How you feel about your appeal as a woman has more to do with your mother than it does me or any other guy."

"You know how weird it is to be my age before you start understanding your relationship with your parents?" She made a face. "Or maybe it's understanding yourself."

Empathy joined the tangle of other emotions crowding him. "There's a reason you're getting hit with it all now."

"I know."

Her attempt to smile reminded him of her essential strength, which in the end was sexier than her fabulous legs or beautiful breasts.

"This isn't really a surprise to you, is it?" he asked.

"Yeah, weirdly, it is." She rolled her eyes in exasperation. "There I go with the 'weird' again. It's just...I've been thinking a lot lately about how I was daddy's little girl and wondering whether that hurt Mom. I assumed he and I had more in common. Only now I'm wondering if I latched on to sports and construction and all the rest because even when I was really young, I could look at Mom and see that, no matter how hard I tried, I couldn't be like her."

"Really? How so?"

She wrinkled her nose again. "I mean, I was a

stork, with these huge feet. I remember this one time I let her buy me these leggings and a top I thought was pretty. Only I got home and tried it on again and saw that my legs were skinny and so long they made the leggings too short, and the top *was* pretty, only what it did was make me look even plainer." Olivia laughed suddenly. "I sound so pathetic, and really I like myself. It's just…" She trailed off.

"You've had some revelations."

She smiled at him. "Yeah. And I probably did look stupid in that top, but I also suspect I disappointed Mom when I wouldn't wear it. When I wouldn't even try. And now here I am, resenting Dad so much I wish I *was* more like Mom. Except I'm mad at her, too. And, yes, I'm officially a mess."

Ben laughed and pushed back his chair. "Come here, sweetheart."

"You think the chair will hold us both?"

"We can find out."

She came around the table and sat on his lap somewhat gingerly, but there were no ominous creaks, so she exhaled and leaned comfortably against him. He closed his arms around her and breathed her in.

"You're the only person who has ever called me 'sweetheart,'" she said suddenly.

"Yeah?" Nuzzling, he explored the sensitive spot

behind her ear and felt her shiver. "Maybe it's old-fashioned."

"It beats 'babe.' I mean, really, do I look like anyone's babe?"

"You can be mine," he said huskily, kissing his way along her jaw until he found her mouth. The kiss started as tender and changed quickly to desperate. He'd been waiting a long time for her.

"We hardly ate a bite," she whispered.

"I didn't come here for dinner," he admitted, then closed his eyes. "That sounds crass, doesn't it?"

"A little."

He opened his eyes to find her smiling.

"I didn't invite you for dinner, either."

"Thank God." Ben surged to his feet, lifting her so that she had to lock her legs around his waist.

"I'm too heavy!" Olivia squealed. "Put me down."

Ben laughed. Girlie. Only girls *squealed*.

"Not a chance." Lust and triumph and a host of other less identifiable feelings gave him the strength of ten men. Carrying Olivia Bowen to her bedroom? No problem.

CHAPTER TWELVE

OLIVIA HADN'T EVEN known she'd made a decision, but the minute he said that—*I didn't come here for dinner*—she knew she had. If she'd still been on the fence, she'd have suggested they go out.

She could not believe he was carrying her to her bed, though. Nobody had ever so much as tried something like that. Most of the guys she dated weren't any taller than she was, or not by much. They'd have herniated a disk hefting her.

She didn't protest, though, given that it was all of about twenty feet from the kitchen table to bedside. And—this felt pretty amazing, riding him like this. His every step had her moving against the ridge that was in exactly the right place to feel best. Olivia wrapped one arm around his neck, because, no, she didn't want to be dropped, and twined the fingers of her other hand in his hair. The texture was thick, unruly, cool. Raw silk.

He kissed her throat, nipped at the side of her neck and stumbled into the door frame, banging her thigh and shoulder.

"Ouch!" she cried.

"I'm sorry." His dark eyes were so intense. "Are you all right?"

"What's a bruise? No, don't stop." She tugged his head forward so that his lips were pressed against her cheek.

He laughed, pretended to stagger but somehow ended up beside the bed, where he lowered her with surprising ease atop the duvet. Then he planted a hand beside her head and leaned there, doing nothing but looking at her.

"You are so beautiful. You've been killing me. You know that, don't you?"

"No." She cupped his cheek with one hand, realizing he must have gone home and shaved again for her benefit. Because he'd expected to end up here, in her bed. And maybe she should be indignant at his confidence, but she wasn't. "What do you mean, I've been killing you? We've gone out once."

"Four times, if you count pizza, sledding and moving day. No, five times. I bought you a burger and fries, remember?"

"You were taking pity on me."

"No. I'd been biding my time ever since you came home. I saw an opening."

"Ever since— Seriously? You were stalking me."

"Maybe." His grin was wolfish. "Worked, didn't it?"

"I don't know. I'm not seeing much action here."

He laughed, but the sound wasn't so much

amused as shaken. "Damn. I can't believe you're giving me another chance."

Olivia stiffened. This was sex. Just sex. Another chance, a real chance, meant more than that to her. It meant trust. Faith in another person, in a future. She'd been short on that even before her father's secret served like a dynamite charge.

"Olivia?" Lines deepened in Ben's forehead.

She slid her hands beneath the hem of his T-shirt and whispered, "Do we have to talk?"

Something flickered in his dark eyes; he must recognize a dodge when he heard one. But he was probably afraid if he pushed it, he wouldn't get her naked. And that part, she was sure about. She had always wanted Ben Hovik. And, yes, now *she* had another chance at him. But this was as far as her commitment extended.

This, she decided, felt really good. Muscles shivered and flexed beneath her hands as she ran them up his back, then slipped them around to feel the washboard tension in his belly and the softness of hair in the middle of his chest.

With a groan, he ripped his shirt over his head, then reached for hers.

Irony: it was her *prettiest* flannel shirt, worn especially for the occasion. Teal and rose plaid and cut for a woman's body. He must like it, because he was careful not to tear any buttons off. Olivia sighed with pleasure when he finished with the cuffs and pushed it off her shoulders.

"Pretty," he said thickly, in an echo of her thought, only it was her bra he was looking at, not the shirt that he'd already tossed aside. And he'd been right; she did still like sexy undergarments. This bra was a teal to match the shirt, satin and low-cut. Even her not-so-extravagant breasts appeared ready to spill over it.

Supporting his weight on his knee and one hand, he cupped her breast with his other hand, an expression of intense concentration on his face. After a strangled sound, he bent and pressed his lips to the flesh above the bra. The next second, he suckled her right through the satin. Olivia's hips jerked in reaction, and she tried to stifle a moan.

"God." Suddenly he was frantic, groping behind her for the hooks. She arched upward to cooperate, wanting nothing more than to be naked for him.

He tossed the bra aside. Dark color slashed across his prominent cheekbones as he gazed for a moment at her breasts before bending to kiss them, first softly, then with more purpose. As he swirled his tongue around her nipple, then sucked, she grabbed onto his shoulders and made unintelligible noises.

Eventually he found his way back to her mouth, and she pulled him down over her, wanting his weight on her. He was no sooner there than she got frustrated at the denim still separating them. As they kissed deeply, tongues dueling, she shoved ineffectually at the waistband of his jeans until he wrenched his mouth away.

"Let me," he growled. Even as he tore open the buttons of his Levi's, she was unzipping her own jeans. "Boots," he muttered.

His clothes were gone. She went still, looking her fill while he swore under his breath and struggled with her bootlaces, finally succeeding in yanking first one boot, then the other off. He peeled off her jeans and panties so fast, she was lucky not to suffer fabric burn.

Then Ben swore again and levered himself off the bed to find his own trousers. *Condom.* Olivia was appalled to realize she hadn't even thought. She was on birth control, but she had always insisted on a condom, too.

"Let me." She reached for the packet, but he shook his head.

"It's been a long time for me, Olivia. I don't want to embarrass myself."

Since his hands had a faint tremor as he ripped open the packet and donned the protection, she didn't argue.

A long time? How long?

But she couldn't have asked if she'd wanted, because he was kissing her again, and one muscular thigh had insinuated itself between her legs. And, oh, one hand was there, too, cupping her, stroking. His finger slid between her folds, and she made more strangled sounds until he lifted one of her legs to make a place for himself and pushed into her. A rumble came from his chest, and he raised his head to look down at her with eyes that were nearly black with desire.

The sensation was indescribable. Pain and pleasure and fullness, coupled with urgency. She grabbed on to him and tried to lift her hips to take him deeper. Taking her response as a *Yes, please, more,* he began to move. At first deliberately, as if knowing the pace that would drive her insane, knowing her pressure points, knowing her, then harder, deeper, until finally he lost it. Ben pounded into her until she simply exploded and felt him do the same, pulsing inside her, a ragged cry escaping him.

Now his weight came down on her as if he was incapable of so much as rolling to one side, and she wrapped her arms around his torso, holding on tight. She hadn't felt anything close to this in so long, it scared her, but it made her glad, too, as long as she only felt and didn't let herself think.

CARSON HAD BENT to tie the laces on his shoe when a hand snaked out of nowhere and snatched his other shoe.

His head came up. "Hey!"

Slagle backed away, waggling his shoe. When Carson lunged, Slagle tossed it over his head. And—*shit.* Of course it was Zurenko blocking the other end of the aisle in the locker room. Somehow all their other teammates had melted away. Carson didn't hear another voice or even a footfall. He couldn't believe he'd gotten so careless; he had let himself be cornered. Or he'd been set up, he thought, his brain working clearly beneath the tension. Bukin wouldn't have gone along with anything like that, would he?

Deciding he wouldn't play their game, Carson lifted his one foot to the bench and finished double-knotting the laces. "If you have something to say, say it."

Zurenko was suddenly in his face. "Make me look bad again, and I'll smash you." Spittle flew. He looked freakin' insane. "Hear me?"

Carson wiped his face with his forearm. "Hard not to."

"And you keep your mouth shut."

"I have so far, haven't I?"

"So far." Zurenko shook his head. "What's *wrong* with you, Caldwell? You want to get in trouble?"

"No," he said. He had difficulty swallowing, and the pain beneath his breastbone almost felt like heartburn. They must think about some of the same things he did. They couldn't be the total dickheads they sometimes seemed, could they? An impulse overcame him. "But don't you ever think about *her*? That girl? Wonder...?"

Zurenko reared back. "She was a piece of ass, that's all. She got what she wanted."

"We didn't have anything to do with it," Slagle put in from Carson's other side.

He looked into Dylan Zurenko's eyes, thinking he'd find, he didn't know, maybe some core of humanity. "You think she wanted to die?" he asked.

Zurenko sneered. "I think this is your last warning. You tell Daddy or anyone else, you're dead." He flung the basketball shoe toward the shower room. "Come on," he said to his sidekick and sauntered away. One of them slapped an empty locker as they went, and the clang echoed in the huge silent space.

Carson was left alone. A brief roar came from the gymnasium when his two *teammates* opened and then shut the door, muffling it. He was so filled with rage and fear, if the shoe had been in his hand, *he'd* have thrown it. Instead he let out a strangled yell and bent forward, his head between his knees, his fingers clenched in his hair.

They'd lose interest in him eventually if he did what they said and didn't talk. Only then he'd have to live with himself, and he didn't know if he could do that.

And Ben— God, he didn't want to see the disappointment in his eyes.

Feeling sick, he hobbled to the shower, reclaimed his shoe and sat back down to put it on.

BEN SAT BEHIND the wheel in the parking lot, waiting for the bus to arrive. He was floating on an unbelievable high. It had been so damn long since he'd made love with a woman. And, God, Olivia. She was even more beautiful than she'd been at sixteen and less inhibited. Hell, he had a clue what he was doing now, too. No, he thought, gripped by exhilaration, what happened between them had nothing to do with know-how. He remembered telling her they'd always been combustible. But even that suggested the glory he'd found in her arms, her body, was all chemical. All physical. He knew better.

He was in love with her. Maybe always had been. He'd certainly never forgotten her.

She must feel the same. She *had* to, or how could she have responded so explosively?

Right now, Ben wasn't going to let himself speculate about her odd expression when he'd mentioned second chances. He felt too good. Apprehension had no place in his mood.

He was momentarily blinded when headlights swung over him. Half a dozen cars had pulled in as other parents arrived, and moments later he saw the school bus lumber into sight. Ben zipped up his down vest and got out, shoving the car keys into his jeans' pocket before heading to the front of the school where the bus would disgorge the team.

He realized he was grinning foolishly, and with some effort he wiped the expression from his face. Even a kid Carson's age would recognize what *that* smile meant. Out of respect for Olivia, Ben had to keep his son from figuring out what his dad had been up to tonight.

With a squeal of brakes, the bus pulled up to the curb, and, after a moment, the doors swung open. Other parents had emerged from their vehicles and wandered over. There was a scattering of applause when the first boy appeared. Carson was the second out, right behind his friend Vadim Bukin. Ben glanced around, not seeing either of Vadim's parents.

He clapped Carson on the back. "Good game?"

"Yeah. Sure." The words were right, the tone subdued.

Ben raised his eyebrows at Vadim. "You need a ride?"

"If you wouldn't mind. No one answered when I called home."

"Sure, come on."

Both boys loped after him, Carson hopping in front, Vadim in the backseat.

Vadim was more talkative during the short drive than Carson was. Yes, they'd won by twenty-five points. Coach had taken out the first string midway through the third quarter. Even so, Carson scored nineteen and he, Vadim, eighteen. Zurenko was the top scorer with twenty-three points. He was mad when the coach took him out because he thought a scout had come to the game.

Ben kind of doubted any serious scouting was taking place at a game between two small rural high school teams, but he didn't want to squash their delusions. If there was going to be any chance for these boys to catch a college scout's eyes, it would more likely happen during the state play-offs. *If* Crescent Creek reached the play-offs. Based on talent, Ben was optimistic that would happen, unless the tensions between teammates torpedoed their chances.

Vadim's parents were parking in their garage just as Ben pulled up in front. "Thanks," he said and jumped out.

Ben pulled away. "Something wrong?" he asked.

Carson's head was bent. "Nah."

"Hard having two games so close together," he remarked. Usually the team played on Tuesday and Friday, but this week they would have only one day off.

"We're okay. And Friday is a home game."

True enough. Ben had trouble getting a grip on his unease, given his full-body sense of well-being. He knew he'd go to bed and think about nothing but Olivia. Wish he'd been able to stay the night. They'd made love a second time, slower, sweeter, but twice wasn't enough.

"What'd you do tonight?"

He surfaced to realize Carson was eyeing him sidelong. *Oh, crap.* That besotted grin was tugging at his mouth again.

"Uh…had dinner with Olivia."

"Dinner, huh." It was not a question.

"You heard me."

Silence reigned until he drove into their garage and turned off the engine. "I really like her," he said quietly.

Neither of them reached for their door handles.

"Do you think that dead girl could really be her sister?" Carson surprised him by asking.

"I think it's unlikely." That wasn't entirely honest; Charles Bowen's insistence on going to the funeral and his death that very night put some weight behind Olivia's fear. "But I understand why Olivia needs to know for sure."

"If she *was* her sister..." He cut himself off. "Why would she have gone into the woods?"

Ben looked at him. "You know there are rumors about a kegger that night."

Not meeting his eyes, Carson gave a jerky nod.

"Could be she was waiting until morning to go by the Bowens' house and some teenagers invited her to come to the party. Whoever she was, the girl likely got to town hitchhiking. Maybe with a teenager up from Miller Falls. An adult would have come forward, don't you think?"

"Unless they're, I don't know," Carson mumbled, "ashamed or something."

"Why ashamed?" Ben heard the faintest of creaks and realized he had a white-knuckled grip on the steering wheel. Nonetheless, he'd kept his voice calm.

"I don't know." Carson shifted. He laid his hand

on the door handle, as if ready to flee. "Like, if the driver came on to her and she said no, so the guy dumped her out."

That was one possibility. Not, thank God, one that could apply to Carson, given his lack of a driver's license or vehicle.

"Okay," Ben said.

"I don't know!" his son yelled, the explosion so sudden it was shocking. "Why are you asking me?" He opened the door and all but fell out, reaching back at the last minute for his duffel bag. Then he slammed the door before Ben could get out a word.

Ben didn't move for a good minute. Fear he'd almost been able to put aside roared through him like a firestorm. Carson flipped out only when one of two topics arose: sex and the dead girl.

HAVING A QUICKIE over the lunch hour the next day gave Olivia a glow of contentment while making her feel a little slutty. She and Ben weren't even in a relationship. At least, not exactly. Well, so what? she decided. It had been really amazing sex. And she knew Ben couldn't ditch Carson every evening, which meant they had to grab their opportunities when they could. Plus…she *had* promised to spend some evenings home packing. In fact, she was on her way now.

Dread had her grateful she now had an escape hatch. She could put in a few hours of hard work—

say, in the attic, while Mom worked on Dad's den or in the kitchen—and then she could take off.

Except…they really needed to talk about Christmas, which was exactly one week away.

Despite being hungry, she was dismayed to smell something good cooking when she went in the front door. Oh, no—that was one of her favorite casseroles, wasn't it?

Her mother appeared from the kitchen. "Dinner is about ready," she said tentatively.

"It smells good."

"I remembered you like my cream cheese–hamburger casserole."

Was she out of the doghouse for some reason? She couldn't tell. They made stilted conversation while they ate. Her mother agreed that maybe they should get together for Christmas.

"Although it's hardly worth cooking a big meal just for the two of us."

"It's Christmas."

"I hope you didn't get me anything."

Olivia glared at her. "Of course I did!" Which was a lie, but what was she supposed to say? And she did intend to. She struggled to soften her response. "But nothing big. I mean, I know you're downsizing." She hesitated. "If you haven't done any shopping, don't feel like you have to get me anything. I don't suppose either of us feels very festive this year."

"No," her mother said softly. "I don't."

Mom insisted on clearing the table and putting away leftovers, so Olivia did end up taking flattened cardboard boxes and packing tape to the attic, where she set to work exploring the stash of winter clothes never brought out of storage this year, plus unneeded furniture and umpteen boxes full of the accumulations of a lifetime.

Making decisions took an emotional toll. A few things, she left out to ask her mother about. But not tonight. Tonight, she'd had all she could take.

She found Marian in her own bedroom, the closet door open and several plastic-lidded storage boxes sitting on the floor and bed. She had something clutched in her hands that Olivia couldn't see. Tears ran down her face.

"Mom?"

She looked up in swift alarm. "Oh! Are you done?"

"For the night." Olivia hesitated. "Are you all right?"

"Of course I am," her mother said sharply.

"Well, then…" She backed into the hall, hating this feeling of rejection. "I'll see you…I don't know. I'll call you."

If Mom said good-night, Olivia didn't hear.

Outside, sitting in her car, she looked at the house that had once been home and realized that even though she hadn't had to bury her mother, she'd lost her all the same. Olivia had never felt so alone.

As LOUSY AS the estrangement from her mother
made her feel, the week that followed—the one
leading up to Christmas, as it happened—was unexpectedly good. She and Ben had lunch together
a couple of times, she had dinner with him and
Carson and the two of them went out one night.
Olivia liked that he shared his worry about his stepson, because in all honesty, even she had noticed
that Carson seemed a little subdued. Apparently he
wasn't so sure there wouldn't be a payback for the
way he'd humiliated two of his teammates. Shar-
ing that fear, Ben was giving Carson a ride home
from practice every day to be sure he couldn't be
caught alone.

The week was busy at the store, and she kept
being grateful for her relationships with her senior employees. They could have resented her and
didn't. After a short meeting with Lloyd, Ross and
Stuart, she sat behind her desk feeling ridiculously
warm and fuzzy because they made her feel as if
they were glad she was there.

She and Ben attended a holiday party at Sabrina's, and she had lunch with two other friends one
day when he couldn't get away.

Which brought her to the startling realization
that maybe she belonged there.

She might have been completely happy if only
Christmas hadn't been looming so near. Except for
her resolve not to leave Mom alone for the holiday,
Olivia had done her best to ignore it. She hadn't

sent out cards, hadn't bought any gifts and could hardly wait until the festive lights and decorated trees disappeared for another year. Dad was such a big part of the holiday for her. As mad as she was at him, she kept remembering how much he loved Christmas. He was like a little kid, shaking his presents, guessing the contents with infuriating accuracy. Disguising what she'd bought him with multiple boxes and elaborate wrapping had become a game.

It had to be those memories along with the loneliness she'd felt after her mother's rebuff that made her so susceptible when Ben invited her to spend Christmas with him and Carson.

How could she resist, even if he issued two invitations: one for Christmas Eve, to be spent with him and Carson, and the other for Christmas Day at his parents' house? Yes, the whole family deal. To top it off, Ben had included her mother in those invitations, too, although Mom had accepted only the one, deciding to spend Christmas Day with some longtime friends, instead.

At least they were spared having to pretend to celebrate with just the two of them. Oh, joy, either in Olivia's student-dig's basic apartment or at the family home her mother was desperate to leave. Instead…wow. Instead, this felt a lot like the way any couple handled major holidays and two sets of parents. Christmas Eve with one, Christmas Day with the other.

Ben's insistence on including her in his family celebrations awakened a yearning in Olivia that she'd been trying really hard not to acknowledge.

The way she'd jumped to accept both invitations told her she'd been deceiving herself about that whole second-chance business. It was just going to be sex; she had convinced herself. Why should she trust him? Anyway, she didn't even know that she'd be staying in Crescent Creek. She could have fun without risking heartbreak.

Sure. Right. Having casual fun with a guy did *not* include spending Christmas Eve with him and his son as well as Christmas Day *with his entire family.*

Oh, boy, what was she doing?

Falling in love all over again with Ben Hovik, that's what, she realized with chagrin.

She hadn't openly admitted to herself that she'd begun to imagine a future with Ben…but now she knew the truth. She wanted to be part of his family. Wanted him to be her family.

Christmas suddenly meant something.

After accepting his invitations, she'd kissed him good-night and gone to bed before she was jolted with the alarming realization that suddenly she had a whole lot of shopping to do, and only five days to do it.

Not sleepy at all, she'd spent a good half hour mulling over ideas for gifts before she discovered she felt something else totally unexpected: anticipation.

THE LIGHTS GLOWED on the Christmas tree, and through the dark window Olivia could see more strung along the eaves of Ben's house as well as on neighbors' homes across the street.

Carson sat on a rolling hassock right beside the tree, where he could fulfill his self-designated job of handing out gifts. Ben lounged on the sofa beside Olivia, his arm resting behind her, close enough she brushed it when she turned her head. And Mom… She sat in the easy chair, her expression almost as bemused as Olivia felt.

Except Olivia was actually enjoying herself, too. Hard to tell with Mom, who was being pleasant but quiet. Of course, Dad had died only…Olivia had to count. Thirty-one days ago. Which made rejoicing somewhat inappropriate.

Only…this had to be better than ignoring the holiday. Imagining how she'd feel if she'd been alone, knowing everyone else was with family celebrating, Olivia realized how lucky she was.

Sneaking a look at her mother, who was shaking her head and even laughing at something Carson had just said, Olivia let herself feel the tiniest bit optimistic. She and her mother had a whole lot to work out, but Mom *had* agreed to come tonight. She'd brought presents for Ben and Carson, as well as for Olivia. And even though they hadn't been talking much lately, Mom had had dinner ready every evening when Olivia went home to help pack.

Surely, surely, she wouldn't suddenly announce she was selling the business, too?

No, we'll find our way through this, Olivia thought, her hope only shadowed a little with apprehension. And…Ben might be in love with her, too. Really in love this time. He'd implied that he had been waiting for her ever since she came home to Crescent Creek. There had to be other single women in the area who'd have been delighted to date him, but Olivia had heard Carson teasing him by saying, "Glad you actually *do* know how to ask a woman out. I was starting to wonder."

Oh—and Carson seemed to like her, another positive. He had even asked if he could come talk to her, like, some day after Christmas. Because he needed advice. Olivia, amused, assumed it had to do with a girl. After all, Dad obviously didn't have a clue, if he'd had to wait until a former girlfriend stumbled back into his life before he could get any.

In the background, a CD played "Silent Night." Ben's big hand closed over hers, and Olivia turned her head to find him looking at her with raw emotion in his dark eyes. She squeezed his hand, aware of the hope expanding in her chest until she felt like a helium balloon, about to rise gently toward the ceiling. Although her butt did stay on the sofa, she blinked back tears and squeezed his hand.

"This one's for you," Carson announced, apparently not noticing the way his dad and Olivia were looking at each other. "It's from me." He laid an awkwardly wrapped gift on her lap. "Merry Christmas," he added, in his deep Santa Claus voice.

Laughing, she murmured, "To all."

And together everyone, even her mother, chorused, "And to all a good night!"

And then she applied herself to tearing open a package that seemed to have been secured with—well, not duct tape, but certainly heavy-duty packing tape.

CHAPTER THIRTEEN

Lounging comfortably on the sofa, Ben reached for his eggnog. "Don't believe me, huh?"

"There's got to be something," his father muttered.

Dad apparently hadn't checked out the TV schedule in advance, because he'd settled in his recliner and reached for the remote as soon as Ben, Carson and Olivia arrived to join the rest of the family. He'd reacted with incredulity to the news that, no, this year not a single football game, NCAA or pro, had been scheduled on Christmas Day.

Amused, Ben watched as his father nonetheless proceeded methodically from channel four on up, sure he'd find some obscure bowl game really was being televised today.

Carson leaned over the back of the sofa. "You sure you want Mom and Aunt Holly to get Olivia alone?"

Ben turned his head. "What do you think they're going to do? Scare her off?"

"There's got to be stuff you don't want them telling her."

"Actually...I can't think of anything." He grinned

when his father snorted in disgust and turned off the TV. "It's not like Olivia didn't know me when I was your age. God, when I was twelve or thirteen."

He didn't let a burst of laughter from the kitchen spark unease. "You go defend her if you think she needs it."

"Maybe I will." Carson straightened. "Geez, you'd think there'd be a game on, wouldn't you?"

"What's the world coming to?" his grandfather asked.

Fortunately, only a few minutes later, Ben's sister announced that dinner was on the table. Instead of the usual family argument—the men wanting to leave the television on so they could follow the game, the women insisting it be off—Ben, Carson, his dad and his brother-in-law, Tom, all leaped up gratefully to join the women and kids at the table.

The turkey smelled amazing, and, as usual, the women had gone all out. Ben had offered to contribute a side dish, but Olivia's offer of the same had been accepted in lieu of his.

"Good thing," Carson had muttered, earning himself an elbow in his side.

Lazily participating in the conversation, meeting Olivia's eyes across the table, Ben felt lucky.

More than lucky. Blessed, he decided, was a more appropriate word for the day. She was here, fitting in as if she had always been part of his family. Teasing Carson, laughing at his father's oft-told jokes, jumping up to fetch something from

the kitchen so that his mother didn't have to. Her
cheeks were pink, her smile merry, and for once he
saw no shadow of grief in her vivid eyes.

Earlier, when he'd said, "The first Christmas
without someone must be hard," she'd started to
shake her head, then nodded.

"It's complicated, but of course it is. But…maybe
if he was still alive, I wouldn't have been able to be
here with you and Carson and everyone." Her eyes
might have been damp when she smiled at him, but
she *was* smiling.

It was his father who proposed a toast midmeal.
"To family," he said simply.

As Ben echoed the toast, he and Olivia looked at
each other. She didn't seem any more able to break
that connection than he was.

OLIVIA SPENT THE Monday morning after Christmas
week poring over receipts to date for December,
positively gloating as she concluded they had made
record profits. Even this weekend's post-Christmas
sale had kept them hopping. Altogether, she was
optimistic for next year…if Bowen's Hardware &
Lumberyard still belonged to a Bowen, she thought
wryly.

If I'm still here.

The usual pang was barely felt. *Of course I will
be,* she thought. These past couple of weeks with
Ben had been wonderful. The only way they could
have been better was if she and Mom had miracu-

lously managed to heal their relationship, and, oh, if it turned out Dad really hadn't confessed to infidelity, and he hadn't died. Only a few minor adjustments....

Okay, that was all unrealistic. What she did wish was that she and Ben had been able to spend more time together. A kid of any age was definitely an obstacle.

And yet, she couldn't even regret Carson. Whether they were related or not, he reminded her of a young Ben and made her laugh whenever they were together.

Speaking of... She checked the time and realized she needed to go. She and Carson were doing lunch today. The sixteen-year-old was free because he was still on break. So was Ben, of course, but after deciding to put off the kitchen cabinet job, he planned to spend a few hours at school this week catching up on things he'd been neglecting. Anyway—she and Carson hadn't invited him to join them.

There was something to be said for being able to walk out the back door, turn right and go one block down the alley to be home. Slush lingered in the unplowed alley, freezing at night and half melting during the day, so she picked her way carefully. She was almost to the stairs leading up to her apartment when she saw Carson sitting on the steps.

"Hey," she called.

He rose to his feet. "I thought maybe you forgot."

"Not a chance," she said lightly, surprised at how guarded he looked. "I even loaded up on groceries. It's make-your-own-sandwich day. Plus I bought cherry turnovers."

"Cool," he said, still sounding subdued. On the way up the steps, he said, "You're coming to the game tomorrow night, right?"

"Wouldn't miss it."

This was to be a home game, with Friday night's an away one, in Stanwood. Ben hadn't mentioned it, so she didn't know if he intended to go to that one or was already assuming it would give them an evening alone. School might be on a break, but the athletic schedule continued at full throttle.

Once she'd let herself and Carson into her apartment and adjusted the thermostat, she faced him. "You want to tell me what this is about?"

Color burned on his cheeks. He suddenly seemed younger, ganglier, his feet too big and even his shrug awkward.

"I sort of need someone to talk to," he said. "I guess I said that, huh?"

"And I was elected. I'm flattered." And she was. "But what about your dad? I've had the impression you two have a good relationship."

He hunched his shoulders and looked miserable. "I thought maybe you could tell me what to do."

Clinging to the hope this was about a girl, she prayed it hadn't occurred to him that she and his dad had made passionate love right here in this apartment numerous times in the past couple of weeks. Carson wouldn't ask anything about that, would he?

"Okay," she said slowly. "But…is this something I have to keep secret from Ben?"

His eyes, blue and desperate, met hers. "Maybe."

THIS WAS STARTING to feel like a really terrible idea. Carson could tell she wasn't very happy at the idea of hiding anything from Ben. And he was thinking, what if she hated him once he told her? Because if the girl *was* her sister…

He cast a look at the door and thought about saying "Never mind" and making a run for it. But he was dying, and he *liked* her. He thought she'd be honest, at least. And who else was there? Grandma or Granddad? He rejected that idea right away. No way he could talk to them about drinking and sex and lying to his dad.

After a minute, he took a seat at Olivia's teeny-tiny table, feeling stiff and nothing like he had that other night, when he and Dad had helped her move in.

She took stuff out of the refrigerator and set it on the table so they could both assemble their sandwiches. He was hungry, like always, but his stomach was so knotted he wasn't sure he could actually eat.

"Talk," she said, waving a bread knife. "What's this about?"

"You can't tell anyone," he burst out.

Olivia froze, a tomato in one hand. "Carson...I won't promise to stay quiet without knowing what you're going to say. You have to know there are secrets I *can't* keep."

"It's...nothing like that," he mumbled.

"All right." Her expression was troubled, but after a minute she nodded. "What I'll try to do is give you time to tell your dad if I think this is something he needs to hear. Okay?"

"Yeah." His voice cracked, something that hadn't happened in a long time. He ducked his head.

She slapped the top slice of bread onto the heaping sandwich in front of her and cut the whole thing in half. Carson still clutched his own knife in his hand. All he'd put on the sandwich was the turkey and Havarti.

He took a deep breath. "It's about *her*. The girl."

Olivia stared at him. "You do know that I think she might be my sister."

Carson nodded. "Everybody is talking."

She didn't say anything for a moment, and he couldn't tell what she was thinking. But finally she said, "All right."

"The thing is...there was a party that night. And I was there. I don't usually go, but these guys asked me and—I think I might have met her." He closed his eyes and said the really awful part. "And had sex with her."

SPOTTING AN OPEN place in the crowded bleachers, Olivia stopped halfway up, but Ben's hand urged her on.

"A couple more rows," he said.

"Really? But…"

"My parents are here."

Appalled, she looked up to see that they were not only there, smiling at her, but they had seats saved for her and Ben. *Oh, no.* What could she do but pretend to be delighted?

"Mrs. Hovik!" She sidled apologetically past the couple separating her from Ben's parents. "Mr. Hovik."

His mother kissed her cheek. "Didn't I tell you to drop the mister and missus?"

"Shari," she said dutifully, very conscious of Ben's possessive hand resting at her waist. She smiled weakly at his father. She hadn't quite been able to call him by his first name, even given the flood of unexpected emotions on Christmas Day.

Erik Hovik was an older version of his son— tall, well-built, dark-haired and dark-eyed with the cheekbones she had long guessed were from Lapp ancestry. Back when they were teenagers, Ben had told her his grandfather had immigrated from Finland. Ben's mother was medium height, plump and cheerful, her light brown hair turning gray without her having made any effort to disguise the effects of age. Olivia had always liked her even though, as a teenager, she hadn't felt very comfortable with her boyfriend's mother. She'd felt even less comfortable on the occasions they'd met after he broke up with her. Spending Christmas Day together had changed that, she had thought. But now—

Now she found herself squeezed in between Ben and Shari Hovik. Ben talked to his parents across her, keeping one arm casually looped over her shoulders.

Panic beating desperate wings, Olivia stared at the court, where the boys were warming up. How could Carson have *done* this to her? She could only imagine how Ben would feel to learn his kid had confided in her and then somehow persuaded her to keep quiet.

For now, she reminded herself. She'd emphasized to him that he *had* to talk to his dad. And not only his dad. Chief Weigand, too.

I shouldn't have promised even that, she thought with a sinking feeling that had a lot to do with the people who sat to each side. Oh, heck, she'd thought the same at least a hundred times since Carson's confession yesterday. But…right or wrong, she had promised. She'd agreed to give him a few days.

It was when she mentioned Chief Weigand that Carson had leaped to his feet.

"No! I can't. I'd get everyone else in trouble."

"Maybe not," she had said slowly. "That depends what they did and saw."

"I told you!" he'd cried. "Some of the guys are

leaning on me. This weekend—" He had stopped suddenly. "They've been afraid I'd talk because they know my dad—my *step*dad—is the principal."

This weekend they had *what?* Threatened him, presumably. Was this an ongoing thing? But she didn't ask. Compassion had mixed with anger into a witch's brew in her belly. "What do *you* think is right?" she had asked him, and he'd only shook his head.

"Please," he had begged one more time.

He'd left after she'd said, "All right. But only for a few days."

And now here she was, spending the evening with Ben *and* his parents, all the while knowing something awful that Carson *had* to tell them.

I shouldn't have promised. But, stupidly, she had.

Tonight's game, once it started, was a welcome distraction. It was harder fought than any she'd yet seen. Lake Stevens was a larger high school with a team that had carried the league championships last year and made it several games into the state championship play-offs before losing.

As in the last game she'd watched, Carson was everywhere, passing, playing aggressive defense, storming the basket and throwing up wild shots that somehow dropped through the net. The only difference was that tonight he wasn't ignoring two of his teammates. His friend Vadim Bukin, the stocky point guard, was almost as hot, and Dylan Zurenko, the center, played surprisingly well considering Lake Steven's center had at least a couple of inches on him.

Olivia's emotions churned every time the ball touched Dylan's hands. *Or* his friend Dex Slagle's. And she knew she wasn't being fair—they were teenage boys, who liked to have sex. For all she knew, they hadn't done anything wrong. Except… if they hadn't, why were they threatening Carson to keep him from telling anyone that there had been a girl at the kegger who *might* have been Jane Doe? A girl Carson had last seen being led into the woods by three laughing, strutting boys—who came back without her?

"I should have gone to find her," Carson had said, shamefaced. "But, man, I just wanted to go home. It was…I kept thinking, why did she go with *them?* I mean, right after we— Except, I know. She didn't seem that drunk earlier, when I—" His gaze had shied from hers.

When he'd gone into the woods with the girl, laid down his coat as a bed, fumbled with enough clothing so he could have sex with her, then escorted her back to the fire. All without ever so much as finding out her name.

As sordid as the whole story sounded, Olivia knew things like that had happened at parties when she was in high school, too. It was a universal story that made her feel sick anyway. She hoped Carson hadn't been able to tell how angry she'd been at him even as she was wrenched by sympathy for his misery.

Beside her, Ben rose to his feet, his gaze trained on the court where Carson led a breakaway. "Yes!" he yelled in triumph as the ball sank through the hoop. Laughing, he leaned past her and his mom to exchange a hand slap with his father. When he dropped back onto the groaning bleacher seat, his arm settled around Olivia as if it belonged there.

She hated the fact that she was keeping such an important secret from him.

What made her maddest at herself *and* Carson was her suspicion that he'd told her everything he had only because he was desperate to get it off his conscience. And, yes, he'd probably hoped she'd say, *There wasn't anything you could do—you didn't kill her. Awful things happen.* And he could go back to feeling good about himself, while what she now knew burned a hole in *her* chest.

His hope of being absolved of all guilt had become clear at the end, when she told him in no uncertain terms that he needed to tell his dad and the police chief, and she saw how resistant he still was.

Oh, dear God—what was she going to do if he didn't at least go to Ben?

Do it herself, of course. And Carson would probably never forgive her.

And there was the sinking feeling again, which told her how much she had begun to count on a future with Ben, one that inevitably would include Carson. Who might come to hate her.

She had gotten *way* ahead of herself, she thought unhappily.

But surely, surely, Ben would understand.

Suddenly everybody around her erupted into cheers, so she did the same even if she hadn't the slightest idea what had just happened. And when Ben pressed a kiss to her cheek, she swallowed the lump in her throat and smiled at him.

MOST OF THE Crescent Creek part of the crowd lingered outside the gym until their winning team came out, grinning and clowning around, to a rousing round of applause. Ben, Olivia and his parents were part of the group. Ben had had time as they waited to wonder why Olivia seemed so shy with his parents tonight. It didn't seem like her.

He put the speculation out of his mind as Carson made his way to them. It took a good while, since he had to accept congratulations all the way. His grandparents both hugged him, and Ben hooked an arm around him for one quick squeeze.

Olivia murmured something, and Carson nodded without quite meeting her eyes. Ben wondered about that, too, but only fleetingly.

"So, if it's okay," Carson said, looking at his dad, "I might go hang out with Vadim and a couple of the guys. I'll spend the night at Vadim's."

Yes! Ben controlled his delight with an effort. "No problem. You need a lift?"

"Nah, the Beardens said they'd drop me and Rob off."

Ben slapped him on the back. "Have a good time."

Carson rolled his eyes. "But not too good. I know." He glanced at Olivia, who had stayed silent. Their gazes held for a moment, and then he turned and jogged away.

"Why don't the two of you come home with us and have coffee and pie?" Ben's mother suggested. "I baked blueberry today."

Pie was not what he had on his mind. Even if it was blueberry. "Uh, thanks, Mom, but not this time." He started a round of good-nights, then put a hand on Olivia's back and gave her a gentle steer.

Behind his mother's back, his father grinned wickedly and winked at him. At least one of his parents had some sensitivity to atmosphere. However, that didn't stop Ben from glaring at his dad and hoping Olivia hadn't seen.

"Will you come back to my place?" he asked when they had reached his Jeep.

Her smile was weaker than usual. "Sure, why not? Unless you think Carson will sneak home to try to embarrass us."

"I think *he'd* be the one who was embarrassed. He asked some questions that made me wonder, but…I kind of get the feeling he's still dreaming about sex, not having any."

Her mouth opened, then closed.

Ben cocked his head. "You think I'm wrong?"

"Um…wouldn't he tell you?"

He laughed. "You're joking, right? Do you think I raced home to tell *my* dad the first time I—" *Well, shit. The first time* we *had sex. His* first time had been hers, too. He'd been a late bloomer. Seeing her expression, it occurred to Ben that he had some reparation to do here. "If I'd told him, he'd have known it was you. There was no way."

She did get into the Jeep once he'd unlocked, but she stayed silent.

That gave him an instant to think—if he had protected Olivia by his silence, who would *Carson* stay silent to protect?

A minute later, he joined the line of traffic exiting the parking lot. After a glance at her, he cleared his throat. "Good game."

"I can't believe they beat Lake Stevens."

"And are leading the league." Damn, he was almost giddy. *My kid is a star, our team is having a kick-ass season, and Olivia and I have the night to ourselves.* Life was good.

It stayed good, except for the puzzlement still niggling at him. Something was a little off with Olivia tonight. He couldn't decide what, except that he'd have expected her to be more relaxed with his parents. She and Carson might have been stiff with each other, too, although he wasn't sure about that. They'd really only had that minute together. And he knew they liked each other. He decided he was worrying about nothing, especially when she came into his arms eagerly the minute he had the front door shut behind them.

He was as stunned as ever at how good she felt there. With those long legs, her body fit against his perfectly. He gripped her butt to lift her just a little, and then rocked his hips. He hoped she didn't want to talk. Blood flow to his brain had shut down.

But she seemed to feel the same, because she locked her arms around his neck and pulled his head down until their mouths met in an explosive kiss that involved tongues and teeth and both of them rubbing their bodies against each other. By the time he sucked in a breath, Ben was wondering if he could make it upstairs. But—

"Damn," he muttered. "We can't do this right here."

She nuzzled his throat. "Why not?" she asked in a low, sexy voice.

God. He backed her against the door and kissed her again. But the same determination clung like a burr. There was always a distant possibility that Carson might decide to come by for something he'd forgotten.

Ben managed to convey that to Olivia.

She whimpered. One of her arms was still around his neck. She had been running her other hand over the erection straining at his zipper. *He* whimpered when she took her hand away, rested her forehead against his shoulder for a moment, then drew a deep breath and straightened.

"Stick in the mud," she said, gave him a wicked grin and tugged him toward the staircase.

He wasn't sure without her towing him he'd have made it. These past weeks, he'd kept thinking he would get something close to his fill of Olivia, enough that he could manage a day at work without constantly getting derailed by fantasies of what he could be doing with her instead. The all-too-many days when they didn't have a moment alone or, worst of all, when he didn't even see her, had gotten to be downright painful.

Once they reached his bedroom, he stripped her with record speed and shed his own clothes even faster. He used his mouth to bring her to climax and, an instant later, was already buried deep within her when he remembered he hadn't put on a condom. Swearing, he retreated.

Her fingers gripped tightly around his upper arms. "Wait! What are you *doing?* Don't stop!"

"Condom."

"I am on birth control."

He froze, gritting his teeth against a surge of lust so powerful, he was going to be lucky to come inside her and not on her belly. "You're sure?" he asked gutturally.

Her lips formed an answer that was almost soundless, but reverberated through him. "Yes-s."

Ben drove into her. No finesse, no tenderness, only need that had him nearly deaf and blind. He wasn't going to last a minute. But, to his shock, she spasmed around him just as he began to lose it. His orgasm felt like a tsunami, slamming into him. All he could do was ride it and think, *Olivia*.

And, damn it, imagine her pregnant with his baby.

He managed, barely, to take some of his weight on his shoulder and draw her with him. Their damp bodies stuck together. He closed his eyes and wondered if she had even begun to imagine wedding rings and baby showers.

MABEL AT THE register waved to draw Olivia's attention. "Call for you."

Olivia had been chatting with Norm Appleseth, who even her father had called an old geezer. He'd been chewing her out for all the gewgaws cluttering up the shelves in a hardware shelf, and had just begun on the subject of clothes that weren't designed for working. But they'd known each other a long time. He patted her arm. "Go ahead, young lady. The day I can't pick out my own paint rollers and brushes is the day that daughter of mine might as well put me in a home."

Olivia laughed and dared to kiss his deeply wrinkled and bristly cheek. "I wouldn't dare make a suggestion."

He chuckled, and they parted. Olivia pointed upward to indicate she'd take the call in her office, and Mabel nodded.

A minute later, she sat down behind her desk and reached for the phone, where the light for line two blinked. She hoped it wasn't Ben to cancel on her. Tonight was New Year's Eve, and they'd planned to go to a party at the home of Seth Pierce, a good friend of his who had bought out old Dr. Dillard's medical practice somewhere about the same time Ben had taken the job here in Crescent Creek. But surely Ben would have called her cell phone—

Or maybe not. Since she didn't seem to have it on her, which meant it still reposed at the bottom of her handbag.

"Hi, this is Olivia Bowen," she said.

"Phil Weigand."

Her heartbeat picked up. "Chief."

"The DNA results came back, Olivia."

She'd swear she could *hear* her heart beat. "That was…really fast." Dumb thing to say. Who cared? *Are we related?*

"You paid through the nose for quick results." His voice was kind. "She's not your sister, Olivia. No blood relation to you at all."

Her breath rushed out, and her whole body sagged. She heard herself making a comment, thanking him, saw her hand carefully place the phone down.

She is not my sister.

This had to be relief she felt. Of course it was. Only…it had seemed to be an answer. A logical possibility. Now…now they had no more idea than ever who Jane Doe was. Whether she had a home, somebody who was missing her, somebody who loved her.

Not my sister.

Who was still out there somewhere, waiting to be found.

Something to think about another day.

The coward in her wanted to wait until tomorrow to call her mother. But…she would surely be relieved, too, wouldn't she?

Her mother answered on the third ring.

"Mom? It's me." Great beginning, only slightly better than, say, *Mom, it's not me.* "Chief Weigand just called. The DNA results came back." She opened her mouth to say wasn't it great how fast it was, and didn't let herself. "She's not related to me."

The silence stretched and stretched, but she didn't deceive herself that her mother wasn't there.

"So you hurt me and your father's memory for nothing." Mom's voice cut like a scythe. "I hope you're pleased with yourself."

Now, she was gone.

CHAPTER FOURTEEN

THIS HAD BEEN one of the lousiest New Year's Days that Olivia could remember. She'd tried very hard to get into the spirit the night before, not wanting to drag down Ben's mood along with hers. She had told him about the DNA results, though, and had been aware he was keeping an eye on her throughout the evening.

Not long after the midnight countdown and a kiss that was more tender than celebratory, he'd murmured, "You ready to call it a night?" Olivia's smile had died. Her "Please" was heartfelt. He had walked up to her apartment, but they had talked instead of making love. Unfortunately, he had to be available to pick up Carson, who had gone to his own party. Part of her bleakness the next day was wishing Ben had been able to stay—or that she had been able to go home with him.

Despite how she and Mom had left things off with their last phone call, Olivia turned down Ben's invitation to go cross-country skiing with him and Carson on New Year's Day.

"You need to do stuff with just him," she had

pointed out, while also praying that Carson would use the day to talk to his dad. If he didn't—oh, if he didn't—Olivia was afraid the time had come for her to betray his confidence.

Midmorning, she rang the doorbell of her parents' house instead of letting herself in. This was not her home anymore, in any sense of the word.

Even a week ago, her mother would have smiled and said, "Why on earth are you ringing the doorbell?" Today, she just gave a sharp nod and let Olivia in. They separated to different parts of the house to pack and scarcely exchanged a word.

Going back and forth to the attic, Olivia found herself pausing in doorways, caught by the unfamiliarity of rooms she'd known her whole life. Every time she came, the house looked less like the home she remembered.

Why was she still coming to help? Because this *had* been home? Out of a sense of obligation? Love? Or because she didn't want to lose Bowen's Hardware & Lumberyard and therefore was desperately trying to maintain a state of civility with her mother?

She hoped the last wasn't the answer, or at least not all of it.

Depressed, she didn't answer when Ben called in the late afternoon. Instead, she waited to listen to his message, hoping he'd say, "That was a hell of a story Carson told me today." She wouldn't even have minded too much if he'd also said, "Goddamn it, Olivia! Why didn't you tell me?"

But, no. Instead, he'd sounded relaxed when he invited her to dinner at his place. "Give me a call," he added.

Obviously, Carson had chickened out, if he'd ever meant to keep his reluctant promise to her at all. Now she was mad as well as depressed.

She never did return the call.

Friday immediately after New Year's Day was slow at the store. Everyone was recovering from the revelry. More snow had fallen during the night, making the roads treacherous. Between the holidays and the season, new construction was nonexistent. Everyone felt broke after Christmas, and the excitement of the postholiday sales was over. The few people who came in were frazzled, buying a washer for a dripping faucet or a pipe to repair a broken one. Hardly a single purchase rang up for more than ten bucks.

In theory, the shortest day of the year had come and gone and the daylight hours were supposed to be stretching, but if so, the change wasn't yet noticeable. She'd have to call Ben tonight, Olivia supposed; she hadn't heard from him all day. But she so wasn't looking forward to the conversation she needed to have with him. In fact…what she really wanted was to talk to Carson first, give him a twenty-four-hour deadline.

She was the last out of the store. Tire tracks left

by departing employees headed down the alley the opposite way she went to her apartment. Even though she'd worn boots today and tried to stick to the path she'd created first thing this morning, she hadn't gone a block before snow soaked the hems of her jeans and her socks above the boots.

Clouds covered the nearly full moon, making the alley awfully dark once she passed beyond the reach of the floodlight above Bowen's back door. The few lit windows in upstairs apartments didn't really illuminate the alley. So it wasn't until she was almost to the foot of her own staircase that she saw the shape lying in the alley—and the stain on the snow around what she realized, in horror, was a person.

She was dialing 911 even before she dropped to her knees in the snow beside him. Beside *Carson,* who she recognized despite a grotesquely battered face.

BEN RACED INTO the emergency room at the small community hospital, his head turning to search the waiting room. Only a young woman sat there with a whimpering toddler, and he didn't know her.

"I'm Carson Caldwell's father," he snapped to the receptionist. "I got a call."

From Olivia. He'd heard what she said but understood nothing but the fact that Carson had been beaten up and was unconscious.

"And your name?"

What difference did it make? He gave it anyway. Unable to stay still, he paced in agitation while she murmured in her phone. It felt like ten minutes, but probably wasn't more than two or three before a nurse ushered him back.

When she pushed aside the curtain for one of the cubicles and he got his first look at his son, a hoarse sound burst out of him, as if he'd taken a hit to his belly. Carson's eyes were swollen shut, his face freakishly distended and discolored.

"Carson?" he whispered.

The boy's head turned as if he was seeking his father's voice. His misshapen lips moved. "Dad?"

Dimly aware that both Olivia and Phil Weigand were present, Ben stumbled to Carson's side. He carefully wrapped his hand around the boy's.

"You've looked better," he said, trying hard to keep his tone light.

Carson made a sound.

"I'm not going anywhere," Ben murmured as gently as possible, "but I need to take a minute to talk to a couple of folks. Okay?"

The nod was barely detectable.

Then Ben pinned Olivia with a hard stare, and he jerked his head toward the curtain.

She and Chief Weigand silently accompanied him into the hall. It was Phil who said, "There's a small conference room this way," and led them around the nurses' station. He paused to tell one of the nurses where they'd be when the doctor came looking for them.

Ben felt mild claustrophobia once the door was shut, not only because of the close confines, he realized, but also because of his visceral knowledge that the room existed for physicians to give bad news to relatives in privacy.

"What does the doctor say?" he asked first.

Olivia looked shocked, her face white. "Probable concussion, definitely broken ribs and arm. He was not only beaten with fists, he was kicked. And..." Her voice shook. "And stomped on. He has a bunch of broken bones in his right hand."

"Jesus." Ben bent forward, elbows braced on his knees, his head hanging. He had to breathe hard, nearly panting, before he regained the ability to straighten and glare at the police chief. "Have you made any arrests?"

"You know I haven't. Carson hasn't told me his side of the story yet. It'll likely be morning before he can. Thanks to Olivia, I have a good idea of at least two of the boys who did this, but I need confirmation from Carson. I can't jump the gun."

Thanks to Olivia. This was the part he hadn't understood from her incoherent side of the phone call that had brought him tearing to the hospital.

He looked at her again. "How is it you found him?"

Her eyes were huge and haunted. "I was the last

one leaving Bowen's. He'd been dumped at the foot of my staircase in the alley."

"Dumped."

"That's clear," Weigand intervened. "There was a single set of tire tracks, but not a lot of footprints, no sign of several people thrashing around. I think someone opened a car door and pushed him out."

"Because they knew where you lived," he said slowly.

"I…suppose so." Her fingers writhed together.

"Did he talk to you after you found him? I thought you said he was unconscious."

"He was." Her lips trembled, and she firmed them with an obvious effort.

Ben leaned toward her. "Then please tell me how *you* know who beat the shit out of my son."

The menace in his voice made her quiver.

"Now, Ben," the chief said. "Let's count ourselves lucky Olivia knows some backstory."

Ben ignored him as if he weren't there. His fierce stare never wavered.

After a moment, her chin came up. "He told me he was being threatened and why. I've already shared that with Chief Weigand."

"He told you." Pressure built in Ben's head. "When?"

"Um…" Now, finally, her gaze shied from his. "Monday."

"Four days ago."

"Yes. I made him promise to tell you. I said I would if he didn't."

"And yet you must have guessed that he hadn't."

"I was…going to call you tomorrow," she said, so softly he barely heard her.

The sense of betrayal went so deep, he was drowning. Rapid-fire, he saw them making love. The perfect fit of bodies. Her in his bed. Kissing him voraciously. Crying out his name as if he meant something.

And all the time she knew—

The only time he could remember being this angry was when his drug-addict ex-wife had talked her fourteen-year-old son into running away and risking his life by hitchhiking to help her, because she thought she needed him. Because *she* was incapable of putting his needs ahead of her own.

"Tomorrow," he repeated with contempt. Ben shifted in his seat, coming close to turning his back on her. He didn't want to look at her.

"Tell me," he said to Chief Weigand, who gave Olivia's stricken face a quick assessing glance before complying.

"Carson came to her in confidence." He paused, as if waiting for Ben to respond. When he didn't, Phil gave a slight nod. "He corroborated the rumors we've heard about the kegger. He admitted to having been there and having sex with a girl he fears is our Jane Doe. Afterward, he saw her going into the woods with three other boys. He believes she was quite drunk by that time." Phil hesitated for a moment. "Carson saw the boys come back to the fire, but not the girl. He now feels guilty that he didn't check on her."

Oh shit, oh shit, oh shit was all Ben could think. Why had Carson dammed all this up? Once word had gotten out about the girl Marsha Connelly found dead, why hadn't he said, *Dad, I think she was at this party last night?*

Because he was a kid. Because he knew Ben wouldn't like that he'd been drinking, that he hadn't been where he had said he would be, that he'd had sex with some girl he didn't even know. *Dear God, please, not unprotected sex.* No, Ben remembered; Weigand had said if Jane Doe had had sex in the recent past before she died, the male had used a condom.

"Dylan Zurenko and Dex Slagle," Ben said grimly, still not so much as glancing toward Olivia, who sat silent partway around the small table.

"Those are the two boys he named when he told Olivia he was being pressured to stay silent. He didn't name the third he saw going into the woods with the girl. I'd like to get that name, too. Carson is a big, tough kid. I suspect it took more than two of them to bring him down tonight."

Nausea clenched in Ben's stomach, a greasy ball he fought to keep down.

A booted foot deliberately stomping down on Carson's hand. Making sure he wouldn't be able to dribble or shoot a basketball. Slamming into his ribs. Fists pummeling his face until blood spurted and he went down.

Ben half rose to his feet, sure he was going to lose the battle to keep from vomiting. But fury proved to be stronger. After a microsecond's hesitation, he sat back down. At last, he looked at Olivia, who stared back with dilated eyes.

"You knew this could happen and did nothing."

Her lips parted, then closed. She swallowed but kept staring.

"I'd like you to leave," he said. "I don't want you near my son."

Her shattered expression should have ripped his heart out, but he had gone so cold inside, he felt next to nothing.

After the briefest of moments, she bent her head in acknowledgment, stood and walked out. The door closed softly behind her.

Weigand shook his head. "Your son trusted her to keep her word. That party was over two months ago. She had no reason to think a few days now were that significant. You're going to regret shutting her out like that."

"If she'd confided in me the way she should have, Carson wouldn't have been battered within an inch of his life and dumped on *her* doorstep like garbage." Ben's voice sounded as frozen as he felt.

The police chief only shook his head again.

Ben was already on his feet and opening the door, on his way back to his son.

OLIVIA WALKED THE three-quarters of a mile or so from the hospital. She had ridden to the hospital in the ambulance, clutching Carson's uninjured hand. It occurred to her partway that she could have asked the police chief to have one of his officers drive her. She could have called a friend… but then she would have had to explain why she *needed* the ride, and she couldn't do that. Not now.

As she stumbled along a snowy road verge, blinded by tears, she knew she deserved to suffer. Having to walk home on a cold night, temporarily losing sensation in her toes, this was nothing. Less than nothing. She didn't blame Ben for his anger. She blamed herself for what had happened to Carson. He could have died, and it would have been her fault. Hers.

Eventually she plodded down the alley behind Bowen's, checked briefly when she almost stepped in the blood staining the snow and dragged herself up the wooden staircase to her door. Somehow she'd retained possession of her purse, thank God. She hadn't even thought about the fact that she wasn't wearing gloves. Her hands were so cold, willing one to function enough to grip her keys and unlock was almost impossible.

At last the key turned in the lock and she all but

fell into the apartment. She dropped her purse to the floor, nudged the light switch with her shoulder, made her way to the thermostat. Her fingers were a strange color, it occurred to her, as an idle observation. She had to use her knuckles to adjust the thermostat upward. Way upward. Then she stood there.

And stood there. She could see the glow of the electric wall heater but couldn't feel any resulting rise in temperature.

I'm in shock, she thought at last. Moving felt beyond her, but she knew she needed to. Somehow she made herself take the few steps to the bathroom and start hot water running into the bathtub that was too small to stretch out in. Until now, she'd used it only as a shower stall.

As the level rose and steam filled the tiny room, she fumbled her clothes off and laboriously lifted each foot into the bath, until she was able to sink down. At first, the hot water felt so good she moaned, and then it *hurt,* and she moaned some more, but slowly life returned to her frozen extremities. When the water cooled, she ran more hot, curling into a small ball to get as much of her body submerged as possible.

By the time Olivia climbed out, toweled herself dry and went to her bedroom for warm socks, flannel pajamas and a fleece bathrobe, she felt almost human. Which meant it wasn't her body that hurt anymore, only her heart.

PHIL WEIGAND HAD had dealings before with Darren Zurenko, who was president of one of the two banks here in town. Zurenko senior saw himself as a Very Important Citizen, so it wasn't any real surprise he'd taught his kid to think he could do anything he damn well pleased. Phil wasn't surprised, either, when Dylan's father was enraged at his son's arrest.

"You're taking the word of that little prick Caldwell?" the father snarled. "If you went to any of the games, you'd know he has it in for Dylan."

Phil's jaw tightened. "Somebody beat that boy bloody and unconscious, broke a dozen bones. You should be thanking providence right now that your son won't be facing murder charges. As it is, the prosecutor may go for attempted murder."

"Attempted murder?" Mr. Zurenko's voice rose to a howl. Then he stuck his face close to Phil's. "I hope you aren't attached to your job, because you won't have it much longer."

Ignoring the man, Phil pushed a white-faced Dylan out the door, down the sidewalk and into the backseat of his unit, feeling no pity at all for the awkward way the kid was forced to sit with his hands cuffed behind him.

After slamming the door on him, Phil walked back up to the Zurenko garage, where one of his officers stood watch over the boy's car. As Phil neared, he saw the fixed way Cody Dixon was staring into the backseat. One more thing that wasn't a surprise: while the seat itself must have been covered, an effort to clean a swath of the upholstered back didn't disguise the underlying brownish-red stain. And when Phil stepped closer yet, he noted that the mats on both sides in the back were missing, leaving behind impeccably clean carpet that had never met the dirty sole of some teenage boy's feet.

He'd have to ask for an extension of the warrant that, at the moment, was only for the car. Somehow he didn't expect that to be a problem. And considering the garbage can stood only a few feet away, he had a good idea where he'd find two small, square, backseat mats, presumably carpeted like the ones on the floor in the front and therefore uncleanable.

As he took out his phone to call the judge, he wondered how the arrest of Dex Slagle was going.

OLIVIA HEARD RUMORS the next day, confirmed in midafternoon by the police chief, who called her as a courtesy. Yes, three boys had now been arrested: Dylan Zurenko, Dex Slagle and Gavin Runyon, a big bruiser of a kid who played football rather than basketball. None of their parents believed their sons were guilty, Weigand said with restraint, but he was holding the boys in juvie in Miller Falls at least long enough to interview all of them thoroughly.

When she asked, timidly, he told her that Carson would likely be in the hospital for a couple of days, but the concussion had been minor and the most significant damage was the broken bones that were giving him a lot of pain and would keep him out of sports for some months.

At the end, he said, "Give Ben time, Olivia. This was a shocker."

"Was it?" She'd had time to think. "He's been really obsessed with those rumors of a kegger. I thought it was because he's such a dedicated school administrator who cares about the kids." Her own mockery had an edge. "Now I think he's been afraid all along Carson was part of it."

The police chief had no rejoinder, which made her smile bitterly. He agreed, but was too diplomatic to say so.

"I'm glad Carson will be okay," she said with finality. "When you see him, tell him I'm annoyed with him but rooting for him anyway."

"I can give you his room number if you want to call—"

"His father was quite clear. But thank you."

At close to five, she was discussing the difference between drum and belt sanders with a customer when she heard a woman asking for her at the front checkout. Leaving the man, who had now picked up a box holding a detail sander, inadequate for the job he'd described, and was reading the small print, Olivia went smiling toward the woman. About forty, brunette, well-dressed, Olivia didn't recognize her. She swung around, her eyes locking on Olivia.

"Hi, I'm Olivia Bowen. How can I help—"

Faster than a snake striking, the woman slapped Olivia, who stumbled back a step.

"You bitch! I hear it's *you* who named my son. You think you belong here because your parents did, but you don't. Go back where you came from," she snapped, spun on her heel and left the store.

Half a dozen employees and customers had seen the confrontation and now stood silent, mouths agape. Olivia's hand crept up to cradle her cheek, which burned and was tender to the touch. A warning twinge told her she'd suffered something like whiplash.

Smiling wryly at the nearest onlookers, she said, "Well, it's always nice to receive these compliments."

A titter of laughter eased the atmosphere. She quietly excused herself to Stu Dodd, who was the nearest employee, and went upstairs to put some ice on her cheek and calm down. She wondered which boy's mother the woman was. *You think you belong here.* The viciously spoken words kept ringing in her ears as she sat behind her desk gingerly pressing the ice pack to her face.

She had been thinking she belonged in Crescent Creek, that she'd come home to stay, she thought bleakly, but it had already been made clear to her that she'd been wrong. The people most important to her didn't want her here. If Ben had called today— But he hadn't. He wouldn't. Silly of her to have started dreaming.

She had been nothing to him but a casual sex

partner who had way overstepped her place. It said it all that she'd been confiding her deepest hurts and fears to him while he kept what he feared most from her. Clearly he regretted ever having introduced her to his son.

Nor had her mother called. At this point, Olivia doubted she would, either. The truth was, probably all Marian Bowen had ever wanted was to sell the damn store, not have to deal with complications brought about by her daughter. Chances were good that, once house and hardware store sold, she'd buy a condo in Palm Springs or Florida rather than staying here in town, since Olivia had seen to it she was humiliated.

I need to start job hunting, she thought. *Let Mom know I won't be staying.* There were enough experienced employees to keep the business running while Mom sought a buyer. A stab of pain in her midsection doubled Olivia forward as she realized suddenly that she'd never been needed. She'd come running home because she wanted to believe she was. *My parents' daughter, the savior, and look what I've accomplished.*

At last she dropped the dripping ice pack into her metal trash can, where it landed with a splat, and went to the small employee restroom to see how bad her face looked before she returned downstairs, smile pinned into place, to help the customers.

The townsfolk who really did belong here, in her hometown.

CARSON PEERED UP at Ben from the hospital bed. "How come Olivia hasn't come to see me?" he asked, the words still slurred.

On a sharp bite of guilt, Ben tightened his jaw and thought about lying. But, damn it, wasn't this whole mess about needing to lay yourself out there and tell the truth?

"I asked her to stay away." Asked? *Told.*

Carson stared at him with eyes that were still barely seen through slits two days after the beating. "But...why?"

Ben already knew he should have called her by now, or gone to see her. He'd felt sick when Phil Weigand had stopped by the hospital last night to tell him about Mrs. Runyon's attack on Olivia, witnessed, from the sound of it, by half the town.

What Phil had said was, "Guess you're not alone in thinking much of Ms. Bowen."

Ben was the one who'd felt too low to live.

Tomorrow, he'd promised himself, deciding it was too late to bother her by the time he had left the hospital. More excuses: his distressed parents had begged him to attend church with the family that morning, and he'd come straight to the hospital afterward.

"Once she knew you were in danger, she should have called me." He sounded more uncompromising than he felt, now that his first anger and sense of betrayal had passed. He'd reacted as if this was all about *him,* and it wasn't. Carson had chosen to confide in Olivia, and if she hadn't lived up to his trust, there'd have been no chance of them having a friendship. The friendship *he* had wanted between them, his son and the woman he loved.

"My fault," the teenager mumbled. "She wanted me to tell you right away. I begged her, and she said she'd give me a few days."

Ben looked squarely at him. "So why didn't you?" This was the first time he'd asked that question. He hadn't been sure he wanted to know the answer. It cut too deep.

He flinched. Was that why he'd been so furious? Because he was *jealous?* God, he hoped not.

Carson had turned his head on the pillow so he wasn't looking at his stepfather anymore. "I didn't want you to know."

"Know what? That you went to a party and maybe got drunk? Had sex?"

"I used a condom."

Ben gently squeezed his shoulder. "Good."

Carson stole a quick look at him. "I lied to you. I mean, about spending the night at Justin's. His mom wasn't home."

"Ah." Ben couldn't help a wry reflection on how many times he'd lied to his parents at that age. Kids did. They weren't about to say, *Mom, I'm going to a party now so I can get loaded.* Or, *I bought condoms today in hopes I can get laid tonight.*

"Do you really believe I'd be so mad about that? That I never got drunk when I was your age?"

Carson peered at him uncertainly. "You did?"

"Of course I did. Puked my guts out the next day, and decided I'm not much of a drinker, but I tried it." He shrugged. "Everyone else was."

"I didn't like it much, either. It made me think about—" He didn't finish, but he didn't have to. *Mom.* That's what he didn't want to say.

Ben touched Carson's shoulder again in silent reassurance.

"It was mostly that everyone was talking about all the girls who'd be there, and they made it sound like all you had to do was pick one and she'd let you…you know. Do whatever you want." Lucky for him, the vivid discoloration of his face didn't allow any blush to show. "And…that's what I did," he said in a final burst. "Only—" his voice had slowed "—then I saw her go off in the woods, you know, with those other guys, and I thought it was some kind of slap at me because I wasn't good enough, so I was mad and ashamed, and I just wanted to go home except I had to wait for Justin." There was a long pause. "And when she didn't come back, I sort of wondered, but mostly I was pretending everything was cool. You know?"

Ben had to clear his throat. "I know." What man *wouldn't* know how Carson had felt?

"And then the next day, when I heard—" His throat worked and he looked beseechingly up at Ben, seemingly unaware that two lone tears tracked down his cheeks. "I thought—I didn't even ask her name."

Oh, damn.

Ben sat on the bed, making sure Carson was looking at him.

"Did she ask yours?"

After a long stare, he shook his head. "All she said was, 'Do you wanna…' Um, you know."

"Would you feel guilty if the girl hadn't been found dead the next morning?"

Carson blinked a couple of times. "I don't know." He thought some more. "Maybe not guilty, but… sort of, I don't know, scuzzy. Like I should have waited until I was doing it with a girl I at least *liked*."

"Yeah." Ben heard the gravel in his voice. "I'm here to tell you sex *is* better with someone you like. It's even better with a woman you love."

If he could call it love when he'd then turned around and hurt her the way he had.

"I just…" Carson was back to mumbling. "I wanted to tell you, but then I blew Zurenko and Slagle off a couple times when they asked me to come to other parties, and they got suspicious. 'Cuz everyone who was there was freaking, you know, thinking we'd be in deep shit, and they thought I was the one who'd have a big mouth because…"

"Of me."

"Well…yeah."

"So they tried terrorizing you into silence."

"I guess it worked."

"Carson, I'm proud of you because you *do* have a conscience. I wish you had spoken out, but at least what you knew has been eating at you. It doesn't sound like anyone else was bothered at all."

"They're assholes. I don't want anything to do with any of them. Not just Zurenko and Slagle, but their friends, too. I just… It felt good they asked me. Because they're like the team leaders, you know?"

"Yeah." Ben lightly bumped his fist against his son's good shoulder, one of the few places on his body safe to touch. "What I think is, you're entitled to make a few mistakes. You didn't do anything so awful. You learned a lesson." He let his mouth tilt into a crooked a smile. "A painful one."

Carson grimaced. "Hell, yeah!"

"I don't say this very often—maybe not often enough—but I love you."

A couple new tears joined the ones Carson's tongue had caught. "I love you, too," he whispered huskily.

Ben gently smoothed the boy's hair back from his head, letting the silence grow until Carson dropped off to sleep, helped along by his pain meds.

Only then did Ben reluctantly rise. He was way overdue to make amends—if Olivia would accept them.

CHAPTER FIFTEEN

IT BEING A Sunday, Ben guessed Olivia would either be at home or at her mother's. He was able to park in the alley about half a block from her apartment and, although he didn't see her car, he climbed the rickety wooden stairs and knocked on her door anyway.

There wasn't a sound from inside. Out of the corner of his eye, he caught a flicker of movement and turned his head sharply. Something down the alley? Or the curtains twitching in the small window he knew was above Olivia's kitchen sink?

He knocked again. Called, "Olivia? It's Ben. Can we talk?"

Nothing.

He might have imagined the movement. She could be at her mother's.

Back in his Jeep, he took out his phone and dialed her parents' number. Marian answered. When he asked for Olivia, she said immediately, "I haven't seen her in several days, Ben. I'm sorry."

He frowned. "I thought she was helping you pack."

"She was." The pause suggested reluctance.

"We...had words." Another hesitation. "No, the words were mine."

He tilted his head back, closed his eyes and thought, *Oh, damn, Olivia. Both of us went off on you.* "You hear about her getting attacked?"

"Attacked?" Marian sounded shocked.

He told her about Carson's assault and the repercussions.

"Oh, dear God. All that, after what I said."

Neither of them spoke for a minute.

"I said some things I regret, too." His voice was hoarse. "That's why I'm trying to find her. To apologize. I went by her apartment, but she's either not there or she's not answering the door."

"Did you try the store?"

"No, but I will." He hesitated. "If you hear from her, would you tell her how sorry I am? And that I want to say so in person?"

"I can try." She sounded stifled.

Mouth tight, he ended the call, got out and walked the block and a half the other direction to Bowen's.

Half the employees he spotted were high school kids, who looked alarmed at the sight of their principal where he didn't belong. There were a couple of women at the cash register, and finally he tracked down Stuart Dodd, whom he knew as a parent.

"Olivia?" Stuart looked surprised. "No sign of her. She usually takes Sunday off. You try her apartment?"

"Yes. I guess I'll just leave her a message."

"Good idea." A solidly built guy maybe ten years older than Ben, Stuart started to turn away but stopped. "I was sorry to hear about what happened to your boy."

"Thank you. He'll be okay, but that was the end of basketball season for him. He's not real happy about that."

"The end of basketball season for Crescent Creek," Stuart corrected him. "To lose three starters…" He shook his head.

That was another conversation Ben had to have, this one with Ray McGarvie, who had left a message yesterday.

"It's safe to say we won't be making the playoffs," Ben agreed. As excited as he'd been, maybe he should feel some disappointment now, but on the scale of things to worry about, how a high school basketball team did in any one season was at the bottom of his list compared to a girl's death, the arrest of a trio of boys who had gotten so arrogant they felt entitled to mete out a vicious punishment to a younger teammate who'd defied them, Carson's pain and disappointment—and Olivia.

What I did to Olivia.

"So," Stuart ventured, "is what I hear true? That those boys may have killed that girl? Or at least left her out there to die?"

"No," Ben said sharply. "There was a kegger in

the woods that night. Nobody even knows if our Jane Doe was at it, far less what happened to her."

Sharp? He must have sounded savage, because Stuart melted away, mumbling something Ben didn't catch. He was left standing there in the plumbing aisle, held immobile by despair.

What if she wouldn't forgive him? What if her mother's rejection and his were too much?

How would Chief Weigand ever determine whether Jane Doe *was* the girl Carson had had sex with?

Ben bent his head and pinched the bridge of his nose. Yeah, and how was he supposed to deal with the parents of three boys who'd beaten the hell out of *his* son? And decide whether to expel those boys?

He ached to talk to Olivia about it, and about everything else, too.

Finally he pulled himself together enough to walk back out of Bowen's to his Jeep, where he dialed her number and counted the rings.

"Leave a message," her voice said.

"Olivia." Words jammed up in his throat. Getting them out was like pushing a stalled car uphill. The silence went on too long. She might delete the message if he didn't get going again. "I didn't mean anything I said. I was scared." He talked faster and faster, now that he'd started. "Scared made me angry, and you took the brunt of it. I'm sorrier than I can say. Please talk to me. Please—"

Beep.

He called again. "I wanted to say that Carson would really like to see you. Will you call him or visit? I know you're mad at me. I don't blame you. But I'd appreciate it if you'd find some time for him. Um, I heard about Mrs. Runyon going after you. You didn't deserve that." Damn, he needed to be eloquent, and nothing was coming out the way he wanted it to. "You didn't deserve—"

Beep.

Enraged, he almost heaved his phone against the dashboard. Instead, his fingers tightened around it until it was a wonder it didn't shatter.

He sat there with his heart thudding and panic suffusing him, making it hard to think. He could call her back— And say what? Please call me? Hadn't he already said that, more or less?

Wait, he decided. He'd try again tonight, if he hadn't heard back from her.

So...now what? Start the engine, get the heat going. Call McGarvie. Check back at the hospital. Go home.

Wonder how he could have been so unthinking, so goddamn stupid, as to lash out at the one person he needed most.

OLIVIA LISTENED TO both messages without feeling moved in any way to call Ben back or see him. She'd been hit too hard by too many people. She didn't leave the apartment on Sunday, even though she could have used some groceries. But shopping meant the possibility of running into people she knew in the aisles or checkout line at Safeway.

No. Right now, she didn't want to see anyone. Not even the sympathetic folks. If Lloyd gave her one of his kind smiles, she'd break down sobbing.

Ben left another message that evening. This one, she deleted without bothering to listen to.

Finally, Monday morning, she did call the hospital and ask for Carson's room. Presumably Ben would be at the high school, not sitting at his son's bedside.

The phone rang enough times, she was about to give up when fumbling noises were followed by a "Hello?"

"Hi," she said. "It's Olivia. Just…checking on you."

"Wow! I thought you were mad at me."

"I am mad at you." She was smiling despite also wanting to cry. "But what happened to you sucks. Do you hurt?"

"Yeah. I mean, not so much, 'cuz I'm on pain-killers, but…yeah."

"Guess that's it for basketball this year, huh?"

"Yeah," he said again. "Coach and Dad talked about forfeiting the rest of our games, but they decided that wasn't fair to the other guys. I guess, once I'm back at school, I'll travel to games with them. You know, just to cheer for them."

"That would be really nice of you. And they

ONE FROSTY NIGHT

might surprise you. A couple of those guys were playing really well."

"Yeah, Vadim is awesome, but we don't have a center except this freshman guy who'll have to be moved up from JV."

She was impressed at his maturity for not saying, *No way can they replace* me. If she had to guess, that's exactly what Dylan Zurenko was saying right now, probably with his parents' encouragement. He'd be hoping, vengefully, that the team would get crushed in upcoming games, so everybody would talk about how all-important he was. Never mind that the team had lost the Friday night game, when Dylan and his buddy Dex were on the court, only Carson missing.

The sad thing was, Dylan's parents would never understand what a disservice they'd done him. Probably Gavin Runyon's wouldn't, either. She hadn't heard anything about the third boy's parents. At least neither of them had marched into Bowen's to confront her.

She and Carson talked for a few minutes. He told her about getting snatched off his bike on his way home after school, and the ensuing panic when he didn't show up to get on the bus for the game.

It turned out he had been missing for something like an hour and a half before Olivia found him lying in the alley. Imagining how distraught Ben had been made her understand his fury.

"Ben said you won't take his calls," Carson said.

"No."

"He was really a creep, huh?"

"You could say that."

"He's a good guy, you know."

She did know. He was filled with nobility, leading the town to give their hearts to a dead girl who had no one else, even as he hid his fear that his own kid had something to do with her death. A generous friend and lover to Olivia, until she got between him and his son.

Disturbed by her bitterness, she decided that the truth was Ben Hovik *was* a great guy—to the people he loved. She just wasn't one of them.

And she was done.

"I wish you'd let him say he's sorry," Carson said unhappily. "I know this is all my fault. If I'd just done what I promised—"

"Carson, if your father and I had had the romance of the century, you couldn't have damaged it so easily." When he tried to argue, she said, "I promise, what happened between the two of us is *not* your fault. Understand?"

"No."

What was she supposed to say? He blew it, not you? But Ben hadn't blown anything important, not to him. What happened stripped away her rose-colored glasses, that's all.

She settled for an explanation a sixteen-year-old boy would understand. "You know I'm not in town to stay. I think Mom's going to sell the business.

I'm job hunting. So anything your dad and I had wasn't going anywhere long-term, okay?"

She hadn't even known she'd made up her mind for sure until that moment, when she said the words aloud. *I'm not in town to stay.* At that moment, she knew: she didn't have a reason in the world to stay. The thought was so bleak, she felt as if she'd been dropped into a barren desert devoid of landmarks. But going back wasn't possible.

"I think he loves you," Carson said hesitantly.

Pain bit into her, almost enough to make her double over. "You're wrong."

She made her excuses after that and decided to go to work despite her desire to avoid most people who lived in Crescent Creek.

After she called her mother.

Olivia was actually a little surprised that her mother answered the phone. The sound of her voice made Olivia stiffen.

"Olivia? Ben told me about that awful woman slapping you."

Oh, that was funny. So funny, she almost laughed. "Did he? He probably sympathizes with her." She restrained herself from adding, *You probably do, too.*

Her mother gasped. "What are you talking about?"

"It doesn't matter." Suddenly she was too tired to care what either of them thought about her. "I called to tell you I won't be staying in town. You need to put the business up for sale unless you plan to run it yourself. I'll stick around for a week to provide some transition, but I'm confident Lloyd, Stuart and Ross can keep it going while you look for a buyer."

"Olivia, I was angry, but I didn't mean—"

"I'm done, Mom. With all of this."

With one hard punch of her thumb, she ended the call, then turned off her phone. And, yes, she cried, which meant she had to wait until she no longer had puffy eyes before she could go to work.

BEN TURNED INTO an aisle lined with tiny bins holding screws, bolts and nuts, and there she was, apparently finishing a conversation with a middle-aged man who said, "Thanks," and walked away with something in his hand.

"Olivia."

Ben felt like crap and sounded like he was coming off a bad bout of laryngitis. He's hardly slept these past couple nights. The atmosphere at the high school this morning had been toxic; he'd fielded half a dozen phone calls from angry parents who thought those "poor boys" were being blamed for that girl's death just because they'd been in a fight, and, as for the fight, boys would be boys. Didn't he know that? Surely arresting them had been an overreaction.

On top of which, it had been clear to him that the only way he was going to have a conversation with Olivia was to confront her in public. So here he was, standing square in her way, alone with her now that the customer had disappeared in the other direction.

At the sound of his voice, she turned, her dismay apparent. And, damn, she looked as bad as he felt, despite the fact he could tell she'd applied more makeup than usual.

Her shiny hair was pulled back in a painfully tight ponytail, ensuring the bones in her face stood out in stark relief. Her eyes looked dull in a face that he might have described as plain, if he'd been meeting her for the first time. The camel color of the cowl-necked sweater she wore over skinny jeans and knee-high boots didn't do a thing for her.

"May I help you?" she said politely.

He took a couple steps closer. "I'm sorry, Olivia. Sorrier than I can ever tell you. I was scared out of my mind. It hurt to think you'd betrayed my trust."

She looked at him as if he were a stranger. "Because I lived up to Carson's trust."

God. "It…took me a day to realize your dilemma. And to accept that you made the right call."

Her expression didn't change at all. "How magnanimous of you."

"I've missed you desperately." His voice came out gravel rough. "Please don't let my temper ruin what we have."

She shook her head. "We didn't have anything,

or you couldn't have lashed out at me the way you did."

"That's not true!" He was drowning, struggling to the surface for one more breath. "People who love each other fight. They say the wrong things. They—"

"Betray each other? Yes, I've noticed." The bite in her words shocked him. "Ben, I understand why you were angry. If we'd been nothing but acquaintances or even casual friends, I'd say I forgive you. As it is, all I can tell you now is that what you said no longer matters. I'll only be sticking around a few more days. I'm sorry things ended this way, but we are done." Steel reverberated in her voice as she finished.

He took another step. He could almost touch her. "Don't do this, Olivia." He was begging. "Please. I love you."

She only looked at him. "Got to say, I'm not all that dazzled by your idea of love, Ben. In fact, I'm not so sure the real thing exists."

"Please." He barely got the word out. He couldn't say, *Give me another chance,* not when she'd already done that and he'd blown it.

"No." That gaze remained steady. "I'm asking you to leave me alone." And then she turned and walked away, going around the endcap of the aisle to leave his sight, and his life.

Ben felt as if he'd just driven off a cliff.

PHIL SAT IN the easy chair and looked at the woman and teenage boy on the sofa, facing him. This was the fourth home he'd breached this evening, with him wishing like hell he could isolate the kids from their parents. What self-respecting teenage boy was going to talk honestly in front of his mom or dad about boozing and smoking weed and having bacchanalian sex around a huge bonfire in the woods?

This particular kid… Phil refreshed his memory by glancing at the open notebook on his lap. Landon Roberts, that was it. Landon looked even more uneasy than the others Phil had seen tonight had, probably because he was not only an athlete but also a four-point student. Keeping his nose clean could make the difference between Stanford University and community college for him. He looked clean-cut, but Phil would be more impressed by that if Landon hadn't gone to a drunken kegger. *And* if the sleazebags Phil had arrested for assault and battery in Crescent Creek hadn't also presented themselves as wholesome, all-American boys.

Practice makes perfect, he told himself, and began his spiel. "Son, I know you've been hearing the talk, but what I'd like is for you to tell me about that kegger you went to out past Crescent Creek. What you saw, with no spin on it."

Unlike most parents, this mother didn't burst into speech to head him off. Expression stern but not angry, Mrs. Roberts only watched her son squirm.

"It was…" The boy's voice cracked. He cleared his throat and tried again. "I don't usually go to parties like that. You know. Where everyone is getting drunk." He shrugged awkwardly. "But the guys said it would be awesome, and I thought, why not?"

Phil nodded encouragement. At least Landon was talking, not mumbling sullen sentence fragments. And, hail Mary, but the kid's mother actually seemed to expect him to explain.

"Did you know most of the other kids there?"

"Well, not all the Crescent Creek ones. And I guess there were some from farther away. Like Marysville or Arlington. But—" He sneaked a glance at his mother. "A lot of the guys were involved in sports. Especially basketball. So…I kind of knew them from games. You know."

"What about the girls?"

"Only ones from Miller Falls. They were mostly girlfriends and cheerleaders. And, I don't know, there's kind of a party crowd." He had developed a tic in his cheek.

"You've seen the drawings of the girl who was found dead in those same woods the next morning." Phil half rose to hand a copy of the already much-publicized rendering across the coffee table to the mother, who studied it and then passed it to her son.

He took one quick look, shuddered and hastily set it down. "Yeah, but I didn't see her. I don't think she was there."

"Did you stay long? Do you feel as if you saw most of the kids who were there?"

"Yeah." He frowned. "There weren't that many. Maybe something like forty? Forty-five? There's this one girl in a couple of my classes who looks like the one who died. She was there that night." His gaze skated over the drawing. "I mean, obviously she's not her, because she was in school the next Monday."

"How would you describe this girl you know?"

"Well, she's tall. Like, five-ten maybe? And, um, the same color hair and eyes and stuff. She could *be* her, except she isn't."

"Will you tell me who that girl is?"

He stared at Phil in bewilderment. "But what difference does it make, since she's not dead?"

Okay, maybe not Stanford.

Mrs. Roberts stirred but didn't say anything, which Phil appreciated.

"I need to know for a couple of reasons," Phil said. "First, it's possible that the kids who think they saw the girl who died really didn't. If she was never there, they may be confusing her for this girl you know. Also, the more people who were at the party I can talk to, the clearer picture I can get."

"We're not in trouble for just being there, are we?"

"You were breaking the law by attending," Phil said gently. "You were all trespassing, for starters. Nobody asked for the landowner's permission.

Also, I'm sure you're aware that underage drinking is in violation of the law." He paused for a long moment. "That said, my only interest is in clarifying whether the dead girl might have been at this party. Just keep in mind in the future that if someone calls the cops and they raid a party like that one, there might be some arrests."

"Oh." Landon nodded with relief. "I didn't have that good a time anyway. Um…the girl's name is Bailey. Bailey Andrist." He spelled it for Phil. She's kind of…" He blushed. "I mean, everyone says…"

"She's easy?" Phil suggested, feeling the need to bail out the poor kid.

"Uh…yeah. Like every guy on the team says he's, you know, had sex with her."

"Have you?" Phil asked, straight-out.

The boy straightened. "No!" he exclaimed. "She's, like, a slut. That doesn't really appeal to me." Now he did squirm. "And I haven't actually, uh…"

Hiding his smile, Phil closed his notebook. If he wasn't mistaken, Mrs. Roberts was amused, too, but kind enough not to let her son see.

He thanked them both with real sincerity and left, checking his watch as he got behind the wheel of his squad car. It was just past eight-thirty, a little late to be ringing doorbells—but, damn it, he really wanted to talk to this Bailey Andrist. Mostly, he wanted to *see* the girl who was tall and looked very much like Jane Doe—and who tended to sleep around. Who was possibly even the type to go off in the woods with three boys.

In fact, this might be an especially good time to catch her at home on a school night. Mind made up, he checked his computer for an address, started the car and pulled away from the curb. The girl didn't live even ten blocks away.

After locating her street, he pulled up in front of a small, shabby house that made him think rental. Through a gap in the drapes at the front window, flickering lights told him a television was on.

The doorbell had tape across it, suggesting it was out of order. He knocked firmly, and a moment later the single bulb of a porch light came on. He heard locks being disengaged, and finally the door opened. A girl appeared. In the background, a male voice growled, "It better not be one of your friends at this time of night."

Phil just stared at her. Landon Roberts knew whereof he spoke. Damned if this girl couldn't *be* Jane Doe. He gave his head a slight shake to clear it, held out his badge and said, "Bailey Andrist? I'm wondering if I can speak to you."

BEN CLOSED HIMSELF in his office the next day and asked not to be disturbed. He had to be here, but he was damn near at his limit.

He'd brought Carson home yesterday evening but talked him into taking a couple more days before he came back to class. He was still in obvious pain, and Ben wanted to see some of the turmoil ease before Carson reappeared. All three boys were still being held at juvenile hall despite the efforts of the attorneys their parents had hired, and even among fellow students, the debate was strident.

Ben wasn't doing much better than his son was. He felt as if he were being ripped in half. He'd accused Olivia of betraying him, when he was the one who'd betrayed *her.* Twice. Once when she was sixteen, the second time Friday night. Why would she forgive him? Or ever trust him again?

The school phone was ringing; lights indicating two different lines on hold were blinking right now, but the secretary, thank God, had taken him at his word and was leaving him in peace.

When his cell phone rang, though, he picked it up. Carson might need him—

The caller was Phil Weigand.

"Phil," Ben said. *Damn, what now?*

"Ben, I have news." The police chief sounded brusque. Maybe as tired as Ben felt. "Don't know if it's good or bad. Lets our three bullies off the hook where Jane Doe is concerned, though."

Ben straightened. "What?"

Weigand described his quest of the previous evening. Apparently Dylan Zurenko and his two buddies were eager to absolve themselves of suspicion in the death of the unknown girl. They'd given names of Miller Falls boys who had also attended the kegger. The chief had eventually tracked down a girl who looked extraordinarily like the drawings of Jane Doe.

"Shook me up when I set eyes on her. I have no doubt she's the girl Carson had sex with," he said. "He was her first of the evening, so he stuck in her memory." His tone was dry. "She also recalls going off with three guys and 'doing'—her word—them one after another. She shrugged and said, 'I like sex. What's wrong with that?' Only she put it a little more crudely than that. Ah—good thing your boy used a condom."

"Yes. Jesus." Ben was relieved; of course he was. But at the same time... "That puts us at a dead end."

Phil grunted. "I'm afraid so. I don't think our Jane Doe was there."

Ben's head was throbbing. "Then what in God's name was she doing out in those woods?"

"Your guess is as good as mine. I'm not giving up, but there's not much I can do unless I find another string to pull."

"I understand. Do I have your permission to tell Carson?"

"I don't see any harm. I'll let the other boys know I've identified the girl and she's not our Jane Doe. Carson, at least, has nothing to feel guilty about."

"He's going to feel a hell of a lot better to find out she's alive and well."

"He may even encounter her again."

"She his age?" Ben asked.

"A senior."

"Thank you for letting me know."

"This has been eating at you as much as it has at me," the chief said. "I can't say I wanted to find out a bunch of our local boys had something to do with that girl's death, but I don't like not being able to find answers, either."

"No."

"Have you talked to Olivia?"

An ice pick stabbed through his temple. "Unfortunately, yes. Forgiveness isn't happening. She's encouraging her mother to sell the business and plans to leave town herself."

"I'm sorry," Phil said quietly, and Ben thanked him.

After ending the call, he stood up and walked out, stopping only long enough to tell the school secretary that he wouldn't be back today but could be reached on his cell phone in case of an emergency.

Her half-frightened, half-avid expression made him wonder fleetingly what she saw on his face. He only nodded and kept going.

Fifteen minutes later, he let himself in his front door.

"Dad?" Carson's head appeared above the sofa back. He must have been lying down watching TV. "What are you doing home?"

"Headache." He grimaced. "Wanted to talk to you."

Circling the sofa, he thought Carson staying

home the rest of the week was a good idea for another reason. Ben had kind of gotten used to the Halloween monster look, but it would cause a sensation in the halls at school.

On the other hand, it might swing sympathy his way, Ben reflected.

His son scrutinized him as he sank down on a recliner. "You look like shit, Dad."

"Thanks."

"No, I mean it."

"Headache," Ben explained.

"Did you take something? I've got these great painkillers, you know."

His chuckle jarred his head and made him wince. Maybe the heavy-duty stuff wasn't a bad idea. The over-the-counter pills he'd taken sure weren't doing the job.

"I think I'll go lie down," he said. "But first— Phil Weigand called. He tracked down the girl you saw at the kegger. She's a Miller Falls student. She described you."

Carson gaped at him.

"She's not our Jane Doe, Carson. Although Phil agrees that she could be a twin."

"She's alive." He sounded stunned.

Ben didn't repeat what she'd said about liking sex. He only agreed, "She's fine."

A raw sound escaped Carson's throat. "I thought—"

Pounding head or no, Ben pushed himself out of

the chair and moved to the coffee table, where he could lay a hand on his son's arm. "I know what you thought. But, thank God, you were wrong."

The boy's body lurched with something like a sob. With his good hand, he swiped at tears. And then he looked at his father.

"But then...who is she?"

"I don't know. We may never know," he said more heavily.

Carson's gaze lost focus. "That's just wrong," he said at last, his voice low. "Doesn't anybody *miss* her?"

Ben had to repeat, "I don't know," the most useless damn answer in the world.

CHAPTER SIXTEEN

"Got a minute?"

Ben looked up from his laptop, somehow not surprised to see his least favorite school board member standing in the door to his office. Hank Meyer was also the youngest member of the school board; his last kid had graduated only two years ago. He was rigid, narrow-minded and opposed to any progressive ideas. Hank had never been a fan of Ben's and had probably voted against hiring him.

Regrettably, saying, "Nope, don't have a minute," wasn't an option.

"Sure, come on in, Hank." He offered coffee, which Hank declined.

It didn't take him long to get down to business.

"We were having a damn fine basketball season."

"We were," Ben agreed.

"I know you're in a tough position, Carson being your stepson and all."

Ben attempted to look puzzled. "I haven't yet made any decisions about suspensions." He paused. "Or expulsions."

"If that boy of yours were to admit it was just

a fight that got out of hand, three of this school's finest athletes could avoid the legal ramifications they're presently facing."

Pissed as he was, Ben strove to sound calm. "You mean, they'd get off scot-free despite having ganged up on a younger boy and beating the shit out of him."

Hank scowled at him. "That's the father in you speaking. I understand that, but I'm asking you to remember you're principal of this high school, too."

Ben let his eyebrows rise, as if in surprise. "As principal of this school, I'm telling you that I consider the most important part of my job to be encouraging the young people of this community to make sound moral decisions, so they can grow into the kind of adults we want as contributing members of society. As neighbors and friends."

"The pride our students and community had in a winning season and a chance at a championship doesn't mean anything to you?"

"The team still has that chance. *Without* the two starters who will be appearing in court to defend themselves against charges of assault and battery." Implacable, Ben held his eyes. "*And* without the starting forward who suffered multiple broken bones in that assault, including damn near every bone in his hand. Which happened when they *stomped* on that hand, to make sure he couldn't shoot a basket."

"My boys got hurt in fights, too—"

Ben shook his head. "This wasn't a fight, Hank. Not by any standard. This was three boys attacking another in retaliation for him having had the guts to speak up about something they should all have admitted to in the first place."

"We don't know that," Hank began.

"We do. None of the three boys had so much as a bruise, in contrast to Carson's serious injuries. I've heard and believe Carson's side of the story, and I understand that Dex Slagle has also admitted that Dylan followed Carson to Olivia Bowen's apartment and stood close enough to the kitchen window to hear what Carson was telling her. The three boys then plotted to 'punish' him. Dex's word."

"Ever occur to you that the Slagle boy may be making something up in hopes of earning some leniency?"

"No." The enamel on Ben's molars was suffering some damage, he was afraid. "That conversation did, in fact, take place in Olivia's apartment. If one of the boys wasn't there, how did Dex know about it?"

The son of a bitch made one more try. "Could be Carson taunted them with it—"

"Feel free to talk to the police chief about his perspective, Hank," Ben said, abruptly disgusted. "I'm also going to tell you here and now that I will support whatever decision my son makes where it comes to holding the other boys accountable for their crime. However, I'd be disappointed in him if he let them walk for the sake of a winning basketball season. In fact, I believe that, as parents *and* educators, one of the most important things we can do is hold our children accountable for their behavior." Hank opened his mouth, but Ben kept talking.

"My only decision as principal will be the question of how to respond to behavior that didn't take place on school grounds or during school hours. Once I've made that decision, I will be very willing to discuss it with the school board in an open session. Feel free to talk to other members and let me know if you want to have that discussion."

The two men stared at each other.

Hank pushed himself to his feet, looking down at Ben. "I think you've blown this incident out of proportion. I can promise you that I will be talking to my fellow board members." He nodded and left.

Ben's anger burned hot in his belly, but he was aware of accompanying shame. He was a fine one to talk about accountability. If he'd put pressure on Carson sooner, or, if he didn't have the guts himself, suggested to Phil Weigand that he lean on Carson a little, all of this might have been prevented. If he'd been frank with Olivia from the beginning, she could have said to Carson, *I think your dad has already guessed at some of this. You might as well talk to him right now. Tonight.* And, yes, if he hadn't been trying to shield his kid, who was dodging accountability himself, he wouldn't have lost Olivia.

Ben groaned and ground the heels of his hands against his closed eyes. If he had to take one more phone call from some parent pissed because the Crescent Creek High School basketball team might not sweep to the long-elusive league championship, he was going to— *What?* he scoffed at himself. Issue another self-righteous lecture, like the one he'd just given? Keep pretending he'd always taken the high road?

Or was it time he started a genuine dialogue? One he opened by saying, "I, too, was guilty of wanting to protect my son even when I knew he was making the wrong choice. When the right thing for me as a parent to do was encourage him to speak up, to admit to his own wrongdoing."

Ben sat without moving, staring at the closed door in front of him without seeing it. The idea had merit—but how could he get everyone else talking, too? The one-on-one conversations weren't working. Nobody wanted to let down automatic defenses.

Yeah, including him.

A town meeting. The idea came, settled in and shaped itself in a matter of a minute or two.

He'd have to get permission from the school board to use the high school auditorium, but he didn't think that would be a problem. Hank and maybe Sam Pruitt excepted. Curiosity alone should ensure wide attendance. He'd encourage parents, kids and even community members who didn't have a kid in the school system all to come.

Maybe it wouldn't work. Maybe his speech would be followed by deafening silence, but he didn't think so. He'd taken this job because he'd believed the people in his hometown were essentially good. This was where he wanted to raise his son. That belief had been challenged some these past few days, but, then, he wasn't proud of himself right now, either.

He turned the idea over in his head a little longer, then reached for the phone. His first call was to Sally Whittaker, school board president.

WHEN A TEENAGE girl came into the store on Wednesday, asking permission to hang flyers for an upcoming event at the front and back entrances to Bowen's, Olivia asked to see it first, as she always did.

Across the top of the bright yellow piece of paper, in huge letters, the banner headline announced:

COMMUNITY MEETING
THURSDAY, JANUARY 8, 7:00 PM
High School Auditorium

It went on to say that there were unresolved questions about the mysterious death of the girl who had been buried as Jane Doe and the possible roles of people in the community. Those questions had allegedly led to an assault on a high school boy and the arrest of other boys.

Let's be honest with each other. Come prepared to listen and to speak openly.

Olivia's lips tightened, but after a moment she nodded and handed it back. "By all means. Do you have tape with you?"

The girl held up a roll.

Olivia forced a smile. "Go for it."

Ben. She recognized his stamp. What was going to be his opening argument? That if Olivia Bowen hadn't kept a secret from one of the boys' own fathers, near tragedy could have been averted? She could hear it now. On open display, the charisma that had persuaded every businessman and woman in this town to contribute to the burial costs and headstone of that poor girl. The warmth and sincerity she had foolishly let herself believe in. Would he massage egos until, once again, everyone was able to go home glowing with a sense of pride in nothing?

As the girl carefully aligned the flyer in the front window, Olivia shook her head and walked away. Tomorrow evening would be the perfect time for a little grocery shopping… Except, if she was going to pack up this weekend and leave Sunday or Monday, she should probably subsist on what she had instead of buying more.

With all her heart, she wished she wasn't still going to be around Friday, to hear the ensuing chatter.

FLOPPED ON THE sofa, Carson gaped first at the flyer, then at Ben waiting to hear his reaction. "You're freakin' kidding me."

His dad's mouth tilted up in a small half smile. "Embarrassed to see your old man stand up in front of the entire town and admit to his own idiocy?"

"If you're talking about Olivia, you deserve it. But—wow—if I was a target before, what do you think will happen *after*?"

Carson was suddenly struck by how worn Ben looked. Until he blew it so badly with Olivia, Carson hadn't seen this particular expression on his face in a long time. Years. Not since he'd been trying to deal with Carson's mom, to keep what he'd seen as promises to her while coming to terms with the fact that she was beyond help. What he looked was *old,* Carson thought, even as he knew that wasn't quite right.

"Do you think this is going to help with her?" he asked. "I mean, do you think she'll come to this meeting?"

Ben sank down on the recliner and squeezed the back of his neck with one hand. "No. I don't think she'll come. I don't expect it to help."

Carson frowned. "Then…what's the point?"

"The point is asking people to think about the stands they're taking. I spent the entire damn day on the phone explaining that, no, I don't think a winning basketball season should be our first consideration. No, I don't think it's okay to let three bullies get away with a brutal attack so we can win the championship. No, I'm not saying that because the victim happens to be my kid." Ben sat forward, his elbows on his knees, his expression intense. "This is a good moment to ask people to think about *why* those boys felt so entitled. And why were you the only one out of forty-plus teenagers who apparently has a conscience?"

"Some of the kids knew that Miller Falls girl," Carson objected. "They probably thought, Weird, she looks kind of like whatever her name is." He wished Chief Weigand had been willing to give her name. It still bothered him that he didn't know something so basic about her.

"Okay, but did any of the Crescent Creek kids know that girl? So what did they think when they saw the drawing?"

Carson shrugged. They both knew what local kids had thought: *Oh, my God, we're in deep shit.* It was like they'd all seen a hit-and-run. Maybe they weren't in the car, but they were witnesses who shouldn't have been where they were. Only— it turned out they hadn't seen what they had feared they had.

Not Jane Doe. The relief felt fresh every time he was reminded.

He did understand what Ben was saying, though. Probably twenty-five kids from his high school were at that kegger. Some of them might not have noticed that girl at all, but a lot of them probably had. And their instinctive response had been to keep quiet. As if her life and death didn't weigh against the possibility of getting put on restriction for sneaking out to a party. Because, truth was, that's the worst most of them would have faced.

Ben's frown deepened. "Their silence makes more sense now that I'm hearing what their parents have to say. Nobody is calling to tell me, 'I'm ashamed my son didn't speak out immediately.' Even worse, the people calling, parents of current students or not, want me to overlook what those three creeps did to you. Not because it was right, or even excusable, but because they're athletes who bring glory to this town."

Carson fixed his gaze on the cast enclosing his wrist and hand. "I'm sorry."

"Sorry?"

"That you have to be ashamed of me," he mumbled. Somehow, in the days since he'd been battered, he and Ben hadn't gotten around to having this talk. Now, here it was.

Out of the corner of his eye, he saw Ben shaking his head.

"I'm disappointed that you hesitated. Wondering

what I did wrong that you didn't trust me enough to come to me in the first place. That—" his voice thickened "—you needed to go to someone else instead of me."

"It wasn't like that!" Carson burst out.

"What was it like?" Ben asked quietly.

How could it not be obvious?

Carson kept staring at his broken hand, noticing in one part of his mind that the ends of his fingers were a creepy blue-purple where they emerged from the cast.

"It's—" He moved his shoulders uneasily, then wished he hadn't because it hurt. "I like Olivia. She's cool. You know? So I thought she could tell me what to do, and you'd never have to know."

Ben didn't say anything. Carson sneaked a look and saw that he still didn't get it.

Oh, man. "Because you're, like, my—" It sounded dorky, repeating what Ben had said, but he had to. "My role model. And I knew you'd never have done something so shitty."

Ben was staring at him really strangely now. "What was it you did that was so bad?"

"That girl! You know." He almost said the word he knew Ben didn't like. "Having sex like that. Just some total stranger, and I didn't care about her at all. And then not saying anything when I thought she was dead."

"Why didn't you say anything at the beginning?" Ben asked him unexpectedly.

He had to think about it for a second. "We were at school, and even before I heard about her, word was being passed around that something bad had happened and we should all keep our mouths shut. And…it wasn't like a threat, not then, but I was thinking it was a big deal that Zurenko and the others wanted me to be part of their crowd." He shook his head, feeling so stupid. How could he not have already known what dicks they were?

Ben laughed. When Carson stared at him, it was to see how much of the strain had eased from his face.

"You're a kid. I've said this before, and I'll say it again. You get a few freebies. You were flattered, and you briefly squelched what your conscience was trying to tell you. Who your age wouldn't have? As for the sex?" He was still smiling. "Most guys' first experience isn't that different from yours. Some fumbling around, embarrassment afterward, plus a dose of exhilaration because, man, now you know what it's all about. The girl was willing, Carson. You didn't do anything wrong. In fact—" with a sigh he rose to his feet "—you did something very right. You had *safe* sex. And you know what? I'm starved. I can do hamburgers fast. How does that sound?"

The dreaded talk was over, just like that. "I'm always hungry," Carson said automatically.

"Good."

"Do I have to go tomorrow night?" he said to his father's back.

Ben paused briefly but didn't turn around. "Nope. That's entirely up to you."

Carson groaned once Ben was out of sight. He so didn't want to go, but now, of course, he had to. Just to prove something to the man who'd chosen to be his father when he didn't have to. When most men wouldn't have. *Yeah,* Carson thought, his eyebrows drawing together, *but maybe I have to prove something to myself, too, not just to Ben.*

He had flicker of understanding: there'd be lots of times in the future when he really didn't want to do something but would make himself do it anyway, because it was the right thing to do. Because…

That's who I want to be, he concluded, with a little twist of sensation in his chest that was hurtful but good, too.

With the forethought and care that was becoming practiced, he maneuvered until he was upright and off the sofa so he could follow his dad into the kitchen.

"What's this about, Olivia?" Lloyd lowered himself to a straight chair on the other side of her desk. At her request, he'd closed her office door to shut them in alone, something she rarely asked for.

She'd put this off as long as she could.

"Saturday is my last day," she said baldly. "I've advised my mother to put the business up for sale, although she'll have to tell you herself what she intends to do."

"What?" He stared at her in shock.

"I was only filling in for Dad. You knew that."

"At first, sure, but—" He shook his head, seeming dazed. "It's a family business. I'd have sworn it's in your blood."

It was. It had taken coming home for her to realize that. But now...

"Damn it!" he exclaimed. "You know business had been declining. Charles didn't have his heart in it anymore." He flushed, hearing his own words. Her father's heart had literally been failing him, even though none of them, including him, had known it.

"I understand what you're saying," she said.

"You've turned the business around. Brought life and enthusiasm to it. How can you leave?"

Olivia looked down at the scarred surface of the old desk. "I don't own Bowen's, Lloyd. You know that. My mother does. She's never been very interested in it. From her point of view, selling out makes sense."

"And that's what she wants to do?" He half rose from his chair. "What if she can't find a buyer?" His stare had become angry. "What then? Has she thought of that?"

I'm dumping all the blame on Mom. Not fair.

"This is...my decision," she said in a voice that didn't sound like hers. "My mother and I don't have the kind of relationship that would allow this to work. Not anymore." Maybe not ever. She didn't have to say that. Because this was Lloyd, she didn't stop there, although she would have with any other employee. She met his gaze, even knowing he'd see how much she hurt. "You're aware of everything else going on. Ben—" She had to take a couple of slow, deep breaths. "All the talk. It's made me realize I'm an outsider now."

When he started to argue, she held up a hand. "Not everybody feels that way, but too many people do. If it was just that, I'd hang on. But it's not. In the end, the people that matter most don't want me here."

"I do," he said quietly, and she broke. He circled the desk fast and held her while she cried. But he couldn't change her mind.

OLIVIA WOULD HAVE sworn she'd meant it when she told Ben she wanted him to leave her alone. *And* when she'd told Mom she was done.

Still, it crept up on her—the knowledge that she had been lashing out rather than strictly telling the truth.

She had wanted Ben to keep begging. And maybe Mom to beg, too, to say, *Please don't leave. I do need you. I like the idea of us as a team.*

Ah, fantasies.

By the time she let herself out the back door of the store in the early evening on Thursday and began the trudge down the dark alley, she felt lonelier than she had in her entire life. Her own mother didn't care enough to fight for them to hold on to any kind of relationship. And Ben— This knowledge hurt even more. He probably thought he was respecting her wishes by staying away. But respect was cold comfort.

She wondered if he'd believed her when she told him how soon she was leaving. Only two more days at the store. Two more days of smilingly helping customers who had no idea that the town's one and only hardware store and lumberyard would soon be changing hands, or even going out of business.

She pictured the block, a significant stretch of downtown, if Bowen's and Swenson's both failed to find buyers and had to close. Would some other kind of business rent at least part of the space? Or would it stay vacant as more locals did their shopping elsewhere and the downtown core became less economically viable? To her, having Bowen's close was like carving the heart out of her hometown, leaving it walking and talking but really already dead.

Most people probably wouldn't even care, she thought, her depression a weight that had her using the handrail to get her up the back stairs to her apartment.

Would she and Mom patch something up later? she wondered. Pretend none of this had ever happened?

Probably.

But Olivia knew she'd never feel the same about her mother again. *Or* her father. Which meant… not her childhood, either.

I'll get over this, she tried to tell herself. *Come out the other side.*

Ben had only really been back in her life for a matter of weeks. Pain that felt raw now would become dull and eventually no more than an almost-forgotten ache. She should have known better than to put her trust in him again.

Shouldn't have rushed home at all.

Good to know, way too late.

She turned up the heat, hung up her parka and tossed her scarf over the back of a chair, then opened her cupboard to study the contents without a lot of hope. Maybe she *should* have gone grocery shopping after all. She could still go out for a burger and fries. She wouldn't have to show her face in a restaurant to do that.

But it seemed like too much effort.

Her gaze strayed to the clock on the microwave: 6:32. Ben would likely already be at the high school, setting up. Had Carson gone with him? She knew he'd been released from the hospital, but she wasn't sure how mobile he was. Or how he'd feel about his stepfather's grand plan.

Not her business.

She'd posted her résumé on a couple of internet sites. She might be lucky enough to have had some response already. She hadn't specified a geographic limitation. There was nothing keeping her in the Pacific Northwest. It might feel more like an adventure, a new beginning, to take a job in San Francisco or Chicago or, who knew, Raleigh, North Carolina. At least Raleigh would be warm.

Olivia settled on a can of soup and a grilled cheese sandwich. She'd have liked a salad but had used up the lettuce last night. She sat at her small table, trying to block out the memory of Carson and Ben here in the apartment. The rumble of deep voices and laughter seemed to hang in the air, almost heard.

She couldn't keep herself from checking the time. Imagining the parking lot at the high school filling up. People talking as they went in, speculating about what the meeting was all about, some grumbling that this was a big waste of time. Ben up front— No. He'd be at the door, greeting people, thanking them for coming.

Then 6:59 became 7:00.

I do not care what he says, she thought fiercely, and she knew she lied about that, too.

PHIL HAD DECIDED to make himself visible but not really part of this gathering. Propping himself against the wall beside one of the exits, he'd be on the lookout for anyone overcome with the intensity of reawakened conscience. Phil almost smiled, picturing the crowd as a congregation swept with the fervor of a religious conversion, rising as one to their feet

to cry aloud, "Amen, brother! Amen." Taking turns
to go to the front and confess their sins.

Watching people arrive, either silent and suspicious or whispering to one another, he shook his
head. Ben Hovik would be playing to a tough crowd
tonight. Phil hoped Ben knew what he was doing
and wouldn't be too crushed if his praiseworthy
effort did a belly flop.

One of the last to arrive was Marian Bowen, who
slipped in as if she hoped no one would see her. Phil
was surprised she'd come at all. A pretty, reserved
woman, she wasn't the kind to go for a public out-
pouring of emotion. She had remained stoic even
at her husband's funeral. Although, come to think
of it, that may have been because of the revelation
about him having had another daughter. Perhaps
she hadn't been grieving at all, or her grief was too
mixed with anger to allow for tears.

She found a spot on the end of a row not so far
from Phil, as if she were allowing for an easy escape.

Almost as soon as she took her seat, Ben climbed
the three steps to the stage and behind the podium.
He'd previously tested the microphone, so he could
start speaking now without any awkward booms
or squawks.

"Thank you for coming," he said gravely, looking around, his gaze seeming to pause on each face.
"I don't want to be the only person up here talking

tonight, but I will start by telling you why I called this gathering.

"It all started almost three months ago, when the weather turned to winter in late October. Snow fell, half-melted, froze again one night. You all know the night I'm talking about. That bitterly cold, frosty night, followed by a puzzle come morning, when Marsha Connelly's dog didn't come right back in when she called, but instead raced into the woods and made her go after him. He'd had a restless night—he knew something she didn't."

Ben had found a cadence that drew in his listeners. Maybe seeing him as a preacher wasn't so far off. He was a real storyteller, Phil realized, finding himself as mesmerized as everyone else seemed to be.

"You know, too," Ben continued, "what that dog and then Marsha found—a teenage girl, inadequately dressed for the night, who had curled up out in the woods by the creek and frozen to death." He paused and searched faces. "At first I thought that tragedy, happening among us, also changed us. Now I believe the girl's death and the many fears surrounding it only laid us bare. Exposed too many of our less worthy impulses."

He held up a hand as if a hum of protest had risen, when in fact the auditorium was utterly silent.

"I was disturbed by the idea of her continuing to lie in a steel drawer. I suggested we make her ours and truly lay her to rest. You agreed. We all felt good about what we'd done." His mouth tightened. "I'm ashamed at how self-righteous I felt," he said in a different voice, one that had hardened. "Because the truth is, all that time, even as I told myself I was doing good, I harbored a worry. I might even call it a suspicion.

"There were whispers of a kegger in the woods that night." He gripped the podium. Phil suspected, if he were closer, he'd see that Ben's knuckles were white. He might hear the wood creak.

"What I feared, what kept me silent, was that my son was out that night, and he seemed…different afterward. I didn't consciously make a decision not to press too hard for answers I didn't want, but I think now I was guilty of not wanting to know a truth that might cast a harsh light on someone I love."

He went on, then, to talk about what truth they now knew and how it had been uncovered, layer by layer. Some by Police Chief Weigand's stubborn efforts, of course. He talked about all the kids who were at the party that night who had maintained their silence. About the threats required to keep them all quiet. About the one woman and one boy who acted on their consciences, and the vicious assault that followed.

"I was taught right from wrong," he said. "What happened was wrong. Perhaps the saddest part is that it turns out the effort to keep a large group of teenagers quiet was unnecessary. So far as we can determine, the girl who died never was at that kegger. Chief Weigand has identified a girl who looks rather like her and was present.

"In retrospect, I'm ashamed of my own denial and silence. I'm shocked by the phone calls I've received this week. Seems everyone wants us all to pretend none of this happened. They want a basketball championship at all cost. They want their sons, or they want boys they don't even know but think they do because they've watched them on the basketball court, not to be tainted by vicious behavior undertaken by these three boys for no purpose but to protect themselves.

"They want us not to say to our children, 'This was wrong. Here is what would have been right.'" His expression changed. "So tonight, far too late, I'm telling you *I* was wrong.

"So far as I'm concerned, the only person who behaved from beginning to end with integrity was Olivia Bowen, though as a consequence she and her mother both suffered from gossip spread without thought or compassion. I became angry at her for all the wrong reasons. Did you know how she's been attacked for naming those boys, speaking for my son, who could not speak for himself after the beating? Our response to her truth telling has forced her to make the decision to leave town. In losing Olivia, we may lose a business that's important to this town, too.

"What I see is that loss has been piling atop loss ever since that frosty night in October, when a girl who we claimed, who still has only us, died." He nodded sharply. "I've said more than I intended. I ask others to tell us what they think. How do you see right from wrong?" He smiled faintly. "If you're one of those callers, come on up and give me hell."

Nervous laughter spread through the auditorium. For a long time, no one moved except Ben, who walked away from the podium but stopped at one end of the stage, perhaps aware he needed to maintain some control of speakers.

Finally a single man stood up and walked forward. Phil's eyebrows rose when he recognized Kirk Slagle, a balding former athlete with some middle-aged spread. Phil tensed, wondering if the shit was going to hit the fan already. Face flushed, Kirk touched the microphone nervously and jumped when it screeched. Then he bent forward.

"I'm no public speaker, but there's something I have to say." He cleared his throat. "My oldest boy was one of the three who beat up Carson Caldwell. I love my son, but for the first time in his life, I'm ashamed of something he did. And I do believe he did it. I want to think he was led by a stronger personality, but I don't know that. What I know is that he needs to be punished, and he needs to accept responsibility for having done wrong if he's going to be the man I think he can be."

His Adam's apple rose and fell. "If he somehow

skates out of legal trouble, I'm here to tell you he still won't be rejoining the basketball team. Because of him, Carson can't play. That means Dex doesn't deserve to, either." He nodded and blundered away from the podium.

Well, now, that *was unexpected,* Phil thought, relaxing his stance.

Murmurs rose. Someone else took a turn. Others stood and waited for their chance. Phil was listening to a woman stridently insisting that everyone was overreacting to typical conflict between some young men when Phil noticed Stuart Dodd walking purposefully to him.

"I have to tell you something," he said in a low voice that shook. "It's…I think I might have had something to do with that girl dying."

Phil nodded and said, "Let's go out in the hall."

CHAPTER SEVENTEEN

OLIVIA WAS CURLED up on the sofa and pretending to concentrate on a book when a knock came on her door. She went utterly still, frantically thinking about people who wanted retribution from her. At nine-thirty or so, the meeting was probably over. Emotions might have gotten heated.

Pulse racing, she tiptoed into the kitchen, where she could just see the small landing outside her door. Would Ben have come—?

She recognized her mother despite the heavy parka and muffler. After a moment, unsure how she felt about this visit, Olivia went to the door.

"Mom."

Under the light from the bare bulb, her mother's face was white and pinched except for her nose, red from the cold. "I know it's late, but…I was hoping we could talk."

"I wasn't getting ready for bed yet. Come on in." She was afraid she sounded grudging.

She took her mother's parka and muffler and put on water to boil for tea. She felt her mother standing behind her, watching as she got down two mugs, found the tea bags, added a teaspoon of sugar for each. Finally she turned. "Do you know about the meeting tonight?"

"I went," Marian said. "I wish you had."

Olivia didn't say anything.

"There was…a lot of repentance."

Olivia believed in that about as much as she did stepping out her door in the morning to find herself looking at a white-sand beach in Kauai.

"Would you like to sit at the table?" she asked politely. "Or in the living room? The sofa isn't too bad."

"Here is fine." Her mother surveyed the tiny confines of the kitchen, including the cramped dining space. "Since there's just the two of us."

Olivia poured the hot water and set the mugs on the table before sitting down herself. Ignoring the cup in front of her, Marian studied her daughter's face.

"I hope it's not too late to say how sorry I am."

Olivia met that gaze unflinchingly. "For?"

"Shutting you out. Not telling you why I was so angry. Not supporting your decision to find out if that girl could be your sister."

"You had your reasons."

"Poor ones," she said bitterly. "Selfish ones."

They stared at each other.

"Ben Hovik said things tonight about the difference between right and wrong. He said the only person who had behaved with absolute integrity from beginning to end was you. He talked about how much he regretted trying to shield his boy from possible consequences of having done something wrong. He mentioned getting angry at you."

Her mom fell silent for a moment, then shook her head. "The look on his face. He said, because of your honesty, we're losing you." Her shoulders convulsed, and she pressed her fingers to her mouth.

Shocked, Olivia waited until her mother had gathered herself again.

"I knew I'd already lost you, and it was all my own fault. For shutting myself in with my rage and hurt, instead of turning to you and even accepting that you had reason to feel angry, too. And—" she took a deep breath, continuing with painful honesty "—a right to love your father, too. As I do."

Olivia couldn't have even said where they were. All she saw was her mother, lowering her pride to bare emotions she usually kept tightly contained. "First, let me say this," Marian said. "Of course you had to submit your DNA. Of course you did. You were right. And, yes, of course I had wondered. By then, every mention of a teenage girl had me bristling. The way your father reacted to hearing about the death—" Tears she seemed not to be aware she was shedding rolled down her cheeks. "Even more, his insistence on going to that damn funeral—"

Olivia jumped up and grabbed a paper towel, holding it out to her mother, who stared at it for a moment with seeming incomprehension. Then she snatched it and wiped her cheeks.

"Oh lord, I'll look like a raccoon."

Olivia smiled, although she felt her mouth wobble, too. "There's only me to see you. And I've seen worse."

Her mother actually laughed. "I'm sure you have. Oh, dear." She blew her nose firmly and wadded the paper towel up in her fine-boned hand.

"I let myself get consumed by hurt." Her voice was thick now. "Sometimes I felt as if it was eating me alive, from the inside out. I *believed* in your father. I thought, he would never—" She faltered and stopped.

"It makes me feel as if I never knew him," Olivia said.

"Yes, but that's something else I need to say. It's taken me a long time. Too long! But I've remembered things I blocked out. It—what happened— wasn't one-sided."

"Him cheating on you?" Olivia said incredulously.

"I'm not excusing that. Don't get me wrong. But...we were having problems, and those were my fault." Her mother's expression had changed, turned inward. Softened, in a way, even as it became troubled. "We wanted more children, you know. I think I did especially. I'm not quite sure, because he didn't say. I suspect he thought dwelling on our failing hurt me."

This laugh was painful to hear. "*My* failing. We tried to keep you from being aware, but we went for testing and counseling. It was me. My uterus couldn't seem to catch hold of eggs. They may have been getting fertilized, but my body just flushed them out."

For a moment her gaze caught Olivia's, shame, hurt, a hundred other emotions laid bare. Then she looked down at the mug of now dark tea. "He was able to father children. Which I guess you figured out. I found myself so furious at myself, my body, and at him. We'd had one miracle—you—and I couldn't understand why there wouldn't be another one. Sex, for me, became desperate, all about procreation and not about love. Your father tried to give me what I needed."

Olivia hardly knew what she felt and had no idea what to say. How could she, even as a child, have remained oblivious to all this?

"It was years before I accepted that it wasn't going to happen. I started refusing to have sex. 'Why bother?' I said. 'You can't give me what I want.' I don't know what I could have said that would be crueler. I didn't let myself see how rejected he must have felt, as if making love never had been about us, about being close, rather than about trying to get pregnant."

"Oh, Mom, I'm so sorry…"

"I think—" red streaked her cheeks when she met Olivia's eyes "—we hadn't had sex for six or eight months at least when he went to that convention in Las Vegas. He…wanted me to go with him. 'We could add a few days, have a vacation,' he said. I had become remote. I refused."

"I suppose you were worried about me," Olivia put in.

Her mother's mouth shaped a smile of sorts. "Speaking of sex…"

"Which I hadn't had yet."

"No, but I knew you were on the cusp, so to speak. I don't remember if I explained that to your father or not. All I know is that he shrugged, packed and went." Now she was seeing a time long ago, a mistake that couldn't be changed.

"Was he different, when he came home?" Olivia couldn't help asking, although she kept her voice soft.

"Yes. I knew something was wrong. I thought it had to do with the business, but he wouldn't talk about it. He was…so sweet, though, so loving." Her mouth twisted. "I'd missed him while he was gone. We…slowly repaired what was wrong. I became resigned, I suppose."

Maybe this wasn't the right time to ask—but when would that time come? "Did you want another baby so desperately because I was more like Dad than you?"

A startled flush spread across her mother's cheeks. She exclaimed "Don't be ridiculous!" but Olivia wasn't convinced.

"Since I came home," she said slowly, "I've been doing a lot of thinking. Realizing how much Dad and I did together, excluding you. I was young and thoughtless, but now I wonder that he didn't realize you might be hurt."

"He was a man." The barb could have drawn blood. "Of course he didn't." Then she made a moue that didn't hide her distress. "There were times, I can't deny it. But most kids take after one parent or another, don't you think?"

"I suppose," Olivia said hesitantly.

"Well, you always trailed behind Daddy. Even when most little girls went through the princess phase, you didn't. You wanted miniature tools. You were good at math. Athletic." She smiled with difficulty, but she did smile. "In one way, I was glad. However I've been acting, I did love your father. You were good for him. After you came home this year, he…revived. We all knew he wouldn't recover, I think, but being able to talk about business and watch NBA games and the NCAA playoffs on TV with you… You made a difference to him."

Olivia couldn't have spoken to save her life. *Oh, Daddy.* Her eyes stung.

"That's why, at first, I didn't tell you," her mother said with obvious difficulty. "I couldn't forgive him, but at least he had you."

"Oh, Mom."

Her mother was crying unashamedly now, as was Olivia. She finally pushed away from the table and took the few steps to lean down and put her arms around her mother. Awkward as it was, they stayed that way, crying against each other for a long time. Olivia was stiff when she did straighten.

They took turns in the bathroom. Olivia washed her face, for what good that did, and brushed her face and braided her hair, something she always did before going to bed.

A thought sneaked into her head, not for the first time. Ben wouldn't approve. He liked her hair loose, to be able to sink his fingers into it. But then, what did it matter what he liked? She might never see him again.

Olivia poured out their untouched tea while her mother was in the bathroom. When Marian reappeared, they sat in the living room, Olivia in a rocking chair she'd brought from home, Mom at one end of the sofa. They looked at each other.

"I believe with all my heart that your father loved me and regretted terribly cheating on me," Marian said suddenly. She'd regained her dignity during the interlude. Her back didn't touch the sofa, and her hands were folded on her lap. "I will have to live with having let him die believing I couldn't forgive him and no longer loved him. But I hope you can forgive me for shutting you out. For letting anger take over my life."

Tears threatened again, but Olivia fought them. "Of course I can, Mom." Her voice came out hoarse. "I love you. I'm sorry I didn't try harder to be the daughter you wanted."

Her mother looked at her in surprise. "But you are the daughter I want! Why would you think any different? I've never been anything but proud of you. Although—I've never been prouder of you than I am right now."

Another sting of tears. "Don't get me started again."

"I need you to know that desperate hunger I felt to have another baby was certainly not because of any dissatisfaction with you."

"Did you ever talk about adopting?"

"Of course we did, but…I don't think your father wanted to. Unlike me, he was…content. For me— Oh, it was some kind of primal need! I don't know if it would have been satisfied by adoption. At any rate, we talked but never did anything about it."

Olivia nodded.

"I want you to stay," her mother said. The eyes that met Olivia's were dark with emotion. "If running the store isn't what you want to do with your life, of course I understand that. But I've had the impression you've been happy since you took over for Charles. I would love it if we could keep Bowen's and even expand it. In fact—" she took a breath "—if that's what you choose to do, I'd like to make you an equal partner now. If, instead, we end up selling, I'll give you half of any proceeds, too."

She only shook her head when Olivia protested, insisting that she had investments to live on, as well.

After a long minute, Olivia said, "I don't know what to say, Mom. I'll…have to think about it. Things with Ben blew up. I don't know how I could stay in town, knowing I might run into him any-time. And community reaction in general…"

"I think you'll find attitudes have changed, after tonight. A lot of people expressed regret." Her mother's expression changed. "I overheard some-thing on my way out. Stu Dodd was telling Phil that he hit something with his pickup that night. You know he and his wife bought the Rolstad place out past Marsha Connelly's."

"I did know. Oh, no. That's why he quit driving his pickup," she realized. "He loved that truck, but he kept making excuses."

"Maybe it had a dent and he was afraid to get it fixed in case the police were looking for something like that. I only caught a bit—they both went quiet when they saw me, and I hurried by. But I heard him say, 'I got out to look, but I couldn't find any-thing, so I convinced myself it was a deer, and it took only a glancing blow but would be fine.'"

A memory came to Olivia. "He asked me about the kegger. I thought he seemed…I don't know, eager, maybe. He wanted to think those boys were responsible."

"So he could believe he wasn't," her mother said,

sounding sad. "I even understand. Ben was right. You've been the only one with any courage."

"Ben didn't do anything so bad," Olivia felt compelled to say. "I was hurt that he didn't confide in me, but I do understand why he didn't. I mean, Carson is family." She had to force the last bit out. "I'm not."

"Then what happened?" her mother asked.

Olivia surprised herself by telling her. All her hurt poured out. Ridiculously enough, she cried again, and had to retreat to the bathroom for mop-up number two.

Finally she insisted on walking her mother down to her car to be sure she didn't get assaulted in the dark alley by someone out for Olivia's blood. They hugged and both said, "I love you," at the same time.

Just before Mom shut her car door, she peered up at Olivia. "Don't hold on to anger too long, the way I did."

And then she started her car and waited until Olivia had almost reached the top of the staircase before driving away.

"THANKS FOR COMING," Ben repeated by rote as people filtered out. Two school board members were among them, both nodding, and Bill Casey saying, "This was a fine idea, Ben. You should feel good about what you accomplished."

He felt stung by the compliment rather than flattered, but he managed a polite smile. "Thank you. And I appreciate you coming tonight."

The last chattering group departed at ten-thirty. Intensely grateful, he followed to lock the front doors, then went back to turn out lights and collect his son.

Carson was sitting on the edge of the stage, feet dangling, his arm in a sling. His bruises had faded but tonight still served as exhibit A.

"I should have told you to stay home," Ben said abruptly.

"What?" Carson shook his head. "I would have come anyway."

"How? You can't ride your bike."

"I could have gotten Mrs. Bukin to pick me up."

Ben walked forward down the aisle, finally taking a seat in the front row, facing Carson. "Did this do any good?"

Carson stared at him like he was an idiot. "What are you talking about? It was insane! I mean, people got up there and said stuff that blew my mind. There were a few idiots who tried to defend being total jerks, but you made most people think." He gave a quirky smile. "And, like you always say, people don't do that often enough."

Ben summoned a smile in response, but his mood didn't lift. "You're right. On the surface, it went well. I just can't help wondering whether everyone won't go home and start wishing they hadn't gotten up and said what they did."

"Even if some of them do, they won't all, Dad." Carson sounded unexpectedly wise.

Ben grunted. "Bill Casey told me I should feel good about what I'd accomplished. Makes me wonder if he was listening to me at all. I'm done with complacency."

"Is it wrong to feel good when you did something right?"

Ben frowned at his son. "Quit trying to buck me up."

"O-kay." Carson went for an Eeyore voice. Gloom and doom. "You're right. Whoever deserves to be happy?"

Ben laughed, swore and yanked at his hair. "Come on—let's get out of here. Wish I didn't have to be back here in—God." He glanced at his watch. "Eight and a half hours, give or take a few minutes."

"You know what? I think I'll go back to class tomorrow." Carson hopped down, but with more care than he would have employed before being injured. "A bunch of kids were here, you know."

"You get a sense of what they thought?" Ben stepped into the control room to flick off the lights.

"They seemed to think what you said was cool."

"Cool. That's me."

Carson bumped his good shoulder against his dad's. "Yeah, don't get any delusions."

Ben felt better for this laugh.

Carson helped turn off lights as they went. Theirs was the only vehicle left in the parking lot, some distance away.

"Mrs. Bowen was here," Carson said.

Ben turned his head sharply. "I didn't see her."

"She was, like, the first one who left at the end, but I saw her."

Pulling his keys from his pocket and unlocking, Ben tried to imagine what Olivia's mother had thought.

"Are you going to try to talk to her again?" Carson asked. "Olivia, I mean."

Ben waited until they were both in before he said, "I don't know. There's a fine line between persistence and harassment. She was…pretty direct when she told me to get lost."

"You're really gone on her, aren't you?"

Ben had inserted the key but not turned it. Now he looked at Carson. "Does it matter, after what I did?"

"If I hadn't been so stupid—"

"I thought we covered this topic."

"Will you try again?"

Ben rubbed his chest, wishing that would assuage the burning but knowing it wouldn't. "Yeah," he said. "I have to try again."

"You'd better do it quick, if she's really leaving Sunday the way I hear."

"I guess so." He started the engine and released the brake. "Can we talk about something else?"

"Um...yeah." Carson grinned at him. "Do you think I could still practice driving? Even one-handed?"

On a laugh, Ben said, "Yes. Carefully. But not tonight, okay?"

"Maybe I could drive to school tomorrow."

"Maybe you shouldn't push it."

His son just grinned, knowing perfectly well who'd be behind the wheel come morning.

STUART DODD SETTLED uneasily in the old wooden office chair facing Olivia's even older desk. "I have something I need to tell you," he said, straight-out.

Olivia braced herself, guessing what this was about. Ironically, she had intended to call him, Russ and several of the other more senior employees in to her office today to tell *them* her decision.

The decision she was now doubting.

"Okay."

He flattened his hands on his thighs. "I think I hit that girl who died with my truck."

There wasn't any point in saying, "I know." "Why are you telling me?" she asked instead.

"I already talked to Chief Weigand last night. But I know you care about finding out who she is and what happened to her. Me, I just kept hoping her dying was someone else's fault."

The shame in his eyes had become familiar to

her lately. So many people not living up to their beliefs in themselves.

"What did Phil say?"

"That she had some bruises." He hunched his shoulders. "Nothing that would have killed her."

Her thoughts jumped back to the first thing he'd said. "You *think* you hit her? How can you not know?"

"I'd had too much to drink." The shame was undiminished. "Wouldn't have driven, except usually there's no one on the road but me between Henry's and home, not at that time of night."

She nodded. Henry's Tavern was on the outskirts of Crescent Creek. Stu wouldn't even have had to pass through town.

"All I saw was movement. Kind of a pale blur. I thought, what the hell is that? It happened so fast. There was a bump, and whatever it was flew off to the right of the road."

"Did you stop?" She had to ask.

He frowned. "Of course I did. But I couldn't find anything. I could tell by touch I had a dent, though. Finally I gave up and went home. Thought it was a deer or maybe a big white dog, but it must be all right."

"And then in the morning you heard about the girl."

He grimaced. "You know what it's like. By the time I got out of the shower, the phone had already been ringing off the hook."

His wife, Olivia recalled, had grown up in Crescent Creek. No surprise she was plugged into the gossip network.

"Did you tell Tina what happened?"

Stu's fingers flexed on his thighs. After a moment, he shook his head. "Should've, but I didn't. I told her my truck needed some work. She didn't think anything about it, 'cept for asking why I was putting it off. I kept telling myself it couldn't have been that girl, until I heard—" His cheeks blazed. "You know. What she was wearing. Real pale colors. Then I knew."

"But now you know you didn't kill her."

He grimaced. "Wish that made me feel better than it does. If I'd called out, kept looking for her, I might have found her. I could have taken her home, given her a bed for the night. Instead—"

He didn't have to finish that sentence.

"Are you hoping this can be kept quiet?" Olivia asked.

He shook his head. "Told Tina last night." There was a long pause. "If it gets around, it gets around. Chief Weigand says I didn't commit a crime." Gray eyes she thought of as steady were red-rimmed. "I understand if you don't want to employ me, though."

She blinked at him. "What are you talking about? I don't know what we'd do without you! Especially if—" It was her turn to break off.

"There any truth to what Mr. Hovik said last night? That you won't be staying?"

"I'm...still up in the air about it," she admitted. "I thought I'd made up my mind, but last night Mom and I had a talk."

"Marian's not going to run this place."

"No, but she might be able to find a buyer."

He was shaking his head. "I don't know. These days, independents like this are a gamble. What if a Home Depot comes into Miller Falls?"

She'd wondered that, too. Right now, she thought Bowen's was strong enough to compete. But for someone looking to invest in a small business, fear of that happening might tip the balance.

"I had the thought that some of the longtime employees might band together—"

He shook his head again. "I'd go for that, but I don't have enough capital. Lloyd is too close to retirement. Russ and his wife are just scraping by, putting their kids through college. I don't see it."

Olivia nodded, conscious of a weight on her shoulders she hadn't wanted to acknowledge. What would happen to all these people if she left and no buyer materialized? Who would hire local teenagers if Bowen's didn't?

Could she get over Ben while living in the same small town?

"I don't know what I'm going to do," she repeated. "Please don't start a panic. Part of me really wants to stay. I've…felt like I've come home. It's just—"

Stu nodded, and she was uncomfortably aware that he probably knew exactly what conflicts were warring within her. There was that gossip network, after all. She doubted she had a single secret to her name. Look what happened when she'd tried to keep one!

"I won't say anything." He gave a faint crooked smile. "Not even to the wife."

"Thank you." Olivia's voice cracked. "I'll let all of you know soon. I promise."

He rapped his knuckles lightly on her desk, said, "Good enough," and left.

Olivia heard him exchanging a few words with Brenda but made no effort to decipher them. She'd resumed last night's brooding.

Was it possible to, oh, smooth things over with Ben? Or even go back to where they'd left off? She knew she'd been unreasonable, expected too much considering what a short time they'd been seeing each other. Some of her anger and hurt, she suspected now, had to do with their history rather than the reality of what had actually happened.

But…what if she stayed and had to watch him date other women? Marry one?

What if he wanted her? Was it in her to trust him that much, given how fragile her trust had been to start with?

Oh, God, she thought. *What am I going to do?*

CHAPTER EIGHTEEN

OLIVIA HAD A busy afternoon, meeting with a couple of reps, dealing with customers and even taking over a cash register for a stretch when they were shorthanded. But everything she did was with half her attention. She tried to block out her internal battle but failed. Each side took turns at winning, the result flip-flopping every five minutes or so. The stress got to her, with her stomach churning as the fight wore on.

Will I or won't I?

In the periods when the *I will* side was in ascendency, she considered practicalities. Would Ben feel an obligation to support the team by going to tonight's away game, even though Carson couldn't play? Would Carson go, potentially leaving Ben home alone?

Once again, she was the last left in the old building after closing. She took her time getting ready to go, part of her still thinking, *Tomorrow might be the last day.*

Deserted but for her, the building held echoes, ghosts. Too many memories. She had no idea how young she'd been when she first came to work with her daddy. She'd simply absorbed his knowledge. By the time she was eight or ten, a serious, skinny beanpole of a kid, she worked cash registers, made keys for customers, mixed paint, answered the phone. She knew the finances, why her father chose to carry this line of tools but not that one. She could have done more, if the primarily male clientele wouldn't have been offended by a child, and a girl, no less, helping them.

Funny, she'd expected more resistance from that still primarily male clientele when she came back to town, and from the very traditional men who now took orders from her, but it had never materialized. Maybe because so many of them remembered the girl who was as much a part of Bowen's Hardware as her father had been.

Her heart squeezed a little as she paused at the back door, breathing in the scents of sawdust, paint, oil, wood pellets and fertilizer, even the people who passed through. So much had soaked into the walls and the uneven floors of this cantankerous barn of a building.

At sixteen, she had imagined going away to college and then, her newly minted business degree in hand, coming home to marry Ben and join her father in running Bowen's. *She* would bring the family business into the modern age. Somehow, she'd just assumed Ben's dreams paralleled hers. He'd talked about becoming a teacher or a college professor. But becoming a college professor would involve him getting a Ph.D., which would delay their future together, so, in her dreams, she decided he'd go for a teaching job here in Crescent Creek.

Locking up at last, she walked the block and a half down the dark alley to where her car was parked behind her apartment. For one moment, she hesitated, but maybe she'd known all along which side would win.

Pride, Olivia hadn't been able to help realizing, was cold comfort.

It would be embarrassing to knock on Ben's door and have him look surprised to see her, maybe uncomfortable. Worse if he had guests. Oh, God—another woman.

No, the rumor mill would have told her if he'd started dating someone else, wouldn't it? Though maybe she should call Stu's wife for last-minute verification, she thought wryly; Tina would know the latest skinny.

Or—I can just do it. Knock, say, I need to apologize for overreacting, although I won't apologize for keeping my word to Carson.

Rigid with anxiety, she decided to go *now*. Get it over with, while she still had the courage.

Fine plan, except she was several blocks away from his house when she realized the SUV that had just passed, going the other direction, was Ben's. Maybe he *was* going to the game. Or to his parents', or...

She rolled to a stop at the curb at the same moment she saw, in the rearview mirror, that the Jeep Cherokee was performing an illegal midblock U-turn. Had he recognized her? she wondered in sudden panic.

The answer was yes. A moment later, the Cherokee braked right behind her bumper, and he got out and walked forward. She felt about the way she would have if she'd been pulled over on the highway by a state trooper. *Roll down my window. Reach in the glove compartment for my registration. Or do they request driver's license first?*

Step one: roll down window. She had stopped about halfway between street lamps, so she couldn't see him all that well when he bent to look at her, only enough to see that he still wore dark slacks and a white shirt, although if he'd started with a tie, he'd ditched it. He should be wearing a coat but wasn't.

"Any chance you were on your way to my house?" he asked.

Olivia nodded. "But it's not that important. I mean, if you're going out…" Of course he was going out!

"I was on my way to knock on your door again."

"Oh."

"Carson went to the game tonight. Why don't you follow me home?"

Her head bobbed again. He retreated to his Jeep. A moment later, she fell in behind him.

He'd been on his way to see *her?* What did that mean?

There was room in his driveway for both vehicles. He was waiting for her when she got out. Olivia thought he was going to say something, but he didn't, only led the way to the front door, unlocked and stepped back for her to go in ahead of him.

She expected to be gestured toward the sofa and given a polite offer of coffee. Instead, two feet inside the door, he said fiercely, "Please tell me you're not here to let me know you're leaving town."

"No," she said in surprise. "Or...not exactly." How could she say, "That will depend on you"? "I came to apologize, that's all."

"Apologize?" Ben sounded stunned. "What would you have to apologize for? I'm the one who should be groveling."

"No." Clutching her bag tightly, she couldn't make herself look at him anymore. "You love Carson. Of course you were scared and upset. He had to come first."

"It wasn't like that."

The small spark of anger she nursed brought her gaze up even as she reminded herself that he'd had good reason to feel she'd endangered his son. As it turned out, she had. "Sure it was," she said anyway. "I won't apologize for keeping his confidence. I will apologize for not pushing him harder to tell you. For...for giving him more time than I should have."

"No," he repeated, then scraped a hand over his face. "Can we sit down?"

She hesitated, then nodded stiffly. Again, he gestured her ahead, and, after shedding her wool coat and letting him hang it up, she perched on one end of his leather sofa. At least she could drop her bag down at her feet, although that left her without anything to do with her hands.

Ben looked down at her for a moment, then sat in an easy chair facing her. "I felt betrayed," he said abruptly.

His face, she saw, looked tired, the lines deeply worn. About the way she felt.

"Betrayed?" Olivia repeated, uncertainly.

"I guess I thought I was owed your first loyalty. God knows why. And, no, the irony hasn't escaped me that I was the one who betrayed you all those years ago."

"You broke up with me. We were kids. We shouldn't even have been talking about forever."

"Probably not, except we were in love." Exhaustion weighed in his voice, too. He couldn't have been sleeping any better than she had been. "I was young and idiotic. Maybe if you hadn't been my first real girlfriend." First girl he'd had sex with, he meant. "I might've had some perspective. As it is, I got to college—"

"I know what you did." That came out sharp, but she didn't want to hear details, thank you.

Ben nodded, those espresso-dark eyes reading

her flash of anger. "Even though I broke up with you, I never forgot you. I told you I saw you play basketball your senior year. That quick, I'd come to my senses, at least enough to sort of think—" His mouth quirked into a wry smile. "But I got just retribution. I found out you were dating someone else. And probably wouldn't have given me the time of day anyway."

No, she probably wouldn't have. Pride and hurt would have made her want to spurn Ben, hurt *him,* if she could have.

"I told myself I had to move on," he said in a low voice. "So I did, but…you were always there."

Emotion swelled painfully in her chest. He'd always been there with her, too. She'd never felt about anyone the way she had about Ben. However ridiculous she'd known that was. Her high school boyfriend. Who knew what kind of creep he'd matured into? she'd asked herself a thousand times.

"I came home to Crescent Creek because of you." He shrugged. "I had other reasons, but it was always in the back of my mind that I'd have another chance at you. What I didn't want to admit, even to myself, is that I was counting on that chance. I knew from Mom you hadn't married. I figured you came home for visits—" He grimaced. "Then you looked at me as if you hardly remembered who I was."

"I remembered." The voice didn't sound like hers.

"Even so, I kept…hoping. I've been waiting for

you for a long time, Olivia. Then I actually had my chance, and instead of you betraying me, I'm the one who betrayed you."

"'Betrayed' is a strong word." Although it had felt like it.

And…he'd been waiting for her? All this time? Was he saying there hadn't been anyone else since he came home to Crescent Creek? Not in three years?

"Not too strong," he insisted. "I lashed out, yeah, because I was scared for Carson. It took me a day or two to realize I was jealous, too. He'd turned to you, not me." He grunted. "That sounds really petty, doesn't it?"

"No, I do understand."

"Thanks for saying that, even if it's not true." He sighed heavily. "But things are complicated for Carson and me. I probably wouldn't have reacted that way if he was mine biologically, but as it is, becoming father and son has been one step forward, two back. Him really, truly believing I love him and will be there for him no matter what. Me believing *he* believes I'm his father. I think…we got there, but underneath I didn't believe it."

Ben sat with his elbows braced on his thighs. His shoulders had a defeated sag, and in his eyes she saw honesty and self-deprecation as well as… fear. Was he really afraid she couldn't forgive him?

"I think…I guessed some of that," she admitted. "But you hurt me. It took *me* a few days to figure out that you'd thrown me back to being six-teen. When I first…started to let you in, this past month, I kept thinking, I trusted him once and look what happened, even though I knew how stupid that was." She met his eyes. "I mean, we were teenag-ers. We both had dreams. It might have been differ-ent if we'd never planned to leave Crescent Creek, but as it was, how could we have stuck together? You were my first serious boyfriend, too." He knew that; she'd been a virgin their first time.

"We can't go back," he said after a minute.

"No." Not that far, but maybe they *could* go back to where they'd left off a week ago. Given what he was implying… Hope choked her. "I'd made up my mind to leave town. I told you that."

He made a raw sound. "I didn't know how I was going to survive it."

"Everything hit me at once." She managed a smile. "Literally, in the case of Mrs. Runyon."

"I heard."

"So Mom said. I guess you two talked."

"Me trying to track you down."

"I gave up on her, you know."

His eyes had darkened, if such a thing was pos-sible. "I'm sorry."

"She went to your town meeting last night. Af-terward, she came to see me. I…didn't even want to answer the door."

His mouth tilted into a half smile. "And often you don't."

She smiled a little, too. She could now. It wasn't only hope she felt. An intoxicating river of relief ran through her. "I've been known to be stubborn."

He even laughed this time.

Olivia sobered. "What you said…got to Mom. She came to apologize. To ask me to stay in town. She offered to make me a full partner in the business. She told me things about her and Dad." She hesitated, wondering how much she should share of what her mother had said. But the darkest part, the infidelity, Ben already knew. Heck, everyone in town knew now. "Back when it happened, they were having troubles. I can't believe I was so oblivious. Or maybe I can." She made a face. "After all, I was a teenager."

She went on to tell him what her mother had said about her crushed hopes for another child, about how she'd rejected her husband, how they'd ultimately healed the breach. "Mom regrets terribly that she let Dad die believing she'd never forgive him. I think she finally has. And I guess she didn't want me to let the one wrong thing he did overwhelm my feelings for him. As a father—" once again she almost lost her voice "—he was amazing. Thanks to Mom, I can let myself forgive him, too."

And you. Not until this moment had she realized how tangled up her feelings about Ben and her father had been. If her father wasn't trustworthy, what man would be? And she already knew Ben wasn't, didn't she?

Only—everyone made mistakes. Even Dad. *Even me. Maybe it should be,* especially *me.*

"So, um, I thought I owed you the courtesy of at least letting you say whatever you wanted to say, too. Instead of dodging your phone calls."

A smile played on his mouth, even as his eyes remained serious. "And not opening your door."

"I knew it was you."

"I figured that out."

Neither of them said anything for a minute. He kept studying her. It was all she could do to sit completely still.

"Well, then, here goes. I know my track record with you isn't great—"

Olivia had to interrupt. "That isn't true. You've been amazing, listening to me through all my troubles. It had to get really old, but you never said so."

"No. It didn't get old." His voice had become even rougher. "I want you to know you can turn to me whenever you're troubled. Whenever you need anything. A shoulder to cry on, a laugh, a listening ear. Patience, friendship—"

Friendship? Her heart sank.

Until he went on. "Passionate lovemaking. Someone to fight with. I want to be the person you call when you're excited or mad or frustrated." A muscle twitched in his cheek. "The person you come home to. Go to bed with every night, wake up next to every morning."

Olivia sat very still, staring at him.

"In case I'm not being clear enough, I'll lay it out. I'm in love with you. I'm pretty sure I always have been."

Then why was he still sitting on the other side of the coffee table? But she saw how rigid his body was. He feared she was going to say, "Sorry, too little, too late. Can't trust you, guy."

What came out was "Then why...?"

"Why what?" he asked, when she didn't finish.

"Did you...give up?"

His jaw tightened. "I was starting to feel like a stalker. Not helped by the fact that I've spent three years watching for you. Not so accidently running into you. This time, you were pretty blunt. You were done. And..." His throat worked. "I deserved to lose you."

"But you were coming to see me tonight anyway."

"Yeah." He shifted. "At first I didn't believe you'd really pack it in—running away isn't your style—but I've been hearing all week that you actually were going. I couldn't let you walk out of my life without trying one more time to get you to listen."

"I love you," she blurted.

"God." Now, at last, he was moving, so fast she hardly saw it happening. He was just there, gathering her into his arms, squeezing her so hard it probably hurt, but she was holding on just as tightly. And either he was shaking or she was. Or both. "Tell me you're staying," he said hoarsely.

"I'm staying. I just…couldn't stand it if—"

He cupped her face in those big hands that had a faint tremor and tilted it up as if he had to look into her eyes before he'd believe she meant it. "I love you," he said again.

She swallowed. "I know."

He made an indescribable sound just before he bent his head to kiss her voraciously, as if he had been starving. Olivia surged upward to meet that kiss with everything in her. Next thing she knew, she'd straddled him. Arousal slammed into her. It was as if she wouldn't believe in anything they'd said until she had physical confirmation. Their bodies fitted together. From the way he kissed her, he had to feel the same.

They wrestled with each others' clothes, struggling to shed them without separating any more than they could help. Ben hoisted her, and his mouth, hot and wet, closed over her bare breast. The pull was strong, insistent, rhythmic. Her head fell back and she moaned, her hips rocking.

He finally had to lift her off him long enough to get rid of his slacks and her jeans, but when she stroked him, he groaned.

"Now," he said in a harsh voice, lifting her back into place. Olivia sank down on him, the need and satisfaction like nothing she'd ever felt. He gripped her buttocks and helped her rise and fall even as his hips slammed upward to meet her. At the end, her body clenched around his as if claiming him, once and for all.

"Love you," she managed to say.

From between gritted teeth, he got out, "Love," even as he pulsed hard inside her.

Afterward, he kept holding her, and she kept holding him. He stroked her back, the curve of her waist and hip, pausing here and there to gently knead. Head tucked in the crook between his neck and shoulder, she was hazy enough to feel herself drifting toward sleep.

Until Ben pinched her butt and she lurched. "What—?"

She lifted her head to find him grinning.

"Thought that'd get you."

"Humph."

He chuckled. "How would you feel about heading upstairs?"

She thought about it. "I'd love to, except— Is it really awful to admit I'm starved?"

Smiling, Ben bent to rest his forehead against hers. "No," he said huskily. "You've been losing weight, haven't you?"

Olivia wrinkled her nose. "Probably. My appetite goes when I'm unhappy. Plus, I've been trying to eat up what I had in my kitchen, and what was left wasn't all that appetizing. I was leaving Sunday, you know."

His jaw spasmed. "Yeah." He rubbed his nose against hers, then kissed her. His mouth was gentle this time. As much as his passion, his tenderness fed her love and filled her with happiness.

"I guess I can go grocery shopping now," she murmured when their mouths parted.

"I guess you can. Except—" He hesitated, something wary in his expression now.

"Except?" she prodded, feeling cautious.

"Don't stock up too much, okay? I won't push. You need time to feel sure about me. But…I hope that doesn't take long, because I want you to marry me. I meant what I said about going to bed together every night and waking up next to you every morning."

"You having a kid *does* make having a sex life challenging…"

Ben scowled. "I want a hell of a lot more than sex with you."

"I know." Smiling, she laid a finger over his lips. She felt as if she were floating on a cloud of euphoria. "And, as it happens, I like your kid."

"Yeah. About that." He cleared his throat. "Do you want children?"

"You don't want to start over again, with him close to college age?" she asked with a pang of dismay. No, stronger than that. A primal shock. *Oh, Mom. I understand.*

"I do," he said, his gaze holding hers. "I want to have children with you. I'm…hoping you feel the same."

She gulped and nodded.

"Good." He smacked a kiss to her lips. "Let's get something to eat. *Then* go to bed. We're working under a deadline here, you know."

They mostly got dressed, Olivia not bothering with her bra, although she did tuck it into her bag in case Carson should come home unexpectedly.

While the hamburgers were cooking, Ben stuck frozen tater tots in the oven to heat. It was a guy kind of meal. Olivia didn't mind at all. She was too caught in wonder.

He'd asked her to marry him. Said he'd wait.

"Did you mean it?" she asked. "That you've been waiting for me ever since you came home to Crescent Creek?"

He turned from the stove, spatula in his hand. "I meant it. I'm a stubborn man."

"I'm a stubborn woman, too."

"I noticed."

"There's something Mom didn't ask me. And you haven't, either."

His eyebrows rose.

"About my sister. Half sister," she corrected herself. "Jessica." She was conscious of her chin coming up. "I'm going to look for her."

"Well, of course you are." Ben sounded matter-of-fact.

"Mom may not be happy about it."

He gave her that crooked smile she loved. "Your mother isn't stupid, Olivia. She knows you."

"You don't mind?"

"Why would I?" He turned back to flip the burgers, his faint surprise convincing.

"With her mother dead, well, I want to make sure she's happy with her grandmother," Olivia said to his back, because she'd already prepared the argument.

"Cheese?" he asked.

"Of course cheese."

He shook his head. "I'm the guy who wrestled a kid who wasn't mine away from his mother because I knew she wasn't doing the job. You expect me to mind if you need to take in your sister? This house has four bedrooms. Carson might freak out, having to share a bathroom with a girl, but he can learn."

She hadn't even gotten that far in her thinking, and he was ready to throw open his home to the young sister she knew only from a short note. There was only one thing to say. "I love you."

Ben flashed a grin over his shoulder. "I know."

The cheese melted, he transferred the burgers to buns and carried the plates to the table. No onions, no tomatoes, no lettuce—but, hey, they were on a deadline. Olivia picked hers up and took a big bite.

IT TOOK TWO months, and, finally, when her own efforts failed, the expense of paying a private investigator, before Olivia had Jessica's last name, address and phone number. By then, her childhood home was empty and had a for-sale sign out

front, her mother had moved happily into one of
the small houses she'd had her eye on at The Crescent and Carson was back to riding his bike and
playing pickup basketball games with his former
teammates.

Crescent Creek High School had not won the
league championships, but they'd come close even
after losing the three starters. Dex Slagle, Dylan
Zurenko and Gavin Runyon were all supposed to
be serving massive hours of community service.
Olivia knew Dex actually was—he'd started by
washing city police cars, then moved on to helping at the food bank. Olivia's mother, still actively
volunteering there, said he was growing on her.
She had reported that he planned to attend West-
ern Washington University. He had also apologized
to Carson.

The Zurenkos had moved away, which broke no
one's heart. Gavin, Olivia had heard, was showing
up occasionally for his community service. She
hadn't so much as set eyes on his mother, thank
heavens. Gavin, of course, was graduating in June,
since Ben hadn't expelled any of the boys. Accord-
ing to Carson, Gavin had been recruited to play
football at Oregon State.

Ben and she had set their wedding for April, during spring break. Hawaii for a honeymoon seemed
like a cliché, but neither of them had ever been so
that's where they were going.

"What difference does it make anyway, when

we're unlikely to set foot outside of our room?" he'd pointed out with a wicked grin.

Bowen's was now officially in the appliance business, and Olivia was eyeing the space beyond it, currently a dry cleaners whose owners were looking to move so they could enlarge. Business was booming.

And she now had her sister's phone number, written on a Post-it note right in front of her.

Possibly my sister, she reminded herself, but had long since realized she had no doubt.

Olivia checked the time again unnecessarily. Jessica's grandmother lived in Pasadena, California. Same time zone. School would have long since let out by now.

Girding herself, she picked up her phone and dialed. By the fourth ring, she was debating whether to leave a message and if she did, what to say. Halfway through the fifth ring, someone picked up.

"Hello?" It was a young voice. A girl's voice.

"May I speak to Jessica?"

"This is her." The girl sounded suspicious.

Olivia took a deep breath, all the speeches she'd prepared gone. She had no idea what the right thing to say was.

But words came anyway. "My name is Olivia Bowen, and I think you might be my sister."

* * * * *

*Be sure to pick up the next book by
Janice Kay Johnson!
Available January 2015 from
Harlequin Superromance.*

LARGER-PRINT BOOKS!

GET 2 FREE LARGER-PRINT NOVELS PLUS
2 FREE GIFTS!

HARLEQUIN®

Romance

From the Heart, For the Heart

LARGER-PRINT BOOKS!

HARLEQUIN *Presents*

PASSION GUARANTEED SEDUCTION

GET 2 FREE LARGER-PRINT NOVELS PLUS 2 FREE GIFTS!

YES! Please send me 2 FREE LARGER-PRINT Harlequin Presents® novels and my 2 FREE gifts (gifts are worth about $10). After receiving them, if I don't wish to receive any more books, I can return the shipping statement marked "cancel." If I don't cancel, I will receive 6 brand-new novels every month and be billed just $5.05 per book in the U.S. or $5.49 per book in Canada. That's a saving of at least 16% off the cover price! It's quite a bargain! Shipping and handling is just 50¢ per book in the U.S. and 75¢ per book in Canada.* I understand that accepting the 2 free books and gifts places me under no obligation to buy anything. I can always return a shipment and cancel at any time. Even if I never buy another book, the two free books and gifts are mine to keep forever.

176/376 HDN F43N

Name	(PLEASE PRINT)	
Address		Apt. #
City	State/Prov.	Zip/Postal Code

Signature (if under 18, a parent or guardian must sign)

Mail to the **Harlequin® Reader Service:**
IN U.S.A.: P.O. Box 1867, Buffalo, NY 14240-1867
IN CANADA: P.O. Box 609, Fort Erie, Ontario L2A 5X3

**Are you a subscriber to Harlequin Presents books
and want to receive the larger-print edition?
Call 1-800-873-8635 today or visit us at www.ReaderService.com.**

* Terms and prices subject to change without notice. Prices do not include applicable taxes. Sales tax applicable in N.Y. Canadian residents will be charged applicable taxes. Offer not valid in Quebec. This offer is limited to one order per household. Not valid for current subscribers to Harlequin Presents Larger-Print books. All orders subject to credit approval. Credit or debit balances in a customer's account(s) may be offset by any other outstanding balance owed by or to the customer. Please allow 4 to 6 weeks for delivery. Offer available while quantities last.

Your Privacy—The Harlequin® Reader Service is committed to protecting your privacy. Our Privacy Policy is available online at www.ReaderService.com or upon request from the Harlequin Reader Service.

We make a portion of our mailing list available to reputable third parties that offer products we believe may interest you. If you prefer that we not exchange your name with third parties, or if you wish to clarify or modify your communication preferences, please visit us at www.ReaderService.com/consumerchoice or write to us at Harlequin Reader Service Preference Service, P.O. Box 9062, Buffalo, NY 14269. Include your complete name and address.

HPLP13R